Mary Tucker Magill

**The Holcombes**

A Story of Virginia Home-Life

Mary Tucker Magill

**The Holcombes**
*A Story of Virginia Home-Life*

ISBN/EAN: 9783744749596

Printed in Europe, USA, Canada, Australia, Japan

Cover: Foto ©Andreas Hilbeck / pixelio.de

More available books at **www.hansebooks.com**

# THE HOLCOMBES.

## A STORY OF VIRGINIA HOME-LIFE.

BY

MARY TUCKER MAGILL.

"Then give me back the times when I myself was forming; when a fountain of crowded lays sprang freshly and unbrokenly forth; when mists veiled the world before me—the bud still promised miracles; when I gathered the thousand flowers which profusely filled the dales! I had nothing, and yet enough—the longing after truth, the pleasure in delusion! Give me back those impulses untamed—the deep pain-fraught happiness, the energy of hate, the might of love—give me back my youth!"—GOETHE'S FAUST.

PHILADELPHIA:
J. B. LIPPINCOTT & CO.
1871.

TO

# VIRGINIA,

MY NATIVE STATE,

This first effort of my pen

Is respectfully dedicated.

If it should prove successful in
rescuing from the grave of oblivion
the memory of her time-honored institutions,
as they existed in the palmiest days
of her prosperity, before she was
scarred and seamed by the
touch of misfortune,
the laborer will
have received
her hire.

THE AUTHOR.

# PREFACE.

It is not my design, in the following pages, to enter the arena in defense of departed institutions, or to provoke political animosities. I have, on the contrary, chosen that period in the history of my State when these discussions had but little place in family interests. In short, it has been my endeavor to present to the world a faithful picture of a Virginia home as it was before the late war.

This period has been chosen particularly, also, because, so far as I know, it is a field yet untrodden by the novelist, though full of interest, as presenting to our view *Virginia* in her palmiest days,—as she was when she first bared her bosom to the sword, and opened her gates to present her sacred soil as the battle-field of the war.

It is the more important that these times should not pass unrecorded, because, owing to the stirring events which so immediately follow them, there is danger of their sinking to a grave " unhonored and unknown." And then, too, when we remember that the most largely circulated pictures of life in our Southern States are taken from " Uncle Tom's Cabin," and like libels upon our people, it ought to be sufficient to arouse the slumbering genius of the South to arise and assert her claims to a position in the nation as a refined, hospitable, cultivated, and benevolent people.

Whilst in these pages I have carefully avoided positive personalities, yet have I earnestly tried to present truthfully the ruling characteristics of *Virginians.* Though no one will be able to blush with indignation at being impertinently dragged before the public, with all of their sacred family affairs, yet the Holcombes do exist, and have ever existed, in our homes through the length and breadth of Virginia.

I say I have avoided personalities, and yet I plead guilty, so far as that humble race is concerned who have been so intimately connected with our domestic relations for centuries. With regard to them, I will say, that each portrait has been drawn from nature,—that great fountain-head of truth. Each one who has found a niche in my gallery of family portraits lives as distinctly in my memory as if seen but yesterday. I have even retained their peculiarities of expression, as essentially necessary to a faithful portraiture of their characters.

The work has been a pleasant one to me, since it has served to recall to my mind those tenderly-remembered days before poverty came to grind, or war and bloodshed to desolate, our homes. My next task will be less congenial, as I propose, should the public desire a further acquaintance with the family, to whom it has been my pleasure to introduce them, to continue their history through a less prosperous, though more exciting, period of their lives.

Until then I make my adieu.

MARY TUCKER MAGILL.

# CONTENTS.

CHAPTER I.

Margaret Holcombe introduces Herself . . . . . 9

CHAPTER II.

Jean Murray introduces Herself . . . . . . 18

CHAPTER III.

Rose Hill and its Inmates.—Jean's Diary . . . . 21

CHAPTER IV.

Margaret's First Impressions . . . . . . 30

CHAPTER V.

"Mary Holcombe, Ladies and Gentlemen" . . . . 35

CHAPTER VI.

Letter from Jean to her Brother . . . . . . 41

CHAPTER VII.

A Family Gathering . . . . . . . . 51

CHAPTER VIII.

Jean's Diary.—A Christmas Morning . . . . . 56

CHAPTER IX.

An Old Virginia Christmas Dinner . . . . . . 69

CHAPTER X.

A Family Consultation, and what came of it . . . . 83

CHAPTER XI.

School . . . . . . . . . . . 97

CHAPTER XII.

George Washington revived . . . . . . . 104

( vii )

# CONTENTS.

## CHAPTER XIII.

PAGE

Harvest . . . . . . . . . . . 108

## CHAPTER XIV.

The Picnic . . . . . . . . . . 114

## CHAPTER XV.

The Angel of Death . . . . . . . . 129

## CHAPTER XVI.

Margaret leaves Home . . . . . . . . 138

## CHAPTER XVII.

Jean's Diary.—Two Years' Gap filled up . . . . 147

## CHAPTER XVIII.

An Important Arrival . . . . . . . . 150

## CHAPTER XIX.

The Family Circle . . . . . . . . . 158

## CHAPTER XX.

Preparations for a Feast . . . . . . . . 166

## CHAPTER XXI.

Miss Holcombe's Début . . . . . . . . 185

## CHAPTER XXII.

The Tournament . . . . . . . . . 198

## CHAPTER XXIII.

Asking Papa . . . . . . . . . . 217

## CHAPTER XXIV.

Dr. Burton . . . . . . . . . . 227

## CHAPTER XXV.

The Devil helps his Own.—A Funeral . . . . . 241

## CHAPTER XXVI.

Fortune Favors the Brave . . . . . . . 256

## CHAPTER XXVII.

A Night Visitor . . . . . . . . . 271

Conclusion . . . . . . . . . . 288

# THE HOLCOMBES.

## A STORY OF VIRGINIA HOME-LIFE.

## CHAPTER I.

### MARGARET HOLCOMBE INTRODUCES HERSELF.

*October 12th.* To-day I begin my new diary, and, as a preparation, I have been looking over the old ones. How glad I am that my precious mother taught me to keep one from the time I was a little child! It is so pleasant to me now to be able to turn over the leaves of my life almost back to the days of pothooks and hangers, judging from the hieroglyphics displayed in my first essays, and the fearful tortures the English etymology suffered in my hands. Parts of it are almost as interesting as a diary I read of somewhere, consisting of such thrilling facts as these : "Got up this morning and washed my face and hands ;" and next, "Got up this morning and only washed my face ;" but still, it is interesting to me. Now, how well I remember my feelings as I made this *entry*, in letters, by-the-by, which stare me out of countenance : "I have had a *grate* sorrow to-day. I fell down and broke my dear Julia's *hed.*" Julia was my big, ugly dolly, over which I was as true a mourner as "Rachel weeping for her children." Well! well! I have made a great step

since then. I can hardly realize I am the same person.
I was eight years old at that time, and to-day I am fifteen.
Then I was crying over the loss of my doll, but since
then I have mourned over my precious mother: all I retain of her are two sweet pictures, one on canvas, but
the sweetest and best in my heart,—for what can I not
remember of her? Her loving heart, her beauty, her
noble gentleness, so far above the commonplace meekness
you see allied to a lower type of humanity, of whom you
hear persons say, "She is so sweet! so lovely! so gentle!"
and you look, and see a little white-faced, meek-browed
being, spiritless as a mouse. What credit does she deserve
for being meek, I should like to know?

I saw such a one in church some weeks ago. She is
a young lady, visiting at Mrs. Campbell's, I think,—a
Miss Murray. I could not help contrasting her with my
own mother, with her noble expanse of brow overshadowing those brown eyes so full of life, fire, and character,
and the gentleness which comes from a chastened spirit.
That is what I want to have. I was so busy drawing
this contrast from the face of Miss Murray that, I am
afraid, I was a little rude in staring; and was only recalled to myself by her blushing face. My own mother
would not have allowed herself to be put out of countenance by so slight a matter,—but is any one like her?
Shall I ever be? Papa says I look like her; but that is
not my greatest wish. I want, it is true, to be her "very
image in fair face," but I want more. I want her mind,
her heart, her spirit: I want to be like her in all things.
I am going to make her my beau-ideal. I remember
saying this to her once; and she said so gravely and
sweetly, "My Margie, would you close your shutters and
read by a tallow-candle, when you could have the glorious
light of God's sun? Why choose me as your model

when you can aim so much higher?" Well, that of course is true; but I do not think it can be any harm to choose an earthly possible aim, rather than one so far beyond me as our Saviour is. Certainly I shall be satisfied if I am only like her.

What a comfort a diary is! I can go to mine, and tell it everything as if it was really a friend. Since mamma died it is the only confidential friend I have had. Papa is so much away, and seems, besides, so much preoccupied: and I always feel afraid that my little cares and troubles would make him smile, though they are as great to me as older persons' are to them. I think it would be a good thing if grown people could realize that. If I ever have children—and I suppose I shall—I will remember this, and encourage them to tell me everything: that will be like mamma.

If I only had a sister! I mean older than myself, or near my age. Now Mary is twelve, it is true; but, goodness, she is more of a boy than a girl, and would rather any time go hunting with John, or play dolls with Lilias, than to listen to me! Then there is Mrs. Bascombe: suppose I should try to make a confidante of her,—"Angels and ministers of grace, defend us!" I did try it once; but she only said, in her stiff way, "My dear, it is a very bad plan to imagine miseries. The sentimental enthusiasms of girls of your age are generally very silly." So, poor snail that I am, I crawl back into my shell, and only confide in my diary. If I am silly, no one knows it, and this dear friend never rebuffs me. I like silent friends. I like to have all the talking to myself, when I am in a talking mood. So this is my birthday! Yes, Miss Margaret Holcombe is fifteen years old to-day! Papa looked quite grave over the fact. I suppose he does not quite like having a daughter fifteen years old, when he looks so young. But men that marry at twenty-one must expect some such inconvenience before they get to be forty. I often wish I could have seen papa and mamma when they were married : they must have been so young and handsome. Just think, mamma was only three years older than I am ! Well, I think that is old enough. If a girl's character is not formed at eighteen, it never will be. Certainly, I expect to feel as old as the hills by that time; but I have more experience than most girls, having charge of the family since mamma's death. Not the charge exactly, but I sit at the head of the table and pour out tea. Mrs. Bascombe and Mammy do the rest pretty much, but still the eldest daughter has to be more womanly under the circumstances. I think it would be better if papa would give me more authority over the children, now that I am fifteen; I am sure I would be prudent and careful; and Mary wants some one to develop her; she is a dreadful tomboy. It would be right hard to bring John and herself into measures, I know, because they do not seem at all to realize how old I am growing, and think themselves as good as I am; and poor little Lilias no one wants to manage, she must always do as she pleases. I will ask papa about this at once. If he will only have confidence in me, and help me, I am sure I can do very well even with John and Mary.

*October* 13*th.* I could not write any more, dear diary, yesterday, because I was *so miserable*, and I had to take it out in a good cry. One feels so much better after a good cry, when they have a great trouble, though I am not very sure I did yesterday, for my head ached and my eyes smarted so that I could do nothing but go to sleep. Fortunately, my troubles never keep me awake, as some people's do. I have tried sometimes to stay awake and cry over them, but sleep always comes in spite of me.

Well, to begin at the beginning: I was so in earnest in the idea of helping the children,—now I am growing so old,—that I put you away in a hurry, thinking that I would soon return to you, and with your help would make my plans for future action. I did not run, because I am trying to get over the habit of romping through the house, but I walked very quickly into papa's study, and found him writing something which he put hastily aside when I came into the room, and met me, as he always does, with a smile of welcome.

"Papa," I said, "I want to talk to you about something *very* important."

"Well, daughter, that suits my mood exactly. You are growing so old now that I shall expect something *very* important;—of course, trivial matters cease to interest young ladies of fifteen." And he drew me down upon his knee, and pushed back the hair from my face. I always know when he does that, he is thinking of my mother, and noting the likeness I bear to her.

"But, papa," I said, "I am not joking. I do not want you to laugh at the idea of my being fifteen. I ought to think seriously about it. My own mother was only three years older when she was married."

"Indeed!" laughed papa, most provokingly, turning up my face to his. "Does this big wheel turn in that direction? No, Margie, I think you are too young."

"Papa, papa, indeed you are unkind!" cried I, while I felt the tears rush to my eyes. "I do not mean any such nonsense. I have never seen the man yet I want to marry." This I said in a very dignified way, because I was hurt that he should laugh at me all the time as if I had been one of the little children.

It had its effect, for seeing me so in earnest he too grew grave, and, putting his arm about me, said,—

2

" Well, daughter, let me hear what it is; I am sorry I laughed at you."

" I came to ask you, papa, now I am growing so much older and more womanly, to let me take more care of, and authority over, the children; they want some one to look after them, and I do not think Mrs. Bascombe has quite the right plan about it, and they are growing too old to be willing to submit to Mammy, so I think no one would care so much about it as I should, if you will only give me the authority. I might have a difficulty with John and Mary at first, but I know it would all come right in time."

Here I changed my position so as to get a view of papa's face; it was very grave and thoughtful, with a shade of troubled embarrassment upon it. He did not speak for full a minute, and then with a manner so full of all I saw in his face that I caught the infection, and felt a shadow of the great trouble which was to come upon me.

" It is true, as you say, my little girl," he said; " I have felt for a long time that some influence was wanting to supply to my children what they have lost. Mrs. Bascombe does the best she can; but that is little. I do the best I can; but that does not at all touch the evil. I see my children, with grief, growing up with many lackings, over which their mother would grieve. Your ideas are kind and worthy of you, dear. I love you for them; but you are too young. I could not, if I wished it, endow you with sufficient authority to govern your sister and brother so nearly your own age. Nor would I, if I could, burden your heart, so young, with such cares. Your influence may do much with them; and I do trust much to it in the making them what they ought to be, but it must be by example more than by precept,

Margie. Learn to rule your own spirit, and then they will respect and admire your mother in you. You give me an opportunity, my child, which I have long wanted, but did not know how to make, to confide to you some engagements I have entered into in which you, in common with my other children, are deeply interested."

"Oh, papa," I said, my face burning with excitement, " I know what it is, and I am so glad : you are going to send Mrs. Bascombe away and get a new governess."

"Margie," he said, as if he were nerving himself to some great trial, " I am going to send Mrs. Bascombe away, and I am going to bring one here whom, I trust, you will all love and honor; and who, I am sure, on her part, will do everything she can to win and keep your love and confidence, as she has mine. She comes, not as a governess, but as my wife."

It was dawning upon me all the time he spoke, but I cast the bated light away. And when the last dreadful word was spoken, and I knew it was true, I tore myself from his arms, and casting myself down upon the floor, wept with passionate and angry grief.

With great gentleness he raised me up, saying, " My child, my darling child, you grieve me bitterly by this."

But I was not to be comforted in this way. I told him that I did not, could not, love him; that he insulted the memory of my mother by putting any one in her place; that I only wanted to go away somewhere and take the children, and leave him and his "old wife;" that *we* never would forget mamma.

"Nor have I forgotten her, dear," he said, so sadly that in the midst of my frenzy I could not help a feeling of tenderness coming in. And when I looked at him, through my blinding tears, he looked as he did the night mamma died, so pale and sad. A thought came into my mind that perhaps he did not marry because he loved, but for the sake of his children. So I crept within his arms again, and, kissing him, said, "Papa, forgive me; I do love you; it was very wicked in me to say such words. You cannot forget my precious mother,—you cannot love another woman as you did her. Don't bring her here. Indeed, I can take care of the children."

"Margie," he said, "you are mistaken; God has so constituted the human heart that the love for one cannot drive out the love for another. And while I shall never forget your dear mother, and all she was to me for twelve years, I do love the woman I shall make my wife with a deep, earnest devotion. I do not marry a slave, to be subject to my will and do my work with no return, but I take Jean Murray into my innermost heart along with your dead mother, and shall cherish her there until death us do part."

"Well, papa," I answered, "you had better send me away, for my whole soul rises against it, and I feel as if it would kill me to see any woman in my mother's place. She shall never have a welcome from me."

"Margaret," my father had never spoken so sternly to me before, and even in the midst of my excitement my spirit quailed before him, "you fill me with forebodings for your future. I insist upon your speaking to me with proper respect, and upon your treating *my wife*, whenever I chose to bring her here, as the mistress of my house, the head of my home, and one whom I have considered worthy to share my heart with your dead mother's memory." And before I had recovered sufficiently to answer him he had left the room. And now I am perfectly miserable. I have to admire papa, even in this; he is right, and I am wrong. But still I hate this woman, this Jean Murray, who is to take my mamma's place  To think of its being the very woman with whom I was contrasting mamma in church that Sunday! I do not blame papa, but I hate *her* and her sneaking, underhand ways, which have entrapped him into marrying her. I know this is all wrong, but I am in that mood this evening when I like to do wrong; because if I do right I will have to forget mamma and love Jean Murray. And then, there is another trial. I called the children last night, and, with many tears, told them. Mary looked grave for an instant, and then said, in that old-fashioned way she has sometimes, "Well, Margie, I think it is the best thing that could happen to us children, to have some one to look after us, we are so neglected;" and John, who always agrees with Mary, said he thought it would be "good fun to have a new mamma," "and he hoped she would make plenty of nice cakes." Senseless animal! to think of cakes at such a time! Even little Lilias wondered if she would undress her and rock her "up and down" as mamma used to do.

Well, it is a great comfort to me to be miserable, if it is by myself. The only person who seems disposed to condole with me is old Aunt Elsie; but of course I cannot let a servant speak to me of papa's faults. So when she came to my room and commenced groaning in her way, "Poor missus! poor children! Well, honey, all men is alike," I answered, quite fiercely, "Aunt Elsie, you must not speak so of papa, he is not like any other man in the world; he has a perfect right to bring who he pleases to his own house." And then I wondered at myself.

I saw papa last night at tea, and thought my swollen eyes and suffering face would have touched his heart and made him repent his harsh words; but he was just as usual, except paler and more quiet perhaps, and after tea advised me to go to bed as the best cure for my headache.

# CHAPTER II.

## JEAN MURRAY INTRODUCES HERSELF.

*November* 14*th.* I sit down to-night, diary in hand, to make my last entry in my maiden life. I have somewhat the feeling which I would have by the bedside of a friend who was on the verge of an unknown eternity; for, let us think of life as we will, whether a "moment's space," or the drifting of a cloud across the sky, it is very important; the moment's space may be fifty or sixty years, and the cloud may drift into blacker darkness, or be first gilded with the light from God's sun and then lost in the full effulgence of brightness; but be this as it may, we all want our lives to be happy and useful, and I do not suppose that there is any time in a woman's life which is more interesting to her than her marriage. An unthinking girl may dash into the new existence with all the gloss of bridal happiness upon her, without a thought of the future, or at least without a recognition of inevitable troubles in store for her. But it is not so with me; in the first place, my sober twenty-four years place me beyond the reckless enthusiasms of early girlhood. I know that no life is all gladness, and then again I know that whilst "my lines have fallen in pleasant places" in some respects, yet in others I will inevitably encounter many trials, to meet which I have no positive knowledge to guide me. I feel like a man wandering in the dark in the midst of pitfalls and precipices; but, thank God, it is not so; I have a hand outstretched, I have a comforting

( 18 )

promise that as my "day so shall my strength be." To Him I commit my way; He has guided me so far, and will to the end.

I am glad Mr. Holcombe has been so perfectly candid with me. He does not promise me a garden of thornless roses, he only promises to do what he can to eradicate the prickles. I can see him now, as he stood in the glow of the firelight, some weeks ago, with the gaslight over his head, saying, "Now, Jean, I do not wish at all to deceive you. I feel that I am asking a great deal of you when I ask you to become my wife, because it is not me alone you marry, but four children, and not four angels, either. I think there is more than an ordinary amount of human nature in my progeny; and of late years, since I lost their mother, the good seeds have been rather choked out by weeds, though there are qualities in the soil of each which will reward the toil expended in the cultivation. I cannot tell you, dear, of the hope with which I look forward to your firm, gentle influence upon them,—they want it so badly." A vague fear filled my heart, and I said, "Is it for that you asked me to marry you, Mr. Holcombe? I could not be a faithful mother to your children with no reward but your cold approbation."

I shall never forget the bright smile which broke over his face as he knelt down on the carpet before me and took both my hands in his, and, looking into my eyes, said,—

"Ah, Jean! Jean! it glads my very soul to catch glimpses of your heart sometimes; you are so very shy of letting me see into its depths. Why, little woman, you are right next the core of my heart. And although I could never have loved a woman who I did not think would be a mother to my children, I do love this one, with the fullest confidence that she will meet my most ardent desires in every respect; but not without some self-reproach, because I am laying my burdens on her slender shoulders." Well, it is pleasant to be loved, even if it does bring cares along with it; and, God helping me, I will do my duty to him and his, looking for help to the fountain of all strength.

There is one thing that ought to be a guide to me in my new duties, and that is, that I know so well what an uncomfortable stepmother is. The troubles which made me an alien from my father's house shall be a lesson to me in my new home,—a lesson learned in England and profited by in America.

This makes me remember the longing I have for my family ties in this hour of my happiness. If my father could only lay his hand upon my head and bid me "God speed," or Robert could be at my side, it would be a comfort; but I must be content with what good I can get, and love my husband all the more that I have so few to love.

# CHAPTER III.

*December* 12*th*. Nearly a month has elapsed since I last opened my diary,—but a month so full of interesting events that I feel as if it had been a lifetime. I can scarce realize that I am the same person I was one month ago. I stood then on the brink of an unknown world, doubting, fearing, wondering,—

> "But the silence was unbroken,
> And the darkness gave no token."

Now how differently I feel from the little, sober-looking bride, in her sober, gray dress, who heard the "dust to dust, and ashes to ashes" of her maiden life pronounced, on that sunny fall morning, in the little church, just one month ago! I suppose every woman remembers her marriage with peculiar feelings. If it turns out happily, she dwells with a tender smile, and eyes that look back far into the past, at the emotions awakened at the time; remembers the strong arm which supported her through it, and the manly strength of the heart upon which she has leaned ever since,—to her it was the development of life,—the door opened into a happy futurity. But if the life begun at marriage turns out unhappily, she thinks of the shiver which passed over her at what she regards now as the funeral of her life of careless maidenhood, an

( 21 )

impulse to leap back from the untried future into the tried past.

I do not know what sensations I shall retain longest, but I now remember the agitation, solemnity, a great deal of hope not unmixed with fear, and a sensation such as I have heard that a drowning person experiences,—a concentration of all the events of life into one moment,— like the Giaour,—

> "When in one moment o'er his soul
> Winters of memory seem to roll."

I seemed to be taking leave of my childhood for the first time, my plays with my brother and cousins, my mother's death and all of its consequent troubles, yet through all of these thoughts I did not lose one word of what the minister said; it seemed distinct, clear, and impressive as a voice from heaven; then it was over, and I was no longer myself, or belonging to myself, but more valued and valuable than I had ever been before. Next followed that journey for which we made no plans, but only went where our will carried us. It was made up of sparkling cataracts, journeys over mountains, lodgings even in the midst of the clouds, calm sails on quiet waters, rests at peaceful farm-houses, in the midst of the loveliness of nature, and every now and then a dip into society, planting friendships for future cultivation, in all of which we were as happy as any other two people ever were, and grew to know each other better each day. But the time came when this holiday-life must end, and we turned our faces homeward. For me this brought a pang, because, first, it recalled all my nervous dread of my future, and because, for the first time in our married life, my husband and I felt differently. He was returning to his home and his children, secure of a welcome; I was a stranger, and in all probability an unwelcome one; and yet I was not without pleasurable excitement. It is a pleasure to have a home to go to, when one has been a waif, a stray leaf, tossed about by winds from every quarter.

Rose Hill, the home of the Holcombes for generations past, is situated in the midst of the mountains of the Blue Ridge. The house is comparatively modern, but the place is known through the whole country as one of those old Virginian estates, passing from father to son with almost the regularity of entail. The negroes have all been born on the place, and have a hereditary attachment to their masters. It struck me as so strange before I came here to hear Mr. Holcombe speaking of his "Mammy." I never could help laughing at it. "Yes," he said, one day, when I was amusing myself at his expense, "you may laugh at me, but you will have to pay her the most profound respect. She is a perfect lady, I can tell you, and a highly-honored inmate of my household. Why, she is a link between us and the past; she has nursed all the children of the two last generations, and played with our grandmothers, and has paid the last offices to the dead of the family for the last forty-five years."

"Why, how old is she?"

"Well, no one knows exactly, but, putting together some facts, we judge she must be nearly seventy; but she is a hale, hearty old woman yet, and I hope will live to teach us what old times were for many years to come."

"But," I said, "I should think it very disagreeable to have an old negress thinking herself so much better than any one else, and to have to make a fuss over her all the time."

"Why, my dear Jean, you cannot imagine a more

perfect servant in everything than she is. She recognizes her position entirely; the smallest nursling is miss or master; nor does she feel humiliated by it. It is a strange combination of the perfect lady and the perfect servant. Just wait until you see her."

The town of C—— is about two miles from Rose Hill, and here the carriage met us. It is a new one, bought for the young bride, though I do not at all realize that I am she. The driver and footman came up, showing their white teeth by way of welcome; and here too I was introduced to my young son. He was first discovered by his father skulking in the distance, and greeted with, "Why, old fellow, what are you doing out there, hiding from your father? Come here, I have something to show you,—a present I have brought for you." But Master John did not seem to appreciate the gift, whatever it might be, and still stood off shyly, with his fingers in his mouth.

"What! You won't come? Well, that is a strange state of things: a boy refuses to kiss his father, when he has been away more than a month. Unnatural son! Ah, 'sharper than a serpent's tooth it is to have a thankless child!' Well, if the mountain will not come to Mohammed, Mohammed must go to the mountain." And so, after a little struggle, my son was presented to me with a very red face, upon a very small portion of the cheek of which I imprinted my maternal kiss, as the rest was hidden in his hands. I think my poor husband was very much mortified at this little episode, as he said to me, as we got in the carriage out of hearing of the child, who preferred to ride with the driver,—

"Ah, little woman, you see how we all want you. A man makes a poor out of bringing up a parcel of children without help. I have tried to do my best, but you see how it is."

I tried to reassure him by saying that I did not think boys ten years old were ever very remarkable for their manners, and I had no doubt we would get on finely after awhile. The ride home through the woods was a beautiful one. Nature had certainly favored us in bestowing a lovely day. The sun was near its setting, and seemed to enjoy the play of hide-and-seek with us through the openings in the trees, now shooting a beam into our very faces, and then darting off to hide in the thickets. At last, the road leading us through the woods into the open country, we came at once into full view of the grand old place. I clasped my hands in delight at the beauty of the scene.

Surely the old Holcombes must have had an eye for the beautiful in selecting the site of their home. I have never seen a place with so many natural advantages. The grove, out of which we had just driven, fronted the house, and now, for a space of about three hundred yards, spreads a perfectly level lawn, around which, in a circle, runs the carriage-road. The lawn stops abruptly at the foot of a hill, which is terraced in three separate falls, each of which is ascended by steps of smooth gray stone. At the top of the third terrace, upon a sort of table-land, in the midst of noble old forest-trees, oak, chestnut, elm, and locust, stands the house, which, from its proportions, position, etc., might have passed for some olden castle, with its white walls gleaming. As we approached it, the setting sun crowned it with a halo of glory, and the windows, from attic to basement, caught its rays, and sparkled as though a bonfire had been kindled within to do us honor; while in the distance the gorgeous flood of crimson and gold impurpled the background of

3

mountains, which reared their monstrous forms, peak
after peak, as far as the eye could reach.

Several persons were visible as we approached: one
slight, girlish figure stood at the top of the first terrace,
with her hand shading her eyes; another, as soon as the
carriage drove out of the grove, started off like an arrow
from the bow in our direction; while dusky forms were
seen either appearing or disappearing hastily in every
direction. It was like the moving figures in a panorama,
only more full of life.

Almost before I had time to ask who she was, the
fleet-footed little girl who was running towards us, impatiently pushing past the footman who was opening
the carriage-door, clambered into the carriage, and then
threw herself into her father's arms, exclaiming, "Oh, I
thought you were never coming, papa!" And this was
Mary, as I found from my husband's greeting, a slender
sprite of a child, with dark eyes, and hair that rippled
and glittered in the light. I am glad that in these late
years the prejudice against red hair has worn away. I
believe Eugene Sue and the Empress of France are to
be thanked for it. To me it was always unreasonable.
I remember once seeing a head of red hair (not dark
auburn, but genuine red hair) pass under a gaslight; it
was at a wedding in a church, and as the magnificent-
looking woman with these rippling waves passed where
the flood of light fell upon it, I never shall forget the
effect; it looked, indeed, like burnished copper glowing
almost to red-heat. I have looked ever since for a sight
like that, and never found it until that fairy-like little
figure came flying down the road with those golden locks
floating in the wind, with her cheeks glowing from the
exercise and her eyes dancing with delight; she was a
picture well worth looking upon.

"Why, you crazy jade, why did you not wait for us at home and welcome us in a becoming manner?"

"Oh, papa, you know I never can wait. It was so long, and I thought you were never coming, and when I saw the carriage coming out of the grove I was off before I well knew what I was doing."

"And now tell me," said her father, "if you know who this is sitting by my side?"

The bright face was turned to me, and as the cold little hands crept into mine, she whispered "Mamma." It was very sweetly done, and I already felt my heart warm and melt as I drew her to me and imprinted my first kiss upon her lips.

The introduction was just over when the carriage drew up to the foot of the terraced walk. The slight figure I had first remarked in the distance now came forward, and submitted to, rather than received, an embrace from my husband, and then gave me the coldest greeting I had ever received,—the heart just warmed by Mary's lips froze to its center; and yet there is something interesting, while it repulses, in the irregular features and sallow complexion of Margaret Holcombe. She looks to me as if she were putting a constraint upon herself all the time,—as if there was a fount of deep feeling under this cold exterior which could be warmed into life. My mind goes back ten years, and I see just such a welcome given. I remember now the image of my dead mother which rose up between me and the lips of the woman I then kissed and greeted as mother. I forgive Margaret on the spot, and pray God that I may never give these children of my husband such cause to curse the day I enter their father's house as that woman gave me.

The last introduction was received beside the glowing

fire in the sitting-room, where two soft little arms stole
around my neck as I knelt before a helpless little figure
swathed in bright-colored flannels, above which appeared
a little flaxen head with spiritual face; it was baby Lilias,
—the darling of the household,—who is cherished with
the tenderer care because the hand of God is laid heavily
upon her. A fall in her infancy has left her a helpless
charge upon her friends,—but such a charge as none would
shrink from. I trust that I, too, may be permitted to
smooth her pathway through life. I feel very hopeful in
my home, there is so much to make me happy, and such
ample room for a life of usefulness as well as of happiness. I have seen the old Mammy too, a stately figure,
with a bright cotton turban, and a white handkerchief
pinned across her breast. I was met by a low curtsy,
and a respectful "Welcome, mistress," which might have
graced a parlor. I was a little annoyed by the grinning
faces which met me at every turn, but one word from this
old queen dispersed the crowd.

"Begone, you darkies! Dat the way *you* shows your
manners to your new mistress? G'long at once!" And a
scampering followed, which cleared the halls pretty soon.

She then led the way to my room. And then I real-
ized what a great lady I had become, to be lodged in this
lovely apartment, with its crimson hangings, rich ma-
hogany furniture, and the luxurious bed with its tempting
white draperies,—over which the bright fire on the hearth
threw a cheerful glow.

Surely, Jean Holcombe, "your lines are fallen to you
in pleasant places." Mrs. Bascombe is a pretty old lady,
part housekeeper and part teacher; she seems a model of
good temper, but not one, I should judge, to fill the place
of governess to such a family as this. Her dignity is so
completely a creature of the moment, that it is, if one may

so express it, a stiff impulse; and I judge that she has been too much a subject of amusement with the children to have much influence over them. Mr. Holcombe says I shall keep her as an assistant in the housekeeping; and he has employed a tutor for the children, who will arrive the first of January. A teacher of music comes out from C—— every other day, and they seem to have so much talent for music that their performance is beyond mediocrity,—though I have no idea that it is due to any especial diligence.

Well, I have before me now the materials for my life's work. I thank God I have only to do my duty and leave results to Him! I am glad I do not look upon it in the light of a trial, neither altogether of a pleasure, but a wholesome mixture of the two. I see my difficulties, and I see the way out of them to be a straightforward, gentle firmness, and a great reliance for guidance on an arm which is stronger than mine.

3*

# CHAPTER IV.

## MARGARET'S FIRST IMPRESSIONS.

*December* 13*th*. The long-dreaded event has actually taken place. I have lived to see my dear mamma's place filled in this house by one so different; and no one seems to do anything but rejoice, except myself. For the last month everything has been a note of preparation; the whole house torn to pieces. Painters and upholsterers at every turn,—new carriage, new furniture, new paintings,—everything new and beautiful for the new bride. Surely it seems to me that what was good enough for my mamma might have answered for Jean Murray.

The children provoke me so; they seem altogether delighted with this new toy; but children all live in the present; I sometimes wish I could too. I wonder how mamma would like me to act! I am sure, if she can see us, she would not like to think that we had all forgotten her, and allowed her to be supplanted in our hearts, as well as in papa's, and our home. No! I must be true to her in spite of everything. Yes; in spite even of the loss of dear papa's affection, which I see will be the consequence. The evening he came I saw, as he got out of the carriage, that he was so anxious to see how I would conduct myself; and it seems to me this perverse spirit, which has possession of me, made me as cold as a stone to him first, and then to his wife. Now, surely, there was no necessity for that,—I ought to have been affection-

( 30 )

ate to him; but, oh! to see him that way with a wife beside him, just seemed to bring mamma up out of her grave,—she rose up before me as plainly as in life. I know Mrs. Holcombe saw it all, she was looking so happy when the carriage drove up, and she turned quite pale; but papa turned away from me, and put his arm around her and led her in,—and in another moment, I have no doubt, she forgot my existence. And, oh! her childish delight with everything, Mary herself could not have been more demonstrative; I think it is so undignified to express so much. It was, " Oh, how beautiful! how bright! how lovely! how kind! how comfortable!" at every step. And there was even old Mammy, deceitful old thing, bowing and scraping and doing the honors, and papa looking as if she was the most enchanting thing that ever had lived,—and the children dancing round,— even Lilias chirping her delight from her chair,—until I was sick of it all, and ran off to indulge in a few tears in my own room.

When I went down to tea, there were more aggrava- tions: in the first place, there she sat at the head of the table, trying to look diffident, and as if she was not old enough to have poured out tea any number of years, and papa, with not a ray of recollection of the past in his face, looking perfectly happy. It made me sick, but no one cared if I was,—no one even saw that my eyes were red. It is a great misfortune to have such keen sensibilities, one suffers so much less when they can forget. Once during tea *she* turned to me and said, with such a would-be sweet air, " I suppose, Margaret, I have you to thank for the arrangement of my beautiful room; it does you great credit." I said, " You are mistaken, madam; I have not even seen it. I suppose Mrs. Bascombe and Mammy did it." I felt papa's eyes on me reproachfully, but I did not look that way, and no one said anything more. Of course she thinks I am very rude, but I was obliged to be truthful, and besides, I do not think she ought to have expected me to fix for her. She must think I am quite destitute of feeling.

I think she has a great deal of taste in dress, everything she wears is of such soft, pretty colors. This morning she came out, looking really pretty, in a flowing, white Cashmere morning-dress, with blue trimmings. Never mind, my lady, by the time you have to come out and go down to the dairy, and skim the cream and attend to the butter, and see the chickens fed, etc., you will get out of your white Cashmere and blue trimmings. It does me good to think of the time when a calico wrapper and white apron will be more suitable. Never mind, when I am married I shall not marry a farmer, to be a slave to his negroes. I will marry a lawyer and live in town. And I am going to have beautiful clothes,—I think crimson will suit me better than blue, I have so little color. I wish I was beautiful! I would rather be beautiful than anything else. What difference does it make about a woman's having sense, every one admires the pretty ones most? Never mind, maybe I will be like the ugly duck, and turn out a swan at last.

I had a chance of making *her* feel badly once again to-day. Mary came running in with a writing-desk, crying, " Oh, Margie, just look what mamma has brought you! just the very thing you wanted." I said, " Take it back, Mary, and tell your mamma I would rather not take it; she had better give it to you." I did not find the satisfaction in this that I expected, because I did want the writing-desk dreadfully, and really could have cried when I saw Mary with it afterwards; and then, too, they brought a quantity of delicious-looking candy; but I would not touch it. Now, if I have a weakness in the world it is for candy, particularly sugar-almonds, and it required a great deal of self-denial not to take some; but of course I should despise myself if I could be inconsistent or submit to a bribe. But, oh! I would give anything if papa would only show me some attention,—if he would only see how I suffer; but he does not. To be sure, he kisses as usual, but there is a constraint about him, and it makes me very miserable; but of course I cannot give up. I heard them talking to-day about the arrangements for us. Papa is going to employ a tutor, and Mrs. Bascombe is to be deposed, but retained as an assistant for this new angel who has just come down from heaven into our midst. My poor mamma never had an assistant, she had to do everything herself; but she was worth two such as this one. I tell you, a woman had better hold on to her life if she don't want to be forgotten.

She remonstrated a little about having any one to help her; but papa said, "You know, *dear*, you are not accustomed to our Virginia country-life, and you would be lost in the maze of things to be done. One day would settle you, I think. By the time Aunt Peggy has run after the food for the chickens, and Bob has been to see if he must kill that calf, and Sucky to 'git out the clof to mek dem boys' cloths,' and Mammy to suggest that you go down and see what ails Chloe's baby, and I put in my tongue about having my dinner ready in time, and the children——" but she put her hand over his mouth, and laughed so gleefully that I almost forgot, and joined her. Papa is so funny, he can talk so exactly like each one of the servants; but I was determined not to be surprised again, so I got up and went out, and left the young people to have their play out, though I should really have enjoyed hearing papa talk longer. I believe I would think she was right sweet if she was not what she is.

We are going to have quite a round of gayety, I believe, in honor of the bride. I wonder they are not all ashamed of themselves,—they used to pretend to be so devoted to mamma. Carriages have been rolling up all day. It seems to me that the whole of C—— must have called. Mrs. Campbell,—I expected that,—then the Grahams, the Tuckers, the Clarkes, the Dandridges, etc. I did not know there were so many carriages in C——. I looked as miserable as I could, until I heard that hateful Sarah Clarke whisper, "Did you ever see such an ill-tempered face? I think it is well Mrs. Holcombe did not see her before she accepted the position; it might have altered matters." After that I went up-stairs, and stayed by myself until Mammy brought me some cake and cordial. I did not ask who sent it, as I wanted it so much; and if *she* had, I could not have eaten it, of course. It is rather a melancholy thought that I am to live this way all my life; but it is not my fault. I cannot ever be very certain what mamma would wish. At any rate, I have begun this way, and I must keep on. So it is no use to torment myself about the right and wrong of it. I was born under an unlucky star, and so will always be miserable; and I might as well make up my mind to it.

# CHAPTER V.

## "MARY HOLCOMBE, LADIES AND GENTLEMEN."

*December* 15*th.* Mamma wants me to keep a diary.
She says it will improve me in every respect. She says
that a diary is not meant for anybody to see but myself;
that it is a turning my heart inside out. She says that I
must put into my diary everything I think; and, if I am
very particular never to put anything I do not really
think, it will help me to be true to myself, because I
would not like to put anything down in writing as my
real feeling, and then talk another way. I don't know how
to say it exactly; but she made it very plain to me that
if I was true to myself I would be true to everybody
else, and a diary is to be a help to me. I told her I
did not know how to begin; and she says she thinks I
might talk a little about myself as far back as I remember; that it will be interesting to me, hereafter, to read
over what I did and thought when I was a little child. I
have not had a very interesting childhood, except mamma's death. I never was very ill, that I remember. Nobody
was ever very unkind to me, though Mrs. Bascombe did
use to scold Johnny and me right much sometimes when
we would go off to the woods and play instead of getting
our lessons; but I don't think reading these kind of
things would be very interesting to me when I get a
woman, as it would only make me remember that I had
not been a very good child, which would not be pleasant.
I think I should like to write a little about mamma's

death. I shall always remember that, though, without
any help from anything. It happened three years ago,
and I was such a little thing, which I suppose is the
reason I did not know it was going to happen,—for she
had been sick for a long time. I did not know anything
much about death, though I saw that little baby of Aunt
Holly's die down at the cabins; but it just looked to me
as if it was asleep.

Well, I used to take mamma's breakfast to her every
morning, and Johnny and I would sit by her while she
ate it. I saw how pale and thin she was growing, and
how her pretty rings would slip backward and forward
on her hand, and then she could not get up out of bed at
all. And then that night that Mammy came and woke
us up out of our sleep and took us into her room, and she
was lying there so pale, with her eyes so big and bright,
and papa was holding her up on his arm, and Margie was
sobbing and crying by the bed, and all the servants were
crying, too. I did not know what it all meant at first,
until she said, so low we could hardly hear, "My little
children, you will soon have no mother; God is going
to take me to heaven to live with Him; you must all be
good children and try and meet me there,—and don't
forget to be good, obedient children to your father, and
love and take care of our dear little Lilias." Then she
kissed us all, and Johnny and myself cried so that we had
to be taken out and put to bed, and Mammy told us in
the morning that mamma was dead; and when we saw
her she was lying so still, with flowers in her white hand;
but I did not feel as if it was my mamma, and was afraid
to touch her, and we never have seen her since.

After that Mrs. Bascombe came to take care of us and
teach us; but it was not like mamma did. Papa says
Johnny and I have been running wild, and I expect we

have. I know I wish I was a boy, it is such a trouble to be a girl, and have to have skirts hanging round you all the time; I never can go out with Johnny without tearing something, and once I was very much hurt by my dress catching on the limb of a tree and throwing me down. Mrs. Bascombe says it was a mercy I was not killed, and all the fault of these skirts. I used to beg Mammy to let me wear Johnny's pants sometimes; but she was very much shocked and said it was unlady-like, and the *Bible* said I must not do it, so I suppose I shall have to keep a girl to the end of my life.

I don't think it will be so hard now I have a new mamma. I like to stay in the house better, and so does Johnny, though he would not speak to her at first; but he loves her now very much. When Margie told me first that papa was going to bring home a new mamma for us, I don't think I was very glad,—it seemed so dreadful to have two mammas; but then I thought how much we all needed some one to take care of us, and I thought papa would not do it if it was not best; and then he told us how sweet she was, and how she would love us all, and so I liked it before she came, and now I love her dearly.

But, oh! Margie behaves so badly, I think; she won't have anything to do with her,—just stays in her own room all the time. And the day after she came, when I took her a beautiful new writing-desk mamma had brought her, she said, so crossly, "She would not have it; I might take it back and tell her to give it to me." I did not like to go back, it seemed so ungrateful in Margie; but at last I had to do it, and tell her what she said. I saw the tears come into her eyes; and papa, who was in there, was very angry, and said he must speak to Margie about the way she was behaving; but mamma caught him by the arm ,and said, "Dear, for my sake, don't do

4

it; leave her alone, she will get over it after awhile : she is suffering now you may depend upon it, poor child; all will come right after awhile." And he kissed her and said she was the blessing of his life,—then she gave the writing-desk to me, and I am writing on it now.

I wish Margie would not do so, she looks so unhappy, and mamma tried so to make us happy,—it is the only thing which keeps us from being so. She sits at the table and never speaks a word, and will not even eat what mamma is helping to. I can see that papa is so angry sometimes; but his promise to mamma keeps him from speaking.

We are to have a gentleman teacher the first of next month, and I am to begin Latin with Johnny, and Eddy and George Holcombe are to come here to school. They are to come with their father and mother at Christmas. Papa is determined to have a family meeting ; I know it is just to show mamma to them all, he is so proud of her,—we will have a nice time I know.

Mamma is so kind to little Lilias, she has had her little bed put in her room, and every night she undresses her and rocks her in her lap. Lilias remembered that mamma used to do that, and asked her if she would. I am sure if our dear mamma can see us from her home in heaven, she is glad that her poor little children have some one to take care of and love them.

It was funny to see how shy Johnny was at first; if mamma spoke to him his face would get red, and he would look as if he wanted to run away ; but since she gave him the pretty-colored ball and the candy he liked to stay with her. I don't mean he liked her for what she gives him, exactly, but that certainly did begin it.

Mammy likes mamma, too; she said at first, when she heard papa was going to be married, she was sorry ;

but now she knows "the Lord sent her here to take care of Miss Catherine's children." Mamma is from the North of England, and that is the way her name comes to be Jean. She was named after her Scottish grandmother. I wish, some of these days, she would tell me something about her life over there. I wonder if the little children play with doll-babies as they do over in this country,—I reckon not, though, way over in England. I don't expect they ever heard of doll-babies.

I think mamma is very good; she went down on Sunday to the negro quarters and read to the people. I went with her, and she did look so pretty and nice in her soft, blue dress, and with her pretty light hair, among the black people. They looked blacker, and she looked whiter, than usual; they sang one of their hymns for her, and she looked right scared when they holloed out so loud; it sounded like they were going to take the top off of the cabin; and then Uncle Armstead prayed and the people cried, and I was scared too. After that mamma and I came away, and she said so seriously, as if she had been thinking of it before she spoke, "And yet the spirit of God may be as truly there as within marble walls." I asked her what she thought of the way they did, and she said, " It seems very strange to me, dear, because I never saw anything of the kind before ; but I shall get used to it after awhile ; some things puzzle me very much." She did not tell me what they were, though I longed to ask.

Well, I have written a long piece in my diary, and I have forgotten to divide the days as I write. I commenced December 15th, and this is December 20th, so I have been five days. I think I will like it very much, though I find it so hard to say what I want. Mamma says I need language and this will help me to acquire it. Margie has been keeping a diary for four or five years ;

but she is a great deal smarter than I am. I wish I knew what she writes about. I am so glad next week my aunts, uncles, and cousins will be here. I think mamma is not altogether glad,—she is a little afraid. I do not wonder; it must be dreadful to have a parcel of people you never saw come to look at you and see if they like you. I am afraid I should run off in the woods with Johnny and hide; that is the way we used to do when we knew Mrs. Bascombe was going to scold us.

# CHAPTER VI.

## LETTER FROM JEAN TO HER BROTHER.

"DEAR ROBERT,—I have been intending to write to you ever since my arrival in my new home, but have been too much engaged with my introduction to my new duties, and becoming acquainted not only with the members of my own household, but my neighbors, among whom I shall find, I think, some very pleasant acquaintances.

"I only wish, dear Robert, you could be here with me, even with my husband by my side. I want some of my own kindred. Just to think, since Aunt Jean's death, there is not a drop of my blood in the veins of any human being on this side of the Atlantic. I am sorry I said that, on my own account. It is a strange, sad view of the case, which never struck me so forcibly as at this moment, and such floods of loneliness rush upon me that they threaten to overwhelm me. In the midst of husband, children, and friends, I am utterly alone; and though I would not exchange my lot with any human being in the world,—I am as happy as I can be, and have so much to be thankful for,—yet there is a void, an aching want; it is as if the hands of my heart were stretching across the barriers of time and space, and I cry out for some link to my childhood, some one to whom I could say, 'Do you remember?'

"My husband, in his tender kindness and watchfulness, sees all this, and feels for me. He unites with me in

4*                                    ( 41 )

earnest entreaty, that you will come to see me. If you only would; and, oh! if I could hope that father would come too,—that I should ever see him again! It was a cruel necessity which banished me from my home, though I would not have it different. And you will smile when I tell you that the reason I have for being willing to look upon my sufferings as a blessing in disguise is, that if I had remained at 'Glen Burnie' I should never have seen Mr. Holcombe. Don't be alarmed, I am not going to be sentimental.

"I know you want to know how I am situated, etc. Well, my home is beautiful, but not at all like 'Glen Burnie.' My early associations are of lovely valleys, murmuring streams, and plays under sheltering hills. But now I have gone up into the clouds. I seem to overlook everything. The place is perfectly beautiful. Mr. Holcombe's first wife must have been a person of a great deal of taste, as the grounds are laid off beautifully. Mr. Holcombe himself takes the greatest pride in it. I tell him that I believe the strongest feeling of his nature is for this home. But he says no,—wife and children come first, then Rose Hill. Have you ever tried to imagine, Robert, your little Jean acting mamma to four children? I cannot tell you how well I do it, but I wish you would come and give me the testimony of an eyewitness. Strange to say, they have their places in my heart already.

"Margaret, the eldest, is fifteen. I do not know her so well as the others, she is more shy with me, does not reconcile herself to my being here so readily. I suppose because she is older and has a more vivid recollection of her own mother. She is not pretty, and yet there is a strange interest about her. Her face is full of intellect, hidden feeling, and undeveloped sentiment. She gives vent to it now with all the exaggeration of her years; but as time rolls on and separates in her mind the true from the false, the real from the seeming,—when she is able to define clearly to herself what her real sentiments and feelings are, she will develop into no ordinary woman. This I learn from her face, for I have had very little intercourse with her, and have not yet been able to break the barrier of ice which surrounds her whenever I approach, or attempt to approach, the citadel of her heart.

"Mary, the second, is a bright, beautiful little sprite, an Adrienne de Cardoville in appearance, an untamed, but not untamable, gazelle-like child, full of warm feelings and fine impulses, and very much devoted to 'mamma.'

"John, my only son, is decidedly a diamond in the rough. You would call him a *cub.* I say he is like most boys of ten I have seen, who think more of animal gratification than anything else, and the road to whose heart lies straight through their stomachs; he has good material to work upon, and plenty of will and energy, a perfect boy in taste and feeling, even to the feeling of superiority to our sex.

"But Lilias, the little flower hanging on a broken stalk, has taken the tenderest hold on my heart. She will never walk, Robert, owing to an injury to her spine, caused by a fall. She is often a great sufferer, though they tell me for months she seems well; languor, however, she suffers from always, and she is utterly dependent upon the tenderness of those around her; a cross word spoken even to another makes her so tremulous that she has to be soothed into quietness again. The night I got here I had her in my arms, and she whispered, 'Will you undress me, and rock me, as my own mamma used to do?' No one heard her, and I established myself as head nurse at once; and truly it has been a labor of

love.    I unswathe the poor feeble little frame every night,
and with the pale little cheek close against my heart, I
sing to her lullabies our mother used to sing to us.    And
in that hour she always seems to come back and sit with
me there; it is almost my sweetest hour during the day.
Of course, all remonstrate against my taking this duty
upon myself, but I would not resign it to any one in the
world.

"The most important person in the family, not excepting
Mr. Holcombe, I think, is the old Mammy.    I believe her
name is Judy, though she is never called anything but
'Mammy.'

"Imagine a very ugly old woman—yes, she is certainly,
though I should not like to say so to Mr. Holcombe, and
I really believe the children think she is beautiful—with
the blackest face you ever saw, surmounted by a turban
of bright-colored cotton.    A dress of striped linsey-
woolsey, with a check apron, and a white cotton handkerchief pinned across her breast.    Mr. H. says she has
nursed the past two generations, and played with our
grandmothers; and certainly they do reward her for it.
She only does what she pleases, which is to rub the silver
and darn the stockings, and occasionally to do up a piece
of lace or muslin.    But if there is a spell of sickness in
the family, she is never known to sleep.    Of course, he
says, she must, but it is sitting by the bedside of the
patient.    No office is beyond her there.    She takes the
whole duties upon herself.    When Mr. Holcombe's
mother died, one of her last requests was that, when
Mammy's time came, she should have a neat coffin, and
a hearse, and be carried to the grave by the children she
has been so faithful to.    He says she was delighted, as
there is nothing they think so much of as a 'pretty
burying.'    Their habits in this respect, by-the-by, are

very funny. My maid, on Sunday last, asked permission
to go to the funeral of her father, who had been dead
sixteen years! They seem to keep these little last offices
until there is a danger of their forgetting their friends,
and then call them back to memory by having *the
funeral*. Is it not strange? But what strikes me is the
numbers there are about the house. Think of having six
women for a family of eight or nine people, and that is
besides the washerwoman and the cook! I have my
maid, who is to do nothing but my pleasure. Lilias has
her nurse, who is always at hand, either sitting by her
with her work or pushing her chair. Margaret and Mary
have their maid; and then there is another who cleans
the house generally; and a little girl to run on errands;
and, besides, there is a man in the dining-room, with a
boy to help him.

"Will I ever get used to these black people? They
are a continual source of wonder to me. The grown ones
are bad enough, but the children are worse. They look
like monkeys. They have all the characteristics of the
negro race unmodified. I wonder if it is mentioned as a
fact in their natural history that their features do not
grow after six years of age; for it seems to me the lips,
noses, and eyes of the children of that age have attained
their full size, and gradually afterward the body grows up
to them. It seems so dreadful for them to be slaves,
worth so much money apiece,—as if money could buy a
human soul. But, after all, the fault does not lie with
this generation, but with those who put them here. We
have just to accept and submit to the fearful responsibility
imposed upon us by our forefathers; there seems no other
way out of the difficulty. To free them now, of course,
would be impossible: such a number of ignorant, helpless wretches, thrown upon our country in a condition of

freedom, would be a curse to both races. It seems to me that, from the present state of things, the master is a greater sufferer than the servant,—here, in Virginia, at any rate. Now, Mr. Holcombe has over fifty men, women, and children. The men do the hardest work in the fields; the women the lighter services, and the cooking, washing, and sewing for the 'hands;' while the children, until they are about twelve years old, are useless and expensive appendages, having to be supported without bringing any profit into the concern. I have been surprised to see how comfortably they are provided for. Their cabins, though rough, are perfectly weathertight and comfortable: the fireplaces almost the width of the end of the houses, and the wide chimneys admitting floods of light all around. It is a scene for a painter to go into one of these places, and see the multitudes of children seated *inside* of the fireplaces upon benches put along the sides, and there the little woolly-heads nod and bob until it is a wonder they are not burned up. But oh, Robert, the wood! You see them bringing entire uncut logs for these fireplaces; and a good fire consists of a moderate sized wood-pile.

"I had an amusing incident last Sunday. I asked Mr. Holcombe if no one ever read to them. He said his mother used to, and his wife also, when she was well enough; and I think he was very much pleased when I said I would follow in their footsteps. So, accompanied by Johnny and Mary, I sallied forth to the negro quarters, where my services were to be held, notice having been issued to that effect and the dining-bell rung to assemble the congregation. I was to officiate in Uncle Armstead's cabin, being one of the largest, and he, being a sort of preacher, was to assist at the services.

"I am sure no stage-panic was ever more fright-

ful than mine when I went into the midst of my con-
venticle. The room was crowded with men, women, and
children, of all ages, sizes, and colors, varying from the
light mulatto to the deepest ebony. Then the dressing!
One young girl, as black as the ace of spades, was dressed
in muslin as white as the snow on the ground, with low
neck and short sleeves.˙ Each one seemed to have honored the occasion with all the finery in her possession.
As I went to my seat, which was ·fixed˙ for me at one
end of the room, I could hear from all sides, ' God bless
her !' ' Our pretty young mistis,' ' Don't she look sweet?'
etc. etc. At first I thought I should have to play coward
and run away; but at last I found courage to proceed,
and asked Uncle Armstead if they would sing. Oh, Robert, if you could have heard that singing ! It frightened
me so in its first burst that I thought I would never rally.
Uncle Armstead would first repeat, in a rapid sing-song
tone, ' When I can read my *titel clare*,' and, running from
the last word directly back to the first, he would lead the
whole choir in singing it, and then, with great rapidity,
take up the second line,—

' To manshuns in the skies.'

It was all indescribable, to see them rock themselves
backward and forward, roll up their eyes until you could
see nothing but the whites, and in tones in which the
nasal decidedly predominated, follow their leader. There
were two figures among the women who particularly
attracted my attention : one, a tall, raw-boned speci-
men of the race, whose voice was like the sound of a
Scotch bagpipe, or the buzzing of twenty hives of bees;
it certainly had the merit of volume and eccentricity. I
never heard its like before, and do not care if I never do
again. She was dressed in all the colors of the rainbow,
but red predominated, prevailing in the head-handkerchief

and shawl, on which she seemed to pride herself particularly. She had, too, a voluminous white pocket-handkerchief, the possession of which article of dress accounted probably for her being easily moved to tears during the reading and prayer which followed, in which the handkerchief was called in requisition very frequently. This person I learned, in answer to a whispered inquiry of Mary, was Aunt Milly, and the other was Aunt Elsie. She must have seen her threescore years and ten, as it is impossible to conceive an older face than she wore; the skin had shriveled away from the negro features, leaving them hideously prominent, and she gave a dreadful accompaniment of groans to the entire services. What annoyed me with both of these demonstrative hearers was that they made the air wail with their dismal sounds at the most touchingly-comforting passages. They seemed in such distress that I purposely chose this style; but they refused to be comforted, and wept and groaned until I did not know what to do.

"At last my duties were over, and I asked Uncle Armstead to close with a prayer. Oh, Robert, the singing was wonderful, but nothing to that prayer! His voice must have reached half a mile; he had collected trite and familiar passages, not only from the Psalms, but from church prayers, and some, I cannot tell where he got them. These he strung together, with very little connection and not much meaning. He prayed for all the white people, his master, and then came my turn. 'God in mercy bress our dear young mistis, who is a ministering to us this day, that she may see herself as she is a standing on the prickly precipices of hell.'

"I must have smiled if I had not been on my knees; but it was a proper lesson in humility for me. Here I thought that I was going to be looked upon in the light of a saint,

and in what a position did I find myself! I confess I was
mortified. You ought to have heard Mr. Holcombe laugh
when I told him. I thought he would never stop.
'Why,' he said, 'Jean, old Armstead thought 'he was
paying you the greatest compliment. The expression had
struck him as an eloquent touch from some admired
prayer, and he laid it at your feet. He never thought of
its full meaning.' And then he began to laugh again until
I too joined him with hearty good will. So ended my first
services in public. I certainly shall never forget the experience; but it has done me good. It may be that God
is as truly present to those poor creatures, with all their
ignorance and simplicity, as in the marble temple where
Dives and the Pharisee go to pray; and when we get
to heaven some of us may find Uncle Armstead, and
Aunt Milly, and Elsie, with a place nearer to God's
throne than ourselves, and we may feel honored to have
a seat even a little below them; certainly, though, one has
a missionary field in such a place as this. May it not be
that this was the end which God intended in placing the
cursed descendants of Ham in this situation, that they too
might receive the good news of salvation in this their land
of bondage?

"Mr. Holcombe says he has studied colonization with a
view to his own negroes, and if he could have seen any
way of bettering their condition he would have sent them
to Liberia long ago, as he should consider himself much
better off without them; but all inquiries tended to confirm the fact that nine-tenths of those thus colonized have
gone back to barbarism. So he cares for them to the best
of his ability until the Almighty sees fit to lift the burden
from his shoulders. He has never bought or sold one,
and, like Abraham in the Scriptures, has had all he has
born on his own land.

"Well, dear Robert, I have written you a long letter, and have not told you half I had to say. My life is so full now that I have no lack of material with which to fill my letters. We are to have a family gathering here, next week, for the purpose of introducing me to my new friends and relations. I desire it and dread it, I don't know which most; but if they are only like my husband I know I will love them.

"I only wish you were here. I am afraid I shall feel more alone than ever.

"Give more love to my dear father than the space I leave would hold, and remember me kindly to his wife. I can feel for her now more than of old, because 'a fellow-feeling makes us wondrous kind;' but I hope I will never be the means of exiling one of my husband's children from his roof.

"Believe me, dear, darling brother, your devoted sister,

"JEAN HOLCOMBE."

# CHAPTER VII.

## A FAMILY GATHERING.

IT is a beautiful custom which sets apart one day in the year on which the whole world may rejoice in the advent of the Saviour of mankind; a day redeemed from the cold and gloom of the winter season, like the hope which his coming sheds upon, what would without it be, the midnight darkness of our lives.

And God himself seems to set his sanction upon it by implanting in each heart an added feeling of gladness. Dark indeed must be the home which does not brighten at the approach of Christmas, and empty indeed must be the purse which cannot gild the day with a token of remembrance.

These festival days in a family circle keep the torch of brotherly love burning brightly,—they link us to our childhood; and it is a touchingly tender sight to see the remaining members of a family circle of the passing generation—men and women—meeting together to spend another Christmas under the old homestead, throwing aside the cares and toils of working every-day life, and living over again the days gone by, with smiles which would be merry but for the gleam of sadness in them,— the tribute which memory pays to the full and filling heads of grain which have gone down beneath the reapers' scythes.

Such a family gathering we will witness in a Virginia

home, in the midst of the hoary heads of the old Blue Ridge Mountains.

Like the woman in the Bible who lost her piece of silver, when it was found "called her friends and neighbors together to rejoice that she had found the piece which was lost," so Mr. Holcombe, thanking God for the new blessing which had come to his heart and home, called his friends together to be glad with him; and the little wife and mother, so happy in her new relations, feeling that upon her rested the happiness of so many, grew lighter under the pleasant burden, and tasked herself to remember what could add to the pleasure of each one. Morning, noon, and night, the busy brain and hands were at work devising and executing. With Mrs. Bascombe's help, the larder groaned under the abundant preparations. Mrs. Leslie, Mrs. Randolph, and old cookery-books of renown were the ruling literature of the day. Jean saw herself developing into a distinguished Virginia housewife. Her ambition in this department was wonderful. The most impossible dishes were attempted with brilliant success. The parlor and chamber were deserted during the day for the storeroom and kitchen, and if Mr. Holcombe wanted to see his wife he had to look for her there, and find her a devotee to cooking,— false to him, and utterly enamored of her new successes.

"Jean, come up-stairs and talk to me,—it is so tiresome in you to spend your whole time down in this hole."

"Oh, Mr. Holcombe, just taste this jelly! Is it not perfectly delicious? And see the icing on this cake. Mammy did it,—ain't she a treasure? and Mrs. Bascombe is making the most delicious——"

"I don't care what Mrs. Bascombe and Mammy do; but you are to come up-stairs with me. I might just as well have married a cook at once. Dolly is much better at it than you will ever be, and I would rather she would cook my dinners."

"You cross old thing! Never mind, you can't do without me, anyhow," was the happy, exulting answer, as she was borne off bodily up-stairs, to the great glee of servants and children.

These were merry times for all, but particularly for the little ones, who, contrasting the season with those which had preceded it, when they, a little motherless brood, clustered around the empty hearth, with no one to lead them in their mirth, were now wild with delight at the preparations made for their happiness. There were sly glimpses into the closet up in "mamma's" room, and the wonderful visions of beauty caught through the half-open door furnished conjecture enough for happiness, which came in floods to all but one brooding heart, nursing in silence a morbid sickness of the soul, jealously putting away happiness with one hand whilst she grasped at her shadowy sorrow with the other,—constituting in her home the "skeleton in the closet," the "fly in the apothecary's ointment;" in the midst of their pleasures, causing an uncomfortable feeling in the hearts of each,—a vague longing to do something to banish the cloud.

Many times would Mr. Holcombe have spoken plainly to her of her wantonness in thus trifling with her life; but the timid, gentle little Jean held him back, because she feared being the cause of disagreement between father and daughter, and would not have herself rudely thrust into the heart of her husband's child. She trusted that as "the continual dropping of water weareth away the hard stone," so her constant acts of kindness and forbearance would at last have the desired effect; and, with her cheerfulness of temper, she saw herself, in the future, rewarded for her endurance of this hard trial, by seeing this child, in whom, in spite of herself, she felt so deep an interest, taking her place too in the domestic circle, and, by her graces and accomplishments, filling up the vacuum her present mood created.

This was well meant, but mistaken kindness. It is never best to heal over a wound on the top, while below, the festering cancer spreads and deepens for lack of an outlet. A few words of kind and gentle firmness, a probing it to the bottom, might have healed what at first was so slight a hurt; but each day increased it, and built up the barrier between herself and her family higher, and the unhappiness,—which at first was more the wayward jealousy of a child, the sentimental nursing of an idea, common at her age,—now began to have substance; for, by her own act, she had cut herself off from the members of her household, and had no place in her father's home. But even she, though in a much less degree, felt pleasant anticipations at the approach of Christmas, because she, too, would welcome with pleasure the arrival of her uncles, aunts, and young cousins; it promised some variety in the enforced monotony of her life.

Accordingly, on the day before Christmas, after the carriages and wagons and everything had been started to the depot for the travelers, she crept down into the parlor with a brighter look upon her face than she had worn for a long time; and Mr. Holcombe, heralding it as a good sign, greeted her with his old tone of hearty affection. Her face brightened anew under the familiar tones, and with some of her old impulse she returned his caresses, and, for a time, was almost like herself, and looked around with surprise and pleasure at the adornments of the room, the festoons of evergreen interspersed with the red berries of the holly, and the bouquets of scarlet sage and bright chrysanthemum. A great deal of taste had been displayed in the entire arrangement of the two parlors; and as Mary and John eagerly recounted how busy they had been, helping mamma, and how Uncle Bob had taken the wagon out to the woods and brought back such beautiful evergreens, a pang of regret that she had missed it all made her wince, and brought back the moody cloud to her face, which was quickly dispersed, however, as the sound of carriage-wheels broke upon their ears, and the whole party adjourned hastily to the piazza to welcome the travelers.

# CHAPTER VIII.

*December 26th.* This has certainly been the very happiest and merriest season of my life. I wish I could be inspired for the nonce that I might transcribe my account of it in such graphic terms that it might always be recalled to my mind with the vividness of the present impression.

These people are so different from any I have ever been accustomed to. I thought Mr. Holcombe possessed his heartiness of manner as a peculiarity, a special gift, but I find I was mistaken; it seems to be a family trait. Now imagine my astonishment when my husband said " Here is my wife, George,"—and I had just prepared my sweetest smile, and made up my mind to surrender at discretion if he *insisted* upon meeting me with a brotherly salute,—to find myself fairly taken into his arms, and embraced with the same enthusiasm as if he recognized in me a sister to the manner born from whom he had been separated for many years; and he had scarcely released me with burning cheeks, before I was handed over to a dear little lady,—my sister Annie, Mrs. Mason,—who welcomed me with " Well, my dear, now it is my time; we won't allow George the monopoly." And then came Mrs. Randolph (Mary), quite young looking, with the remains of considerable beauty. And her husband, a handsome man, but decidedly more formal than the rest

( 56 )

of the family; then came claimant after claimant for
" Aunt Jean ! Aunt Jean !" until the poor little woman felt
perfectly bewildered and soon saw nothing but a crowd
of figures all bleared together.   From this I was rescued
by a soft hand which I afterwards found to belong to
Cynthia Marshall, my. sister Annie's youngest daughter,
who is married to a young lawyer of Richmond, and is the
triumphant possessor of the only baby in the party; besides, there is Mary Mason, a fine, bright-looking woman,
about my own age I should judge; Ellen Randolph, about
the age of Margaret, and two sons of Mr. George Holcombe.   What a party to be introduced to all at once !
But, thanks to their kindness, in half an hour I knew
them all, and loved them, too. · My two sisters attracted
me particularly; they seemed to see at a glance the
embarrassment of my position, and kind, motherly sister
Annie was by my side, with my hand·in hers, talking
about "the boys," meaning, as I soon found, *her brothers,*
as if they had been children.   She is much the eldest
of the family, and more like a mother than a sister to
the others; then sister Mary, with her pretty young
face, looking more like the sister than the mother of her
pretty young daughter.

Brother George is younger than my husband, and
somewhat like him, but not so good looking in my opinion; they all think him a great genius.   He is the literary man of the family, and writes beautifully ! I confess
to being a little afraid of him, both because I know he
will think me so very stupid, and because he looks to me
as if he was going to tease me all the time, as he does
the others; but I suppose he feels sorry for me, and
spares me. I told Mr. Holcombe, privately, that I was
very glad he was not a genius ; at which he seemed, or
rather pretended, to be vastly offended, and protested that

he had laid claims successfully to the character all his life, and now saw himself suddenly stripped of his hard-won honors by his own wife; and think of his telling on me at the table, and demanding the sympathy of his family! It was too bad. I almost felt like crying.

Cynthia Marshall is a bright, happy little thing. She is so distressed that her husband could not come,—proud young matron that she is, she thinks everything incomplete without him.

"Have you learned to manage Uncle Ned yet, Aunt Jean?" she said, as we sat together after tea. I disclaimed any such intention.

"Pshaw!" said she, laughing, "I don't believe that; every woman tries it, and most of them succeed. Men are so easily fooled: a little extra petting, and the day is carried. Now my husband is so sweet-tempered I have a very small field for the exercise of my prowess. He has but one weakness in the world, and that is—*lard.*"

There was a general laugh, and cries for an explanation; so Cynthia took the floor.

"Everybody that has kept house at all knows how quickly lard goes—it just seems to melt; particularly in winter, when so much is used in cooking. Well, I don't know what Charles thinks I do with it; but he certainly crumples up his forehead and looks very black when I tell him 'the lard is out;' and I am so much afraid of the consequences that now I watch the firkin with the greatest anxiety, and scrape the sides very diligently, before I admit to myself that it is out. And then comes the breaking it to Charles,—I assure you, mamma, it takes me a whole day to prepare for it. I dress my room up in the most attractive manner,—put a white counterpane on the bed and my ruffled pillow-cases,—have the brightest sort of fire kindled on the hearth, flare open all the

window-shutters,—because, like all men, he delights in a
glare of light; then I have the most tempting dinner prepared, with his favorite dessert (he is a perfect baby
about sweet things), I get out the best china and silver,
and my company table-cloth and napkins; when all is
exactly right, I dress myself in my most becoming dress,
with blue ribbons generally, because blue is his color;
and, after surveying myself in the glass, with the same
pride and confidence with which a general would view a
well-disciplined army, I find myself prepared for action.
As soon as I hear his step in the street, I rush to meet
him with my brightest smile of welcome, don't let him
wait one moment for his dinner, listen in the most interested manner to his dull details of business,—what the
judge said,—what this witness said, and that witness
said,—all ending in how he ought to have gained his case
and how he did not; but I comfort him until the crumples
are all smoothed out of his forehead, and then wile him
up-stairs, get his slippers for him, make him lie down
while I comb his head; and after I have wound him up
to the seventh heaven of delight, I whisper in his ear,
'Oh, honey, the lard is out!' He sees through all
my manœuvres then, but he has not the heart to scold,
so he laughs his merriest laugh, and says, 'By George,
Cynthia, it does go quickly!' But he is getting so
smart now I will have to fall on some other plan;
for whenever he comes home and finds me a little fixed
up, he throws up his hands, and says, 'You need not tell
me, my dear—I know the lard is out!' But baby is waiting to be put to bed; so, Aunt Jean, I leave you to digest
my matrimonial experiences for your own benefit." And
off she ran, leaving a great laugh behind her at her story.

Her mother says she is as happy as she can be, though
Charles is by no means rich, and Cynthia has to exercise

very close economy in her domestic arrangements; but it
does not seem to trouble her at all. She takes life very
easily, and thinks herself the most fortunate woman in
the world.

Christmas morning had scarcely dawned before I was
wakened by the shouts of the children in the hall, as
they went from door to door, calling "Christmas-gift,"
and compelling Somnus to vacate his throne long before
his abdication was legally due. In an instant I was on
my feet, dressing myself, eager to be ready for their first
summons to me; this I did in spite of Mr. Holcombe's
remonstrances, who grumbled, sleepily, that I was nothing more than a child myself; and indeed I can't think
I was, either. I am sure no one of the children felt a
keener relish than I did for the fun. It seemed such a
change in my lonely, cheerless life. I felt as if I had
just begun to live in earnest; and I am going to take
every enjoyment which God sends me with as much youth
and zest as I can. Indeed, it has been resolved in a
family conclave, the night before, that we should all put
off our years like old garments for the holiday, and
resume our childhood. Brother George said he intended
to ignore all of his years but twelve, and chose the
longest and biggest stocking to hang up for himself,
insisting upon our following his example, until the table
was piled with the well-filled garments. I heard his
voice, with the others, approaching my door, and hurried
my preparations for their reception. Little Lilias was
by this time awake, and as much excited as I was, and
whilst I was dressing had been giving me an animated
description of a visit St. Nicholas had paid her during
the night; and as a proof of the reality of the apparition
she drew out her well-filled stocking from under her
pillow.

Just then I opened my door to join the rioters, and found a crowd of revelers collected outside, foremost among which was a burly figure dressed to represent St. Nicholas, with his long white hair and beard, fur cap and coat, and long snow-boots, with a pack slung over his shoulder, from which protruded the legs and feet of numberless stockings (it had been decided that the gifts should be reserved for the Christmas-tree at night). My appearance was greeted with a huzza. And St. Nicholas, handing over to me a long-legged stocking, chanted, in brother George's voice,—

> "Here's a Christmas greeting for Madam Jean,
> The presiding fairy of the scene."

A renewed shout applauded the impromptu couplet, and St. Nicholas in stentorian tones demanded, "Ned and Lilias Holcombe at my hands." An eager response from Lilias was the answer. And through the half-open door the little flaxen head was seen pushed forward as far as her helplessness would allow.

"Ah! ha! here she is! I knew she would be ready. St. Nicholas left her stocking under her head last night. But who is that lazy hulk who dares to try even to sleep on such a morning as this, when Christmas comes but once a year?" And at once he pounced upon my luckless husband, who, still intent upon his morning nap, had covered up head and ears in a vain attempt to shut out the merry-sounds.

> "And here's my greeting for lazy Ned,
> Who spends Christmas morning lying in bed,"

said the incorrigible St. Nicholas, shaking the recumbent figure with a hearty good will.

"Oh, George, will you have done? Will nothing ever make a man of you?" was the unappreciative response, as

6

a tousled head appeared from beneath the bedclothes and looked around at the crowd in sleepy surprise.

"Will anything ever make a boy of you?" retorted George. "Who wants to be a man when he can be a boy, I wonder? I dare anybody to call me such names on Christmas-day! I am just twelve years old, and very young of my age. Pelt him, boys! He is fair game."

Instantly the whole tribe was on him, until he cried for mercy. Sisters Annie and Mary had joined the group by this time, and Cynthia, with baby in her arms, crowing and laughing in as full enjoyment of the scene as her elders,—even she had her little red sock in her hands, which she was sucking with great enjoyment.

At last, in self-defense, Mr. Holcombe had to promise to get up, if his room was vacated, as he declared this French style of receiving visitors in his bedroom, though it might suit the ladies, was not to his taste.

St. Nicholas then led off his party to the negro quarters, and, after calling nurse to take Lilias into the next room and dress her, I donned my india-rubber shoes and wraps and followed them. I never shall forget the scene. The ground was covered with snow, which glittered under the beams of the sun, and through the unbroken mass tramped these Christmas revelers, their feet crunching through the icy surface at each step. And heading the party was St. Nicholas, looking more than ever in character with the scene. Their numbers were swelled as they went along, and cabin after cabin poured out its contribution to the procession, and "Christmas-gift, marster!" "Christmas-gift, mistis!" resounded on all sides, mingled with exclamations of amazement and wonder as they caught sight of the long white beard and hair of St. Nicholas, with his pack thrown over his shoulders.

"Who's dat ole marster dar? It mus' be Christmas

comin', sho nuf. Well! well! I do bleve it is Mars'
George! It's jist like him. I knowed him jes as soon as
I seed his eye! Christmas-gift, Mars' George!" And
the showers of sugar-plums, which followed the appeal,
established the identity of "Mars' George" completely.
It was too laughable to see the little woolly-heads bob-
bing up and down on the white snow in search of the
missing sugar-plums. At last Mammy's house was
reached, and we found the old lady, with her best turban
and apron on, ready to welcome us, while through the
half-open door we caught the hospitable gleam of a real
Christmas fire. Mammy looked more than ever as if she
was concentrating the entire dignity of her master's family
in her person. Her appearance was picturesque, if not
handsome, as she welcomed us with her lowest curtsy,
and insisted upon our coming in.

"Come in, my dear children, to the fire. You will,
every one of you, cotch cold, and den you will have to
have old Mammy to nus you. But who is dat? Lord,
ef it ain't Mars' George! Bless your heart, honey, what
a figure you dus make of yoursef!"

No one felt disposed to decline the hospitable invitation, as the biting northwest wind made the glow of the
fire very tempting. And in another moment we were
standing around the bright, blazing hearth. A coffeepot
was at our feet, and the steaming contents were soon
presented to us,—Brother George and myself being
honored with cups of fine French china, the remains of
an old set, as she informed us, which her old mistress
used to have, and which she had given to her. And
while we enjoyed the delicious beverage, the old woman
went from one to another of the party, feeling our feet,
to see if we had suffered from the expedition; and Brother
George spent the time, to their mutual enjoyment, in re-

calling other scenes of which this Christmas reminded him; while she stood behind his chair, laughing at his humorous recollections, and no entreaties could induce her to be seated "while the white people was there."

"Law, Mammy," said he, "how this reminds me of the times I used to come down here and eat your breakfast for you after I had finished my own at the house! I always liked yours the best."

"Yes, honey, so you did; but there never was a nigger on your father's place that did not have enough and to spare. And I never lost nothin' by it. You was sure to bring me somethin' before the day was out. There never was a stingy one of the name. And your mother, law! she would have give' the last mouthful she had to keep anybody from bein' hungry."

"Yes, so she would, Mammy; but she used to make everybody stand about."

"Of course! And so she ought. Darkies must be kep' in their places. There wasn't never no marster no mistis any better than mine. But I would jest like to see the nigger that would be darse to give one of them a word of imperence. And all the children was jest like 'em. Why, law! Miss Ann, don't I remember the time that you seed Dolly going out to the wood-pile, when the snow was on the ground, in her bare feet, and you sot down and took off your own shoes and made her put them on. But it wasn't that Dolly didn't have any shoes, but she had left them down at the cabins, 'cause the children never likes to wear they shoes."

"Well, Mammy," said George, winking at me as an intimation that he was drawing her out, "have you got any free negroes round here now?"

"No, thank the Lord, Mars' George; they ain't many of that trash about now; dey ain't no better den poor white folks. I ain't got no use for 'em nohow. Give me a darky what has been brought up by the quality."

"Why, Mammy, Ned and myself want to give you freedom. Would you not like to be free?"

"Free! What I do with free? I been b'long to white folks all my life, and I will die b'longst to 'em. Niggers don' kno' how to take kere of theyselves nohow."

"But, Mammy, there is a fine country you can go to across the ocean, which belongs to black people—*Liberia*. I expect they would make you a queen over there."

"I tell you what, Mars' George, nigger is a very big fool, but not that big, and the niggers in your *Library* can get somebody else for they queen. I ain't never going where I won't see none but black faces. I ain't overly-fond of niggers nohow."

"No, indeed, old lady," said George, as we all rose to go; "and we wouldn't let you go either. The children you have nursed are going to take care of you as long as God lets us; and then we will put a white stone over your grave, with writing on it, to tell how faithful you were to us all. Good-by, Mammy; make haste and come up to the house; I want to drink your health to-day."

And "Good-by, Mammy, good-by, Mammy," was echoed through the crowd, until we lost sight of the old figure standing in the door, looking after us, with her eyes full of tears, while the rest of her face smiled her adieus.

Breakfast as a breakfast was rather a failure this morning, as the young people had dived into their stockings, and looked upon Dolly's flaky rolls and omelets with an expression of disgust born of satiety; and even the older people were too full of talk of old times and present plans to take much interest in so prosaic a matter as the morning meal presented.

The Christmas-tree was to be arranged during the morning, and the two sisters, Mary Mason, Cynthia, and myself formed ourselves into a committee of arrangements; Margaret and Ellen were invited to come with us, but the former refused, haughtily, and Ellen, after casting a longing look at our party, followed her.

The children were made perfectly happy by a whisper from me, that I had had a tree set up in the wash-house for the little negroes, and they were to have the entire responsibility of that, as I had arranged everything for it on a large ironing-table in the room.

·Off they went, Mary, with the key in her hand, heading the party; and I do not think that even their own tree gave them the pleasure which this did.

In the mean time we grown children adjourned to the library, which is at one end of the suite of apartments, of which the two parlors form the center, and the large dining-room the other end. Here we found a beautifully-shaped tree fixed in the middle of the room; its base formed of a large box, which was entirely concealed by moss-covered rocks. Upon a table beside the tree each member of the family had deposited their gifts; and, as each one was to surprise everybody else, each gift was wrapped in white paper, with the direction upon it; besides these there were various ornaments for the tree, cut out of gilt paper, and a number of colored wax candles.

The only children admitted were the baby, who rolled about in good-humored content on a sheepskin spread on the floor, and Lilias, whose chair was placed by the fire, where she could be amused by what was going on. Every one seemed to throw over them a veil of mystery; and

Cynthia amused us very much by her droll guesses at the contents of the various packages.

"Gracious, Aunt Jean! I am jealous of you. I never saw anything like the packages I have tied up for you. I tell you the Holcombes are trying to make a good impression on you. I only hope they will be able to keep it up. Ah, at last I see something directed to Cynthia Marshall; I was afraid she was forgotten. Let me see; it feels like——" but she was deprived of any further opportunity of finding out by having the package taken possession of by Mary, who tied it far out of her reach at the top of the tree.

"Cousin Cynthia, is there anything for me?" said Lilias, from her easy-chair.

"I should think so, Dame Lilias; at least a dozen additions to your family. How many babies have you now?"

"Oh, I don't know; but there is still room for more. I have not had any new ones for nearly a year, and it is time for me to have *reditions*, ain't it?"

"Well, I think once a year ought to satisfy any reasonable woman. And here is a long package for Baby Annie. Gracious! I do believe I am going to be a grandmother. I hope it is made of digestible materials, for she will swallow it whole before it is a day older, won't you, Baby?"

Baby laughed, and showed her two little white pegs by way of an assurance that her appetite was fully whetted.

"Oh, Jean," said sister Mary, "I wish you could have known my mother. She was the greatest hand at a Christmas frolic. I have known her, after she was an old woman,—indeed, up to the time of her death,—dress herself up to represent St. Nicholas and astonish the

children, and she always would have all of her descendants under her roof once a year. We all had to come
when she told us. I tell you, sister Annie, we will
never have any one to care as much for us again; there
is no love like mother-love after all, and she did more for
the enjoyment of the children than anybody else will
ever do, unless her mantle falls on Jean, here. I am
glad that the Lady of Rose Hill promises to be a Lady
Bountiful. This is more like our old family gatherings
than any we have had since mother's death."

And so the morning passed: in a mingling of gay and
quiet talk, interspersed with such sketches of the characters of those who were gone as formed pleasant intro-
ductions to me. At last our work was done, and we
stood off and surveyed it with perfect satisfaction, and I
felt as if I could hardly wait until the evening to see its
full results.

# CHAPTER IX.

## AN OLD VIRGINIA CHRISTMAS DINNER.

It does not seem to be much the fashion in Virginia either to give or accept invitations for dinner on Christmas-day; it is essentially a family festival, with which the stranger does not intermeddle,—so that we had no invited guests for the day; but this fact did not prevent a good deal of anxiety on my part about the success of my dinner, and my other duties and pleasures were interspersed with frequent runs down into the pantry and kitchen to see how everything was getting on; each turn, however, convinced me more and more that matters were in the hands of abler administrators than I could ever be, and I could only look around and admire. There were huge pyramids of cake, looking like mountains of snow; and the sparkling jelly, shaking its amber sides in the white foam of cream; Charlotte-russe; blanc-mange; mince-pies, etc. I was just flattering myself that I was quite successfully hiding my ignorance with regard to the *modus operandi* of these things, when I espied a queer-looking dish, made up of about a dozen hen's-eggs in the midst of preserved lemon-peel, cut to imitate straw.

"Very pretty," thought I; "but, goodness, who wants to eat boiled eggs at dessert?" So I very humbly ventured to say, "Mammy, are the eggs boiled hard or soft?" She looked at me for a minute, and then burst into a hearty laugh, and said,—

" Why, law, missus, where is you been livin' that you
don't know about hen's-nests? Why, them ain't real
eggs, them's 'blank mong' hardened in egg-shells."

I felt very much like the king of England who puzzled
his stupid brain to find how the apple got into the dump-
ling ; but I was too much crestfallen to ask any more
questions, and retired up-stairs, feeling that I had lost
caste with the directors of the lower regions, at any
rate.

At last dinner was announced by Robin, and I thought
I had never seen anything so beautiful as the table
stretched from one end to the other of the long room,
with its rich array of silver and china, set out so taste-
fully on the cloth of the finest damask, which fairly glis-
tened in its snowy whiteness,—whilst the sun, peeping
through the half-closed shutters, threw a thousand rays
of refracted light through the cut-glass decanters and
tumblers.

I suppose I shall see many such dinners if I live in
Virginia much longer, but certainly this was the very
best I had ever seen up to that time. It was none of
your French affairs where the food is brought in by piecemeal, and you are forced, for politeness' sake, to make a
gourmand of yourself by eating long after your appetite
is satisfied ; here everything was set on the table at once,
and surely it was enough for a regiment,—the immense
saddles of venison and mutton, the huge turkeys, ducks,
etc.,—for it would take a week to describe it all. I
would have been appalled at the waste if Mr. Holcombe
had not told me that on Christmas-day every servant on
the place had a piece of the Christmas dinner, so it must
needs be a bountiful one. The sweetest incident of the
day, in my opinion, occurred just after the first course
had been removed. I was beginning to wonder what

was the cause of the little pause in the operations, and why George and Harry Holcolmbe and Ellen Randolph had left the table, when the folding-doors opening into the parlor were thrown back, and the three absentees stood in the vacuum, and the sweetest childish voices I ever heard sang the following verses, written, as I afterwards learned, by my brother George:

### WELCOME TO THE BRIDE.

"Then welcome, thrice welcome we bid thee, sweet lady,
  To the land of the loved one who sits by thy side,
To the halls where his gathering clansmen are ready
  To cheer with their welcome the bonnie young bride.

"Here are sisters and brothers, and kinsfolk and friends,
  No tless leal and true-hearted and honest than thine,
Whose soothing caresses can make you amends
  For those yet more dear whose loss you repine.

"Though fair be the fields where in childhood you've played,
  And though bright be the skies of your dear native land,
Yet our mountains and valleys are also arrayed
  In nature's rare beauties with liberal hand.

"Then welcome, thrice welcome we bid thee, sweet bride,
  Let affection's kind offering thy spirit beguile;
Forget for a moment who sits by thy side,
  And your minstrels reward with your beautiful smile."

How sweet! how kind! to welcome the stranger thus, I was thinking, and then memory traveled back, back through the long years, many a mile away across the ocean, to my old home. But I no longer felt like a stranger in a strange land. These warm-hearted people had taken me to their hearts, and mine responded warmly to the greeting. I was roused by George's voice, saying, laughingly, "Why, Jean, little sister, I did not mean to make you cry." And then I became conscious, for the first time, that my tears were falling rapidly.

"It is but a shower in the sunshine, which is more of a

smile than a tear. Brother George," said I, driving away the drops, "this is truly the sweetest surprise I could have had."

Next followed the Christmas toasts, to which each one of the family was expected to contribute a mite. Mr. Holcombe's was the first, delivered with a great deal of feeling,—all, of course, standing around the table "To the memory of our parents. May their descendants emulate their virtues, so that in their turn their children may 'rise up and call them blessed.'"

Mr. Randolph.—"To Virginia, the mother of statesmen. May we, her children, live worthy of her name, that like the mother of the Gracchi, when asked for her jewels, she may be able to point to her sons."

Robin had been dispatched for Mammy, who now entered and stood behind brother George's chair; *he* gave—"Our dear old Mammy, whose fostering care was over us in our infancy and youth, and whose tender faithfulness has soothed the dying hours of so many of our loved ones. May she long be spared to be a blessing to us all and to teach the present generation that a faithful servant can well be an honored friend."

Sister Mary.—"To the stranger within our gates. May the mantle of her predecessors descend upon her, and like them, may she live in the memory of the children of her generation as the great heart and bountiful hand of their childhood."

Sister Annie.—"Whilst we are enjoying these blessings, may we none of us forget whence they all come; and let us also remember that our great rejoicing on this natal day is over the gift of God to the world in the person of his Son Jesus Christ our Lord."

Ellen Randolph.—"Many happy returns of the season. May each one find us wiser, better, and happier."

Cynthia Marshall.—"My husband! whom everybody else forgets. May I never sit down to another Christmas dinner without him."

Margaret.—"My mother's memory. May she ever live in the hearts of her children."

George Holcombe, Jr. — "To Christmas-day. Hereafter may we be blessed with two such seasons in the year instead of one."

Mary Mason.—"Rose Hill, the kindly roof which always extends a hospitable welcome to us all. May it ever live in our memories as the scene of our happiest days."

Harry Holcombe.—"To the absent members of our circle: though absent in the body, may they be present in the spirit at this our Christmas gathering."

Mary Holcombe.—"To mamma. 'Her children rise up and call her blessed. Her husband also; and he praiseth her.'"

Johnny.—"To this good dinner. May we never have a worse,—and always have the teeth to eat it."

Jean.—"To the Holcombe clan. May their loving kindness to the stranger be returned sevenfold into their own bosoms in time of need."

Lilias.—"To you all, ladies and gentlemen."

I have not attempted to describe the scene as sentiment after sentiment was given out. Such an April day, made up of clouds and sunshine, I have witnessed. Johnny's essay probably excited as much merriment as any other; particularly when the explanation was given that he had been a perfect martyr to toothache for some time past, and was even now "holding his jaw."

But I must not linger too long over this part of my story, for the door is thrown open, and I cannot suppress a scream as Robin makes his appearance in a blaze of blue flame.  One moment shows me that he is bearing in his hands the enormous plum-pudding, and the fire which so alarmed me is only licking up the French brandy with which it had been saturated.

The dessert was beautiful and beautifully served : and I sat by, receiving the compliments on the success of the dinner, with the preparation of which I had had so little to do.  I could not resist whispering to sister Annie the account of my *faux pas* about the hen's-nest.  She laughed very much, and kindly relieved my curiosity about how the blanc-mange got into the shells.

The eggs are broken very little at one end, and the contents discharged through the hole.  The blanc-mange finds its ingress in the same way; and when it is hardened, the shells are taken off, and the pretty mould is laid in its nest of candied lemon-peel.

I wonder if I will ever be a good housekeeper ?  I am going to try, because I cannot always expect to have Mammy and Mrs. Bascombe to do everything for me.

But at last the dinner is over, and we all adjourn to our rooms to rest awhile before the enjoyments of the evening commence.

"Why, Jean," said Mr. Holcombe, following me into my room, "my little wife has won golden opinions from all sorts of people,—and what did you think of it all ? Ain't Christmas a grand time in our Virginian mountains ?"

"Yes," said I; "and if all the people in the world were like you dear Holcombes, I would not care to go to heaven."

"Well, little woman, you see the sunny side of us now. We are pretty much like other people, only possibly a little more buoyant and light-hearted; but we have our troubles too.  But ain't George a glorious old fellow ?"

"Indeed he is; and that 'Welcome to the Bride' was the sweetest thing I ever heard. How beautifully those children sing!"

"Yes, they begin almost before they can talk, all of them. George and his wife both sing: and they hear music from the time they are born. I think that, probably, has a great deal to do with it."

"What kind of person is his wife?"

"As different from him as you can well imagine two people to be. She is the most quiet, gentle person you ever saw. Very tall, fair, with a soft voice and perfectly placid countenance. George teases her all the time. And she takes it so calmly that you would think that he could find no enjoyment in it,—but he does. She is very proud of him, and, I suppose, devoted to him; but she never shows it to any human being. She has what is always styled 'one of your enviable tempers;' and I suppose it is, though I confess to liking a little more mercury. Now, I know a diminutive piece of humanity who hardly needs language, because you have only to look into her face to read all she feels at once. Now, tell me the truth, little woman, did you cry or laugh most to-day?"

"Well," she answered, "I could with great propriety ask you the same question; for I saw your tears more than once, and you are an older soldier than I am."

"Well, I plead guilty," said Mr. Holcombe; "the fact is, a smile and a tear lie very near together sometimes. And such seasons always bring back father and mother so vividly, but not painfully. I would not have missed this Christmas here for anything: it has been the very best introduction you could have had to the 'Holcombe clan.'"

## MARY'S DIARY.

*December 27th.* . . . . . But I think of all the merry
times of this Christmas the two Christmas-trees were the
best.   Mamma said that we children might fix the tree
for the people while they fixed the one for the "white
*folks.*"   So off we ran to the wash-house and found a
great big tree in the middle of the floor, and a table by it
piled up with all sorts of things.   There were all the
things Lilias and myself have been working on for the
last ten days.   The bright-colored tarlatan bags filled
with candy, with the names of each one of the people on
them.   Bachelor pin-cushions, little flannel needle-books,
little doll-babies, bags of colored marbles, balls, hand-
kerchiefs, cravats, ribbons, etc.   Oh, the laugh we had
over the collection : and then the fun we had putting them
up on the tree !   Harry Holcombe said he knew there
was not another tree in the whole world which bore at
the same time head-handkerchiefs and bachelor pin-
cushions, oranges and apples ; but it certainly did look
pretty when it was done, with Uncle Armstead's red
comforter on the top branch, and Mammy's new turban
just below it, and the doll-babies sticking their heads
out between the green twigs in every direction.   We
wanted to put wax candles on the tree, but mamma said
we had better not, because there was so much *combusti-
bles* about it that she was afraid of fire, so we put a row
of candles on the mantel-piece behind it.

And then, when everything was lighted up, and we
opened the doors and let all the people in, it was too
good.   Everybody on the place was there, from old
Mammy and Uncle Bob to Chloe's baby ; all dressed in
their new winter suits, and looking so nice.   They had
none of them ever seen a Christmas-tree before ; and I

don't know what they could have thought of it, but they certainly were pleased: nobody could think anything else that looked at them; their eyes were as big as moons, and their teeth as white as the palings around the garden.

And when Harry and George and Johnny mounted up and took down the things, and called out their names, they must have heard them laugh in the house, and you heard all over the room, "Thank ye, marster. I knowed you wouldn't forgit me, marster."

Aunt Annie said we could understand now what the Bible meant by "it is more blessed to give than to receive," because we enjoyed this part more even than our own tree, which was really so much more beautiful.

After the tree was stripped, I told all the people that papa said Sam and Ned might get their banjo and fiddle, and all of them could have a dance in the wash-house. So off they went, and soon tables, tree, and everything were cleared away, and I ran off to tell mamma, because she was so anxious to see them dance. She looked through the door opening into the kitchen, because she was afraid she would embarrass them if she went in the room. She says it was like a picture. There was Sam with his banjo, and Ned with his violin, playing in front of the fire, while Jim and Bill stood on the hearth by them, clapping to the tune, and Sandy had his bones. Mamma thinks the clapping is very wonderful, the time is so perfect; and they beat themselves on their breasts, knees, feet, sides, and the back of their hands without getting out once. You could tell the tune without any instrument to help; and mamma thinks the dancing is so much prettier than white people's dancing, because they are so free in their movements, so active; and when they dance up to each other, with their arms akimbo, and then cross over and go down in a line, and stop and shuffle, it is certainly pretty. But mamma had to laugh at Rachel: she jumps up and down, and then round in a ring, all the time, and looks so awfully solemn, it is like she was at a funeral.

Mamma and Cousin Cynthia Marshall stayed there a long time, but at last we all had to go in to tea, and after tea we had our tree. But I am too tired to write about that now. I will have to do it to-morrow.

*December 28th.* We knew the time had come for our tree when Robin came in and lowered all the lights, and then the folding-doors were opened, and there was the great big tree with wax lights, twinkling from one end to the other, and no end of cornucopiæ and bundles wrapped in white paper; and there stood Uncle George in his white beard and fur cap, with a long stick in his hand. He stepped forward as the door opened, and repeated the following verses in a very loud voice:

> "At this his own season St. Nicholas comes,
>   To give you a merry greeting;
> He has left the gay towns and luxurious homes
>   To attend this family meeting.
>
> "Dull Care is bidden to quit us with haste,
>   Nor deem himself one of this party;
> While Business withdraws, showing thus his good taste,
>   And leaves us to merriment hearty.
>
> "In times that are old, St. Nick, you are told,
>   Always appeared with a pack,
> Which was stuffed just as full as it ever could hold
>   With knick-knacks, and strapped on his back.
>
> "But in these times we call later, so travelers say,
>   In a land far over the ocean,
> They've discovered a tree, which each Christmas-day
>   Hangs loaded with many a notion.

> " A root of this plant I contrived to procure you,
>   And have watered and nursed it with care;
> Its results are apparent, you see them before you,
>   Come forward and claim its fruits rare."

And then we all went in the other room while Uncle George took off the packages with his stick and handed them to each of us. Everybody found just what they wanted, and everybody looked as happy as possible. Mamma had more, of course, than any one else, because she is the bride and the newcomer, but we all got beautiful presents.

Mamma gave Lilias such a beautiful little work-box, with the tiniest little scissors and thimble, and everything she could want in it, and papa gave her the Rollo Series, or, as she calls it, her "Rollo serious."

And John has "Tales of a Grandfather," and a splendid knife, and some gardening-tools.

Margie has a pretty little watch from papa, and I a pair of bracelets, and mamma gave me Sir Walter Scott's Novels, beautifully bound. Uncle George gave Margie and myself an album apiece, with some verses in them, as a dedication, he says. I don't know exactly what that is, but the verses are very pretty. Margie's are these :

> " Go, pretty book,
>   And when upon thy snowy page
> My fair shall look,
>   Tell her whose love I would engage
> That to my partial eye she seems to be
> More pure and spotless, pretty book, than thee !

> " Tell her, when treasures rare,
>   Fair volume, in thy page shall meet,
> That then I will compare
>   To her own mind thy tessellated sheet,
> Where taste and heavenly poesy combine
> To make mosaic of this page of thine.

"Or tell her that I send
. An empty casket to her care,
And bid my friend
 Store it unstintingly with jewels rare,
Culled by young Fancy from the heaps that lie
In the full treasures of fair Poesy.

"Or let me liken thee
 To the smooth surface of a lake,
In which we love to see
 The stars of heaven reflected back,
When night unrolls to the enchanted eye
The spangled curtain of the dark-blue sky.

"Above the rest resplendent,
 The bard of Avon's nameless star
Shines lord of the ascendent,
 And shoots his blazing meteors far;
While next great Milton's sapphire rays
Pour on the eye the bright empyrean blaze.

"But, ah! the attempt were vain
 To number all the starry host
That in her splendid train
 Bright-eyed Poesy can boast,
These glimmering faintly, while with powerful ray
Those shoot abroad as genial as the day.

"Disdain not yet the beam
 That Genius scatters from his glittering car,
Although it may not gleam
 From Byron's sun or Moore's bright morning star,
But, gathering all their rich and varied dyes,
Shine like a rainbow in the vernal skies."

The verses in mine were called

### AN ALBUM A FEAST.

"An Album should be like a ladies' feast,
 Where many sweet and dainty dishes meet,
And, from the greatest even to the least,
 The guest expects to find each dish a treat.

" Then let me, Mary, as a friend advise
 What kind of dishes you should here prepare;
But first I'll bid you, if you would be wise,
 Be sure to choose your cooks with special care.
Admit, I pray you, men of taste alone,
 Whose *haut gout* teaches to select with skill,
And with discernment season what's their own
 With spices, Attic salt, or what you will.

" The cooks selected, be it next your care
 The viands suited to the board to choose,—
To cater for your guests the tempting fare
 Fastidious appetites will not refuse.
And, first, as tongue's excluded from the table,
 Why, you must try to make it up with brains,
With brains of living bards, if you are able:
 If not—why, then, of those whose deathless strains,
 Breathed from abroad, have reached our distant plains.

" Some folks there are—and such you often see,—
 Who, poor and proud, or stingy (fie upon it!),
Serve up hot water, and miscall it tea,
 And give soup maigre in a washy sonnet.
Another offers you a hollow puff
 Of empty praise—it was not worth his pains;
This gives acrostic kisses,—wretched stuff!
 That turns the stomach with his puling strains,
 Or cudgels mazy nonsense from his barren brains.

" Others there are who fain would see a part
 Of your fair pages with religion graced,
Nor think the aspirations of the heart
 Wedged in with trifles are at all misplaced.
I think not so! Religion's sacred lore
 To her own holy books should be confined;
Her sovereign balm, that every ill can cure,
 That cleansed the leper and restored the blind,
 Is not for albums more than feasts designed.

" Let no untutored scullion undertake
 To serve your board, to bake your household bread,
To make your pasties that one's teeth will break,
 And sodden puddings, heavier than lead,
 In form and substance like the dunce's head;

> But men who of fair Avon's stately swan
>     Are well content to make a standing dish,
> Who draw their nectar ever and anon
>     From Milton's sacred fount, nor better wish
>     Than from Lord Byron's piscary to fish."

I don't understand mine as well as Margie's. It seems to me it would do as well for a cookery book as an album,—all about puddings and fish and cooks, etc. I didn't like not to look pleased when Uncle George was so kind as to write it for me; but I can't help being sorry he put that kind of poetry in my album, it looks as if he thought I was so fond of eating. I feel like putting my book away, and not letting any one see it. I wonder if he did mean I liked eating too much? I hope not.

# CHAPTER X.

IT was the day after Christmas, and Mr. Holcombe had proposed an adjournment to the library after breakfast. The invitation was accepted by several of the older members of the party, including.Mr. George Holcombe, Mr. and Mrs. Randolph, and Mrs. Mason.

The gentlemen lighted their cigars, and lounged in what we must confess to be true Virginia style, with their chairs tilted back, and their knees considerably higher than the laws of grace would demand; while the ladies each had her work or knitting at hand, and Robin piled the andirons with huge sticks of hickory-wood, which sparkled and cracked in the most convivial and chatty manner.

"Look here, Ned," said Mr. George Holcombe, turning to his brother, "what is the difficulty with Margaret? She does not look or act like herself. I hardly know the child. It has been worrying me ever since I came."

The blood rose to Mr. Holcombe's cheek, showing that the subject touched upon was very near to his heart, and could only be stirred delicately. He did not reply for a minute, and then it was in rather a low tone.

"The fact is, I have been debating with myself whether it would not be better to consult you all about that very matter, which is a great trouble to me; but I don't much like to talk to any one about my own child."

"I don't think you ought to feel that way about us, Ned," said Mr. George Holcombe. "I don't think there

( 83 )

is any great difference between one's own children and those of one's brother and sisters. I am leaving my two boys with you, old fellow, believing this from my heart." ·

"Well, the fact is, Margaret has never become reconciled to my marriage. She undertook to oppose it violently at first, which I was not very much surprised at; but I confess I did expect that after—after the change took place, and she knew how much I had acted for the happiness of all parties, her good sense would lead her to rejoice in it. But I have been disappointed. She has preserved this moody, uncompromising manner throughout. I don't think she has ever voluntarily spoken to Jean, and, when forced to do so, has—— Well, it had better not have been done at all."

"Yes, I have observed it ever since our arrival," said Mrs. Mason, "and grieved over it. I think she is the victim of a morbid idea, which, if not cured, may do her and all of you great harm."

"And have you never spoken to her on the subject?" said Mrs. Randolph, turning to Mr. Holcombe, in surprise.

"No, I am sorry to say, I have not since I first broke to her the news of my intentions. The scene then was so painful that I did not care to repeat it. It is true, I have been near it more than once, when her manner to my wife was unbearable almost. But Jean is so opposed to my saying anything, and, indeed, has exacted from me a sort of promise that I will leave the cure to time."

"Kindly meant, but unwise, you may depend upon it," said Mrs. Mason; "the disease is growing worse instead of better; each day increases the evil. Of course, she has no tangible ground of complaint. I have never seen any one occupy the position of stepmother more gracefully than Jean does. Their own mother could not do more."

Mr. Holcombe reached out his hand, and, with a smile, pressed that of his sister in his own. It was a slight action, but showed his sensitiveness to anything which concerned his wife.

"Thank you, Annie. I don't know how anybody can resist her; but Margaret does most successfully. The fact is, Jean is the more sensitive on the subject, because she suffered misery from a harsh stepmother herself. She never told me very much about it; but I am sure it was her positive unkindness which caused her to accept her old aunt's invitation to come over here and make her home with her; which she did nearly nine years ago. And she lived with her up to the time of her death, which happened about two years since. Mrs. McDonald left her a very ample support, and her father and brother were anxious for her to return home. She would probably have done so in the end, but I made other arrangements for her. These circumstances of her life make her of course more sensitive than she would otherwise be about her position here. And she becomes so nervously anxious every time she thinks I am going to speak to Margaret that I really could not do it: and I should not be surprised if she had endured more even than I know."

"Well, Ned," said Mr. George Holcombe, bluntly, "I don't think any man has a right to allow his wife to be insulted even by his child; and if I were in your place, Miss Margaret should either behave herself or I would send her out of the house."

"Oh, George," said Mrs. Randolph, "don't talk so harshly. There is no one in this world so indulgent as you are, or who allow their children to walk over them

8

more completely than you do. I know it is all talk, but I don't like to hear it."

Here the laugh turned on Mr. George, who was not at all remarkable for the good discipline of his household. A laugh in which he, too, joined.

"But I would not be surprised if to send Margaret away for a time would be the true solution of the difficulty," said Mrs. Mason. "I think the danger to her is greater than to Jean if she grows morbid and reserved and nurses this idea; but if she goes away to school, you may depend upon it, she will think of her home very differently. I think Jean feels naturally on the subject; and I have a good deal of sympathy with Margaret too. She was very much devoted to her mother; and it is naturally a trial to see her place filled. I think a great deal of patience ought to be exercised towards her."

And this idea would undoubtedly have been carried into effect if it had not been for the interposition of Jean, who opposed it with all the vehemence of her nature. It was agonizing to her to think of Margaret being banished from her home on her account. It seemed her own story over again; and she wept as bitterly as if she herself had acted the harsh stepmother, bringing discord into her husband's house, and scattering his children. So the plan was abandoned.

Mrs. Mason spoke to Margaret tenderly of her duty, but with no apparent effect. She looked stern in her composure, but only said, softly,—

"It is impossible for any one to judge for me, aunty; I am obliged to do what I think right, no matter what the consequences may be. Meanwhile I forgive you; I know you have acted for the best."

"Bless the child!" said Mrs. Mason, as Margaret left the room after having imprinted her kiss of unasked forgiveness on her cheek. "I don't want any forgiveness; I don't understand what she means. She seems to have built up a wall of fancied duty and fenced herself in with self-approbation, until she imagines all the world is wrong and she alone right. Well, well, when young people get to that pass they have to be left to their heavenly Father's unerring discipline; He will bring it all right at last if it is through much tribulation."

Monday morning saw the dispersion of the happy party at Rose Hill. Everybody was sorry to go. Mr. George Holcombe declared himself perfectly demoralized and unfit for any useful employment.

"You must make Ned bring you to see us, Jean," said he, as he took leave of Mrs. Holcombe. "I want you to know my wife; she is a great deal too good for me, and I only wonder she was ever willing to take charge of such a scapegrace as I am; but come and judge for yourself. She is such a perfect Mrs. Micawber that she never can get away from home. We cannot promise you such a welcome as you have given us, but we will try. The fact is there is something in the air of old Rose Hill which makes it different from any other place in the world to me."

Mrs. Mason, Mrs. Randolph, and Cynthia were equally urgent for her to return their visit, and so they went off, leaving the whole party standing in the wide porch waving their adieus; and, as the carriage drove into the grove, Cynthia stuck baby out of the window, upside-down, as her final farewell.

For some days after their departure everything was dull enough. Jean went very hard to work with her lessons in housekeeping, while Margie confined herself more than ever to her own room. Mary tried to while away the time by reading her new books; and Lilias, surrounded by her innumerable family, diligently employed herself with her new work-box, which she pronounced "certainly the most *dispensable* thing she had ever had."

The boys meanwhile lived out of doors, snow-balling, rabbit-snaring, and squirrel-hunting, and all looked forward to the advent of the new teacher as some relief from present stagnation.

Mr. Holcombe was probably the greatest sufferer from the vacuum which the departure created, as a gentleman farmer in Virginia does not have very full employment, particularly during the winter season ; so he engaged his time in debating with himself what course he had better pursue with regard to Margaret, and fully decided that matters should not stand still any longer.

An opportunity for bringing matters to a crisis was afforded him about a week after the dispersion of the family party.

They were assembled at the breakfast-table one morning when Mr. Holcombe said,—

"I received a letter from Mr. Williams this morning ; he will be here to-morrow. So now, Mr John, you may prepare yourself for action. I shall expect him to be very strict with all of you."

"Indeed," said Margaret, in her loftiest style, "I hope, papa, you do not expect me to make an obedient pupil. I am afraid you will be disappointed if you do."

"I certainly do, my daughter," he said; "and I hope you will always be too much of a lady to *force* any great exercise of authority from a gentleman teacher."

"He will be apt to fail if he tries it, papa," she said, with the most perfect calmness. "I certainly never intend to submit to any one in the world but you."

"I don't think you are very remarkable for *your* submission to me, young lady," he said, very sternly; "but I insist upon some additions to your list of sovereigns, myself and to whomsoever I choose to delegate my authority; your mamma first and then your teacher."

She bent her eyes on her plate, and her cheek paled slightly; but she said, daringly,—

"I have no mamma, sir."

"Leave the table, Margaret, and go to your own room."

She got up and left with the same stolid look upon her, and the children, with awe-struck faces, soon followed, and Mr. Holcombe was left alone with his wife, whose tearful eyes showed how much she felt the insult. He put his arm about her and said,—

"My darling wife, I want you to release me from the promise I made you some time ago; I must talk to that wayward child, and see if something cannot be done; this state of affairs is getting beyond endurance."

"Oh, my dear husband, please don't; let us try a little longer," was the answer, as she clasped his hands nervously, and her voice took a tone of passionate entreaty.

"Jean, this is almost childish in you; there, forgive me, dear, I did not mean to be harsh; but you get yourself into a state of nervous agitation about this matter which is unnecessary and unlike you. Margaret is nothing more nor less than a willful child, who, because she has been crossed, is indulging her temper at the expense of the happiness of the entire household; and I cannot stand it any longer: you must see yourself that our present course is unproductive of good to any one of the parties concerned. Instead of improving, she is growing more and more insolent; and in a few days we will have a stranger added to our family circle, who will draw most unpleasant inferences from the evident condition of affairs."

8*

"Oh, Mr. Holcombe," sobbed Jean, "I ought not to have married you. I might have remembered that step-mothers are never welcome. You should have told me of Margaret's opposition."

"And do you think you would have been justified in refusing me because of Margaret's opposition?"

"Yes; I never would have married you in the world."

"I am sorry, Jean,"—and Mr. Holcombe's voice assumed a grieved tone,—"that I made the happiness of my life at the expense of yours; but it is too late to think of that now, we must patch up this place in our domestic affairs before the rent is made worse. I shall speak to Margaret this morning, with or without your consent. I have listened to your timidity long enough, and now I must act according to my own judgment."

"Betsey,"—to a servant who had just entered the room, —"go up-stairs and tell your Miss Margaret I want to speak to her in my study." And kissing his wife very tenderly, he left her to keep his appointment.

Jean had not offered any further opposition after she found it would be useless; and, indeed, if she could have reasoned at all on the subject, she would have found herself agreeing with him; but it was a matter of feeling and not of reason,—she hated to be canvassed even by her husband and his child, whose judgment she knew would be so unfavorable.

In the mean time Mr. Holcombe waited in his study for the interview with his daughter; but he waited in vain. Presently a knock at the door, and Betsey appeared. Miss Margaret begged to be excused, she was so busy this morning. This was indeed passing the point where endurance ceased to be a virtue; he was a most indulgent man to his children, but had always received from them, hitherto, the respect due to his relations with them, and the angry blood flamed in his face at this cool disregard of his wishes. .

"Is she in her room ?"

"Yés, sir."

"Then I will see her there. You need not wait."

And he strode by the woman, and mounted the broad staircase with quick, determined strides. Without the ceremony of knocking, he opened the door. The refractory young lady was seated before the fire, a little pale it is true, but not otherwise discomposed.

"Margaret, did you understand that I wished to speak to you in my study ?"

"Yes, sir ; and I told Betsey to say that I hoped you would excuse me, as I was very much occupied this morning."

He glanced at her idle hands, and said,—

"And pray, Miss Holcombe, what were you doing that was more important than attention to my wishes ?"

She cast down her eyes for a moment, and a half smile, partly of daring and partly of embarrassment, discomposed her lips; but she said nothing.

"I do not wonder," Mr. Holcombe continued, and his voice shook with anger, "that you hesitate to acknowledge the subterfuge to which you resorted in order to avoid an explanation with me ; an explanation, let me tell you, which I do not intend shall be longer deferred."

The bright black eyes were raised at once, and she said, very coolly,—

"And who, sir, is to blame that I fear to meet my father ?"

Her composure exasperated him ; and this tone of injured innocence threw him off his guard—he felt he was losing ground.

"Surely," he said, "you cannot ask such a question

for information ? I return it to you, and demand a candid and truthful answer.   Who is to blame ?"

The long, slender fingers interlaced themselves, and the nails seemed almost buried in the tender flesh in the intensity of the clasp; but there was no answer.   Mr. Holcombe eyed her keenly for a moment, then went on:

"You refuse to answer me, then I will tell you.   For nearly three months now you have failed, utterly failed, in every filial duty.   You have alienated yourself from the family circle and from our hearts.   My first-born child, from whom I expected so much in the way of influence over the younger children,—you have set them an example I pray God from the bottom of my heart they may never follow.   You have done everything to bring discord into our household,—failing in that, you have succeeded in administering a drop of unhappiness to each one of us; and to yourself more than all.   And why has all this been done ? what excuse do you offer for it ?"

She would have answered; but he put up his hand and stopped her.

"Because I refused to allow you to dictate to me my course in life ; because, forsooth, I chose, in opposition to your wishes, to take what happiness and good God in his bounty vouchsafed to me ; because I placed at the head of my house one in every way worthy to fill the position, and in the choice of whom I was influenced scarcely less by a consideration for the happiness of my children than my own."

A scarcely perceptible smile of incredulity broke the stillness of the obstinate face,—it provoked him sorely.

"I know the excuse you make to yourself is reverence for the memory of your mother..   Foolish child—and do you imagine for an instant that an angel in heaven is moved by the petty jealousies which torment us here?

or has her nature, which was eminently unselfish, so changed in heaven as to cause her a pang because I can be happy again, and her poor little children have some one to take care of and love them?"

"I could have done it as well, papa."

He had spoken with so much passion himself that the cool response which met him added fuel to the flame, and he replied, with bitterness,—

"Your self-appreciation must be high indeed, to lead to the expression of an opinion so replete with vanity and conceit as this last; but I do not agree with you. One so utterly wanting in self-discipline as yourself could never be a safe guide to any one. I am thankful that your sisters and brother are not dependent upon you. I trust them with perfect confidence to the mother who so kindly consented to take the charge of them."

"Yes, sir,"—and at last the tears flowed, and the voice became tremulous,—" and I alone am left to remember my mother; except for me her memory would die entirely : even her own children have forgotten her."

"Foolish child! these heroics are utterly out of place, they exhaust my hard-tried patience. You imagine two conflicting duties, and make yourself a martyr to an idea. You feed your foolish heart in solitude until you build up a false strength for resistance to the real call of right and happiness. But let me tell you, Margaret, if an angel in heaven can know unhappiness, if our dead friends are permitted to watch over us from their home in the skies, your mother grieves over you this day, and if she could speak to you would advise you very differently from your present course."

If he had only taken her to his heart then, as a mother would have done in like circumstances, all might have been well; for, for the moment, the barriers of pride were broken down. But he was a man, and a man too, deeply incensed, and did not choose to open his arms to her until she acknowledged her wrong. And so the soft place in the strong young heart grew hard again as she said,—coldly,—

"Papa, it is useless for you and me to argue this point. I am very sorry, but we can never agree, and I cannot command my heart any more than you can. I acknowledge I was wrong in what I said this morning,—consideration for myself and for you will keep me from offending in that quarter,—and I suppose you have a right to direct my actions in other things, so I will do what you bid me if it does not come in conflict with my truthfulness."

Mr. Holcombe saw that he had lost ground, but very dimly guessed how; she was in some way master of the field, which he could not regain, so he had only to make the best of what liberty she allowed him.

He said, "I insist, then, Margaret, that you no longer absent yourself from the family, and that your conduct to me and—your—my wife, be perfectly respectful and courteous, if you cannot make it affectionate, and that the gentleman whom I have employed as your teacher shall never have cause to complain that you act with regard to him other than a 'perfect lady;' more than this I cannot ask, since it includes all that a high-bred woman and a Christian can do. I leave you, Margaret, to your own conscience and your God. Your present course is a sore disappointment to me; I had many hopes centered in you."

Again the tears dropped from under the drooping lids, but she made no reply.

With a deep sigh, Mr. Holcombe turned away. Was there ever a greater failure than he had made? Were not matters even worse than before? Perhaps, after all,

Jean was right, and the cure of the evil had better have been left to time. Actually that calm manner of hers, so unlike the impulsive, passionate child she had always been, had left him with an uncomfortable feeling of being himself in the wrong. . It was this feeling which impelled him to turn back again and say,—

"Margaret, of what do you complain? what do you wish?—help me to unravel this vexed skein."

The answer might have been frozen before it reached him, it brought such a chill with it.

"Thank you, papa, I shall do very well, I expect. I have nothing to ask,—that time has passed."

And so he went, disappointed, grieved, wondering what had so suddenly developed this mere child into a woman.

As the door closed, two arms were reached forward for an instant, as if to stay him. But no voice came. And throwing herself on the bed, Margaret cried herself to sleep.

Meantime Mr. Holcombe repaired to the library, and finding his wife alone, said, "Jean, what is to be done with a girl of fifteen who, after behaving as badly as a child of six could do, suddenly, to your surprise, assumes the bearing of an injured woman, and leaves you, in spite of your convictions to the contrary, with an uncomfortable feeling that you have in some way been to blame?"

Jean could not help smiling at the evident beaten look he bore, but would not say, "I told you so."

He recounted his interview with Margaret, and said, "I know I did not manage it at all well, but I was so angry at her refusal to come to me in the beginning, and then her expression of calm forbearance threw me off my guard, and I let her get the better of me from the first. I declare it is too provoking to think of the martyr look she assumed when she announced her intention of obeying my 'behests' as a matter of duty. I certainly ought to have conquered her before I left, but I did not, but beat an ignominious retreat, leaving her complete mistress of the field. May be you were right, little woman, at last, and I had better have let the matter alone."

"Certainly the way it stands now does not promise much comfort for any of the parties concerned," was the quiet answer, "and I am afraid I cannot do much to help you."

"I believe now it would be best to send her away to school," said Mr. Holcombe. But the nervous flush which mounted to his wife's face stopped him; and he had learned by this last experiment to distrust his own convictions, and did not insist upon his view of the case.

Margaret slept heavily until dinner-time, and then went down, feeling utterly stupefied by the exhausted passion, in the first place, and then by the long sleep. So the meal passed without any very decided exhibition of what her own rôle would embrace; at which all parties were disappointed, as Mr. Holcombe had some curiosity to see what he was to expect. There was rather an elaborate attention to any expressed wish of his, but, except this, there was no indication of what her proposed course would be. Jean was beginning to watch the contest between these two with an interest not unmixed with amusement; and she could not but see that this wrong-headed, spirited girl was more than a match for her easy-tempered, indulgent father, whose chivalrous ideas reduced him to tortures of self-humiliation by having to use harsh words to a female, even though she was his own child, and one who sadly wanted a firm spirit to discipline hers.

She did not dare to ask herself what was to be the end of all this, but, Micawber-like, contented herself with watching the domestic horizon, hoping that something would turn up to prevent the denouement she so much dreaded.

# CHAPTER XI.

MR. WILLIAMS arrived the next day, and was soon installed in his new duties. He was the son of an old friend of the Holcombes, and brought with him the recommendation, which always carries weight with a Virginian, that he was born a gentleman.

I am aware that we have been much laughed at about this idiosyncrasy, and admit that it is often carried to an unfortunate and ridiculous extent; but I do not think that the heritage of a good, great name can be surpassed. And though it may be true, and doubtless is, that as high-minded, honorable gentlemen have risen from the lower ranks of life as can be found connected with any of the most highly-esteemed families in the country, yet it must be that the pride of birth, and a name which can be traced back for generation upon generation without its bearing the shadow of a stain upon its fair escutcheon, has something ennobling in it: it must act as a soul-tonic in the time of sore temptation.

Be this as it may, Mr. Williams's birth carried a recommendation to Mr. Holcombe, and his appearance increased the favorable consideration. He was a gentleman in person and manners. He had chosen the profession of teaching, as he frankly confessed, because the wheel of fortune had gone round, and he was not yet able to get his profession. In the mean time, he was very glad to find himself so pleasantly situated, and commenced his duties with considerable zest in consequence.

9          ( 97 )

A room in the yard had been fitted up as a schoolroom, and the Holcombes, and one or two children of some poor neighbors, constituted the school. Most families have their peculiar characteristics; and that of the Holcombes seemed to be great activity of mind and body. They were wide-awake children, as Mr. Williams found, much to his gratification, and not at all hard to teach, though most of them were very backward; for, as Margaret expressed it, "Mrs. Bascombe had untaught them for two years."

Poor old lady! She was much more in her element making pies and cakes in the storeroom than teaching the young ideas to shoot in the schoolroom.

Mrs. Holcombe petitioned that Lilias might be left under her care. And as she was too delicate to allow her education a place of first importance, it was easily decided to leave her to "mamma" for the present; and she proved a great source of interest and entertainment to her. Often, too, she was too unwell to do more than lie still in her little crib and listen either to reading or singing,—generally the former,—as her mind, more active than her body, drank in with avidity whatever food was presented to it.

Her chair was so arranged that, when she wished it, a kind of circular shelf could be fastened to the two arms, and so she could have her playthings or work placed within her reach; and here she would sit day after day with her "family," consisting of eight doll-babies of various sizes, for all of whom she had names, and of whom she spoke as familiarly as if they were real personages. She had an amusing way of making them responsible for her own misdeeds.

Jean had left her one day to prepare her lessons, and returned to find her absorbed in her work-box, with her books closed beside her; before she could begin to reprove, the winning little face was raised to hers, and laughing in her most seductive way, she said,—

"Mamma, Nelly is a very bad girl to-day; she will not get that *Gogafry* lesson, all I can do. She says she would so much rather sew; and Betty has not learned one word of her *Multification*. I don't know what to do with these children."

"Why, that is a very bad state of affairs, little mamma," was the answer; "but we must never give up to them, must we? regular habits for little girls, you know."

"Yes, that is a fact, mamma; but holiday once in awhile does everybody good, and it is a good thing for Nelly to learn to sew, too; suppose we indulge them for this day,—'all work and no play makes Jack a dull boy,' you know."

"Yes; but I remember, too, that 'all play and no work makes him a mere toy,' so we had better put the workbox out of reach, so that Nelly and Betty won't be tempted to forget duty for pleasure."

This was as much management as the gentle, timid, little invalid ever required. So Jean's task was easy.

In the schoolroom, Mr. Williams soon found an interest in his bright pupils. Margaret and George attracted him particularly, being further advanced, and both ambitious. George was the steadiest worker, but Margaret the quickest mind. She was apt to flag and become discouraged, however, and her teacher soon found the spur which would rouse her, and used it to his own advantage. At first she took a great dislike to Latin, and positively declined to prepare the lessons. Mr. Williams, to her surprise, seemed to chime in with her ideas without difficulty.

"I do not see much use in your studying it," he said.

" Why not ?" she asked.

" Oh, well, you know a woman does not require the intelligence a man does."

" I don't agree with you," she said, indignantly.

" Don't you ?   Oh, I beg your pardon, I thought you did."

" No, I don't; I believe a woman is just as capable of learning *everything* as a man is."

The only answer was a slight shrug of the shoulders and an incredulous lifting of the eyebrows, as if politeness alone prevented the advance of strong arguments on the other side.

" I wish you would talk, Mr. Williams, and not look in that provoking way."

" Well, Miss Holcombe, a woman generally finds more use for her needle than her Latin.   Do you know how to sew ?"

" I don't see that the two things conflict; and I know I can learn Latin as well as George."

This was the point he wished to reach, so he dropped the conversation, and never had any difficulty with Miss Holcombe's Latin lessons afterwards.

Nor did she find herself so out of place under a teacher as she expected; it is true, her lofty spirit sometimes came in contact with his, but he always seemed to know by instinct the best way out of the difficulty without any departure from his usual courtesy; and generally succeeded in managing her without her finding it out.

The discipline was good for her in every way.   And she at last fell into a more natural manner in the household; the winter evenings around the bright wood fires, where George and herself either worked out their examples together, or she played chess with Mr. Williams, were very pleasant, though there was still a cloud be-

tween herself and the older members of the family. Her
submission to her father's wishes were often little less
than an impertinence. And if she held any intercourse
with Mrs. Holcombe, she was sure to leave a sting behind
her; but in spite of all this, everything went on much
better than could have been expected; and spring opened
upon the family of Rose Hill more peacefully than the
stormy winter promised.

Mary and John labored up the ladder of learning in
company with Harry Holcombe,—finding it rather stupid
work,—and John felt inclined to change his amo, amas,
amat, into odior, oderis, odetur.

One of Mr. Williams's accomplishments was reading,
which he did with rare expression and beauty; and the
long evenings were enlivened by the congenial company
of Dickens, Shakspeare, and many lesser lights. So that
Jean Holcombe always looked back upon this first winter
of her married life as the happiest, though as we have
seen it was not free from care.

Hunting was a famous amusement with the boys at
Rose Hill, and often Mr. Williams would accompany
them. Sometimes, too, they would go off swimming.
Every holiday was spent in this way, and Mr. Williams
gained their love and confidence by always making one
of the party, and enjoyed the expeditions as much as they
did.

"Mr. Holcombe," said Jean, one day, "it always
frightens me so to see the boys going off with their guns,
or to go to the water, they are so rash. Suppose some of
them should get hurt."

"Well, Jean," he said, "these are risks boys must run.
They have to learn to take care of themselves and other
people too; it would never do to keep them out of danger
all the time, it would make perfect milksops of them, and

9*

the time may come when they will need all the hardihood and nerve their present lives can give."

"Yes, I know all that, but I am never easy when I see them go off on these expeditions. I always expect to see one of them brought home by the others. I think it would be better if they would learn to swim first."

"Learn to swim first!" exclaimed Mr. Holcombe, laughing,—"in a wash-tub, I suppose. You women are all alike; I never saw one of you that did not make some such mistake as that. My mother, who was as strong-minded a woman as ever lived, told us one day that she positively forbade our going into the water at all until we learned to swim, and it was not until we laughed that the absurdity of the proposition struck her."

Jean joined in the laugh against herself, and said,—

"Well, I am glad to be in such good company as your mother, at any rate. You are sure not to think anything she does very foolish."

"But there," said Mr. Holcombe, looking towards the woods, "I think I hear their voices now."

It was a habit of the boys, whenever they left home for the day, to stop at a large tree at the end of the lawn, which they called their sunset tree, because from there the view of the sunset was always most beautiful, and here they sang their sunset song. It was a custom they had taken from their fathers, who had told them of how they used to go down to this spot for the same purpose.

The hunting or swimming was always hurried over then, in order not to lose their meeting at their sunset tree, and their arrival was heralded to their friends at the house by their voices singing their evening song, which had been written by their grandfather so many years ago.

As Mr. Holcombe spoke, the clear voices rang through

the evening air. And both Jean and himself went out into the porch so as to hear them more distinctly.

Their voices blended beautifully, and they could distinguish Mr. Williams's deep notes, mingled with the more childish tones of the boys, and even at the distance at which they were the words were easily distinguished.

### THE SCHOOLBOYS' EVENING SONG.

"Come, come, come, come to the sunset tree,
    The day is past and gone,
The schoolboy now is free,
    And his daily tasks are done.
The twilight star to heaven,
    The summer dew to flowers,
And a holiday is given
    To us by the evening hours.

"Sweet, sweet, sweet, sweet is the hour of play
    To the boy let loose from school,
After delving all the day
    At some puzzling grammar rule.
Oh, then, how sweet to all
    Are the triumphs of the race,
And the merry game at ball,
    And the turf our resting-place!
                Then come, come, come.

"Light, light, light, light are our spirits now,
    While bounding o'er the green,
And our friends assembled near
    Enjoy the lively scene.
And when our games are o'er,
    And the hour is past for play,
Then, sitting at the door,
    We'll sing our roundelay.
                Then come, come, come."

# CHAPTER XII.

## GEORGE WASHINGTON REVIVED.

"PAPA," said John, running into the library one morning in early spring, where Mr. Holcombe was lying at ease on the lounge with a book in hand reading aloud to his wife, who sat at her work by his side, "do you remember the young pear-tree you set out last spring?"

"What, the one at the end of the walk?"

"Yes, sir."

"Of course I do; what of it? I saw it yesterday; those grafts are doing remarkably well."

"Well, papa,"— John had commenced his interview with a very beaming face, but this had given place to an expression of doubt and uncertainty, which induced Mr. Holcombe to lay down the book he was reading and to repeat with an increased appearance of interest:

"Well, what of it, my son?"

"Papa, I—I—somebody has cut it down."

"Somebody has cut down my young seckel pear-tree!" ejaculated Mr. Holcombe, in astonishment, getting up from the lounge and standing before the child. "What do you mean, John?"

The tears began to roll over Master John's cheeks; but he made no answer.

"Well, this is the strangest thing I ever knew. I must get at the bottom of the mystery. What do you know about this, John? That you are in some way concerned in it I see, of course; but how I cannot imagine. Do you know who did it?"

" Yes, sir," sobbed John.

" Well, tell me. Of course I shall be very angry; but you need not be so much frightened. I am no ogre."

" Papa, I did it."

" You cut down my pear-tree !" said Mr. Holcombe, in profound astonishment. " In the name of all that is reasonable what could have induced you to do such a thing?"

" You told me——"

" I told you,"—and Mr. Holcombe drew a long breath expressive of suppressed impatience,—" I told you to cut down my pear-tree ! Well, either you or I have lost our senses. For goodness' sake, stop that crying, you great baby, you, and tell me what you mean !"

" Stop a minute, Mr. Holcombe, you frighten the child," whispered Jean. " Come here, Johnny; tell us all about it now,—I know you have not meant to do wrong."

Her gentleness calmed the sobs in a minute, though it was still with considerable difficulty that he managed to say,—

" You know you told me I must always tell the truth."

" Of course I did," said Jean, holding his face towards her so as to keep from him the view of Mr. Holcombe's impatient movements as he put his hands in his pockets and strode up and down the room.

" And papa said that—it was when he was talking to us about Uncle Randolph's Christmas toast, about the great men of Virginia; and he said we must try and be like them."

A smothered ejaculation from Mr. Holcombe, " Heaven grant me patience ! But what have the great men of Virginia to do with my pear-tree ?" was very near upsetting John again; but a few more words of encouragement, and he said,—

"And I was trying—but George Washington's father said he was willing to lose the cherry-tree because he told the truth !"

This was too much, and Jean put her hands over her face and shook with laughter. Mr. Holcombe had not caught the low-voiced explanation, and looked from one to the other with amazement.

"There, go out, John," said Jean, wiping the tears from her eyes, "I will explain to papa; it is all right."

And, as the door closed upon him, she gave full vent to her amusement, in which Mr. Holcombe joined most heartily when he understood that George Washington and his successful raid upon his father's cherry-tree had been John's guiding star. "But how I must have disappointed him !" said he, at last. "Instead of acting the proper and moral papa, like old Mr. Washington, of whom, by-the-by, they make a perfect old prig, I almost frightened the life out of him. Well, I would willingly lose the pear-tree for the sake of the good joke; it will last John for a lifetime. I must write to George about it. I wish I could tell him and hear him laugh."

"But do pray go after John now and comfort him," said Jean. "But, Mr. Holcombe," as he was leaving the room, "I—of course you know more about the children than I do; but, if you would only not go too far in the opposite direction, explain to him about things, don't let him think you esteem it a privilege to lose your tree."

"Yes," said Mr. Holcombe, "I am going to act old Mr. Washington to perfection. 'Poor Johnny,' I am going to say, 'my son, I would rather have lost'—— But I am afraid I cannot be as effective without the big white cravat and shorts."

"Pshaw, Mr. Holcombe ! Don't do so. I really think it is right serious; you may do the child an injury," said

Jean. " I never saw such people as you are. I believe a good joke would reconcile you to anything, and you fly from one extreme to the other."

"Yes, that is a fact, Mrs. Jean; but I am going to make it all right now. I'll take his knife away from him as a punishment, and tell him. that I know he did it for the best, but I hope he won't do it again." And he left the room laughing, leaving her still with a slight feeling of uneasiness, and not a little wonder how he ever managed to bring his children up as well as he had done.

The fact of the matter is men are not fond of that kind of business, and if they can find any excuse for shuffling off the trouble and responsibility, they are very apt to do it.

John appeared at dinner in a very composed state of mind ; peace was evidently made, and without the loss of the knife, as Jean observed, and privately determined to impress the lesson on the young man herself.

But John did not escape so easily as she thought. The two boys, George and Harry, got hold of the story, and called him George Washington ever afterwards.

# CHAPTER XIII.

## HARVEST.

"JEAN, you know next week my wheat will be ready to cut, and you will have any quantity to do for harvest."

Jean laid down her work, and looked up at her husband in surprise. She had never thought of her having any duties to perform at harvest.

"Oh, yes," he said, laughing at her bewilderment. "I expect you to go out in the field and help to bind up. You will make a splendid Ruth."

"Of course, I know you are laughing now," she said; "but what is to be done, really?"

"Why, you have to prepare the greatest quantity of pies, and cakes too, I expect. The hands all must be fed up during harvest."

"You don't make the women go in these hot suns, do you?" she asked.

"Well, Jean, I give you leave to keep them at home, if they want to stay. I assure you, harvest is a perfect jubilee. I have to make the women take turns to stay in and cook. Even the children are crazy to go."

"Well, I should think it would kill them to be out in the broiling sun all day."

"It is hardly fair to judge them by yourself, Jean. In the first place, a negro from his nature can stand more heat than ten white people. I assure you, I have seen Rachel wrap herself up in a double blanket, and lie down in front of a fire which would roast an ox, and sleep like an infant cradled on its mother's breast. And

(108)

then they, of course, from their position and lives, are inured to hardships,—it is obliged to be so. I could not keep them all like ladies and gentlemen; and what you consider a hardship they look upon as the greatest pleasure."

"I would like to see them at work," said Jean. "Would that be possible?"

"Oh, yes; when they get to the fields near the house, you can go out; or you can ride out with me any time. You will be very much interested,—it is a pretty sight. How many of the women about the house can you spare?"

"Will they want to go, too? I never thought of that," she said.

"Of course, they will all want to go; but that don't make any difference. You will have to keep enough to do the work; but I suppose you can spare one or two. The fact is, the wheat is very ripe, and I am anxious to have as many hands as possible, so as to get through soon, while the fine weather lasts."

Jean thought that at least two-thirds of the house-servants could be spared; but she found that was out of the question. Nanny must stay with Lilias, and two other maids; and Robin, of course, would have to stay in the dining-room, since Mr. Holcombe could not stand a woman round the table.

The weighty matter was at last settled, and harvest commenced.

It is a trying time to all housekeepers,—though less so, probably, in an old Virginia household,—where there are so many supernumeraries in the way of servants. But even Jean felt the inconvenience. The carriage could not be gotten out, because the driver was in the field; the dinner in the house was delayed, because the hands

10

must be provided first; the weeds were permitted to show themselves in the beautiful garden, because Sandy was harvesting. And thus, in many little ways, she was constantly reminded that harvest was progressing; and often, too, she would hear the voices in the distance singing their harvest songs to the music of the swift-moving cradles. They had commenced at the farthest extremity of the farm, and worked in towards the house; so that it was not until the end of the week that Mr. Holcombe announced that they were near enough for the ladies to visit them. Jean preferred to walk, as she was too timid about riding to venture. So, in company with the whole family, she started out one bright afternoon, about an hour before sunset. The voices of the singers grew louder and harsher on the ear as they progressed, and presently they came in full view of the whole party. Certainly it was a beautiful sight. There were about thirty hands altogether, of all ages and sizes. The men displaying the bone and sinew of their muscular forms to the greatest advantage in the movement of the cradle, while the women in their blue cotton dresses, with uncouth-looking head-dresses surmounting their craniums, formed picturesque additions to the scene. Each cradler had two binders; and the rapidity of their movements Jean thought wonderful: The golden grain was swept by the unerring scythe; the wide sweep of the arm baring an incredible space at each throw, so that the beautiful field, which, at their coming, had nodded a welcome with its million of heads, soon showed for a great distance before them nothing but the short stubble, forming a groundwork for the richly-piled sheaves which dotted it from one end to the other.

"Look, mamma, here comes Aunt Ailsie to speak to you," said Mary, as a queer-looking old figure appeared in a short cotton dress, which displayed to disadvantage the coarse shoes and not too neat-looking hose, while the hood of faded gingham, which sheltered her from the beams of the sun, failed to improve the negro features of the withered old face.

"Why, Aunt Ailsie, are you here, too?" said Jean, in surprise. "I thought you were too old for the harvest-field!"

"No, mistis, thank the Lord! I is been in the harvis-field all my life, and I hopes to die in it while the Lord spares me."

"Well, how do you stand it, old woman? Ain't you tired?"

"Oh, yes, mistis, but I'm still spyarin', — tumblin' over the clods—on pleadin' groun',—thank the Lord!" This medley of congratulations was almost too much for Jean's gravity, and the boys laughed outright.

"There seems to be a fine crop this year," said Jean, for want of a better remark.

"Yes, mistis, He dun sont a 'bundant harvis to 'rich He land. Thank Him for it!"

But the conversation was brought to a sudden stop by the old woman's catching sight of several woolly-headed urchins making a raid upon her tin bucket of provisions, which she had hidden under a sheaf of wheat; and she made a dash at the depredators, leaving the "white people" to laugh at their leisure.

Mr. Holcombe now rode up for a moment to speak to them; and when Jean told him of their interview with Ailsie, he said, laughing,—

"Unfortunately, Jean, those pious-talking ones are not always the best; they take it out in talking. When I hear one of my negroes descanting eloquently on the subject of his religious experience, I always keep my eyes about me. There used to be an old woman named Hetty, and my mother always said, when she would bring the yarn in, which she had been spinning, to have it weighed, she always knew, if Hetty's mood was particularly pious, that the yarn was a hank short."

But as the sun was looking his last just before bidding the world good-night, the whole party turned their faces homewards. As they made their way through the woods which lay between them and the house, Margaret and Mary, accompanied by the three boys, made the grove vocal with their imitations of the music of the reapers:

> "Where now are good Brother Danel?
> Way over in de Promis' Lan'.

> "He got cotch in de den of lions,
> Way over in de Promis' Lan'.

> "Where now is Medrach and Bednigo?
> Way over in de Promis' Lan'.

> "They went fru de fiery furnace,
> Way over in de Promis' Lan'."

"It seems to me," said Mr. Williams, "that one of the shining lights is neglected in that memorial."

'Oh, no, Mr. Williams," said George, "they make a cunning combination of Shadrach and Meshach, making it Medrach; their metre would not allow a further concession to history."

"Oh, mamma," said Mary, "look at Aunt Milly! Don't she look handsome?"

She certainly looked picturesque as she stood on the brow of the hill, her tall figure clearly defined against the sky, and her voice coming to them mellowed by distance, crying, "Come, come, come."

"She is calling the cows," said John; and there, way off across the meadow, they came at her bidding, one after another, making a pretty feature in the landscape as their graceful forms blended with the softened hues of twilight.

It was decided to go home by the "cuppin,"—a "nickname," John said, "for cow-pen." So they turned off into the green meadow, and reached the brow of the hill just as the three milkmaids were emptying their first buckets of the foaming white fluid into the large tubs.

The cows stood patiently within an inclosure made of rails, while the calves ma-a-ed discontentedly on the outside,—a useless expenditure of eloquence on the subject of their defrauded rights, which their master, man, failed to recognize.

The scene was as new to Jean as the harvest-field had been, and she was very much amused to hear the milkmaids talking to the animals, as if they really understood them.

"You Bet! stan' roun' here!. Don't you hear me? I ain't goin' to take none of your ars!"

"I see you, old Whitey! You is jest gittin' ready to kick dis here bucket over, en as sho as you dus, you will git it, now min', I tell you."

At last, much to their gratification, the work of *spoiling* was over, and the calves were let in to their mothers, to take the remnant of the feast, which, after the long waiting, was most joyfully received.

"What are they going to do now?" said Jean, as she saw the women lifting up the tubs. "Surely they never can carry those things on their heads;" but she found her mistake as, rising up under their burdens, and placing one hand on the hip, while in the other they carried a full bucket, off they went, singing at the top of their voices, the tubs poised gracefully, and the burden-bearers looking as much at ease as if they carried no weight at all.

10*

# CHAPTER XIV

THE regular vacation at Rose Hill was arranged for the winter, though, during the hottest part of the summer, extempore holidays were allowed in order to recruit the exhausted energies of teacher and pupils.

One was proposed soon after harvest, as Mr. Williams had not been very well, and required a relaxation.

"Suppose we make up an expedition to Hawk's Nest," Margaret proposed; "Mr. Williams has never been there, and we can all go and see the sunset,—it is worth a ride of twenty miles."

The proposition was unanimously carried, and taken to the Upper House; which, instead of vetoing it, further suggested that sunrise was as well worth seeing as sunset, and that they had better get up a picnic party which would last two days.

Now Mr. Holcombe had a farm just at the foot of the mountain, and it was at this time without a tenant,—what if they took possession of the house for a few days for the variety of the thing!

This plan was of course delightful, though Jean declared herself unable to go, as Lilias, who had suffered much from the warm weather, was more unwell than usual, and could not of course leave the comforts of home. Mr. Holcombe immediately announced his intention of remaining also, though with characteristic determination not to acknowledge danger of trouble, he said he knew

( 114 )

there was nothing the matter with Lily more than she suffered from every summer.

Mrs. Bascombe, with Rachel and Ned as assistants, were dispatched on Wednesday with everything necessary for the comfort of the party, though one of the great enjoyments was to consist in the absence of the luxuries of home.

Thursday proved as bright a day as any one could wish, and a trip to Europe could scarce have claimed more abundant preparations: there was an extensive supply of worsted-work, etc. for the girls, and guns and fishing-tackle for the boys; books enough for a party twice the size of theirs, to last them twice as long; besides chessmen, backgammon, and every variety of game. It was determined to stay until Saturday evening.

Uncle Bob made his appearance with his inevitable cart, which presented a strange medley when it was all packed to start.

"Who dares to take a slate?" said Harry Holcombe, holding up one to public scorn, which he had just ferreted out from the loose baggage. "I don't care whose it is, it ain't fair to take anything belonging to school."

"It is mine, Harry; give it to me," said Mary.

"And what upon the earth do you want with it? you are not generally such an enthusiastic mathematician."

"I wanted," said Mary, blushing, "to learn to draw, and thought I would begin on a slate."

The laugh was too general for Mary's comfort, at the idea of drawing from nature on a slate.

"Never mind how much they laugh, Mary," said Mr. Williams, "it shows their ignorance. I could tell them of a celebrated sculptor whose talent was discovered by a figure he drew on the top of a firkin of lard; but it is just as well for you to leave the slate at home, as Harry's feelings are so sensitive. I have everything you will want in my portfolio, and I may be able to help you too."

"Oh, thank you! thank you!" was the eager response, as Snowflake (so she had named her pony) was brought to the door, and her father came forward to help her up.

"Why, you are not more than a snowflake yourself," he said, as she sprang into her seat with scarce any help from him. "If you don't take care of this young lady, Mr. Williams, she will go up on the wings of the first wind which comes along higher than the old woman who was tossed up in a blanket."

Margie was already mounted on Brown Bess, and never showed to such advantage as in her present position, with her lithe, young figure set off by the tight-fitting riding-dress of some black material, and the broad-brimmed hat tied down under the chin. She was perfect mistress of her horse, and as she patted the arched neck, the pleased movement of its pretty head showed the touch to be a familiar one.

Mr. Williams bestrode black Festus;—Mr. Holcombe's fine Arabian,—and the boys were mounted on the refuse of the stable. George having chosen a scrubby, rusty-looking mule, whose antics caused no little amusement to the party, and Harry and John mounted on one horse, and were to take turns in holding the reins.

"Good-by!" "good-by!" resounded from all sides.

"A good riddance of bad rubbish!" called out Mr. Holcombe as they rode off.

"Good-by, Uncle Ned," said George. "Bucephalus presents his compliments." And he touched his steed behind, which sent his heels high in the air, by way of a farewell greeting.

Mr. Holcombe and Jean stood watching the happy party as they rode into the grove.

"They are certainly a merry set," said he. "I wonder if time is going to let them stay so all their lives. It seems right hard to think of their growing old and dying careworn."

"Yes," said she, "if life was everything; but——"

"Ah, well, don't let us get on such doleful subjects. I am never going to look forward. I believe we will all do as they do in the story-books,—live in peace, and die in a pot of grease."

A ride of three or four miles brought the picnickers to the little white cottage, built almost under the mountain, and there stood Mrs. Bascombe in the door to welcome them.

There was a long porch in the front of the house, from which you entered two rooms: one, the kitchen, where Mrs. Bascombe, with Rachel to help her, superintended ovens of various sizes, with glowing coals on the top and underneath, before a fire of huge logs, such primitive modes of cooking being necessary owing to the transient nature of the settlement; the other room (the largest of the two) served as dining-room, parlor, etc. It now presented a very seductive appearance to the hungry equestrians, in spite of its lack of furniture, for in the center of the room was spread the supper-table, made attractive by the beautiful white cloth, blue India china, and highly-polished silver, whilst in the center, the tempting pat of yellow butter, with its crystal lump of ice on the top, gave a promise of good cheer at the evening meal.

A flight of stairs landed in the room, and Mary at once proposed to Margaret an inspection of the entire establishment. So the two lady hostesses disappeared; their merry laughter soon drew the rest of the party after them, and they found the upper floor to consist of four tiny bedrooms, with beds spread on the floor, and boxes fixed in the corners, covered with white draperies, to answer the purpose of washstands and dressing-tables.

"I speak for this room," said Harry, rolling himself over the bed in the largest room. "The rest of you have my permission to do as you please."

"You have fairly won it, Harry," said Margaret, "as no one wants it after you have rolled over it. But don't flatter yourself that you are to have it alone. George and John occupy it with you. This one is Mrs. Bascombe's, that Mr. Williams's, and Mary and myself will take this, at the head of the stairs."

"Good gracious, Margie!" said John, "sleep in the bed with those two boys! Why, Harry kicks, and George has an uncomfortable way of throwing his arms about."

"And I think," said George, in comic dismay, "that I shall forsake the populous assembly and repose on the porch."

"Do," responded Harry; "and if you are cold, just shut the front gate."

Mr. Williams settled matters by offering disconsolate John an asylum in his room.

Just then the odor of steaming coffee reached them, and they descended the stairs to find the dainty meal prepared for them, and Mrs. Bascombe was duly complimented on the masterly manner in which she had met the emergency.

Mary declared the bread and butter to be the best she had ever tasted, and the broiled chickens met with universal approbation.

The evening proved too warm to stay in-doors, so the whole party adjourned to the green outside the house, and lounged contentedly on the grass, whilst the moon beamed upon them complacently.

" Did you ever see anything so beautiful as this moon ?"
said Mary.

" That shows the greatest ingratitude for past favors,
Mary," said George. "It is just as bright every full
moon as it is now. It seems a pity to me that we always
have to be denied something. The moon, for instance, is
such a jealous jade she will not countenance a rival,—she
puts out the stars every time she shows her face. It
would be so much prettier if we could have all together."

" They did at the siege of Corinth," said Margaret; "at
least Byron says so. By-the-by, Mr. Williams, is not that
passage open to criticism ?"

" What is it ?"

Margaret repeated :

> "'Tis midnight on the mountains brown ;
> The cold round moon shines deeply down ;
> Blue roll the waters, blue the sky
> Spreads like an ocean hung on high,
> Bespangled with those isles of light,
> So wildly, spiritually bright.
> Who ever gazed upon their shining
> And turned to earth without repining,
> Nor wished for wings to flee away
> And mix with their eternal ray ?"

" Well, no," said Mr. Williams, when she stopped ; "at
least it would be hypercritical to raise such an objection.
Except when the moon is at its full, stars can be seen :
and even to-night you can see them dimly."

" Yes, but not ' wildly, spiritually bright.' And he does
say the ' round moon.' Now the moon is never round
but when it is full."

Mr. Williams laughed. "You are a young critic, Miss
Margaret, and if Byron could only hear you he would
give you a niche in his ' English Bards and Scotch Reviewers.' "

" Why, Mr. Williams ?" asked Mary.

" You know at the commencement of Byron's career he wrote some poems called ' Hours of Idleness,' and though there are some of the pieces which have merit, taken as a whole, they are not worthy of his genius. The ' Edinburgh Review' was a magazine published at that time, and it took up these poems most savagely. Among other things it said, I remember, the poesy of this young lord belongs to the class which neither gods nor men are said to permit. Fortunately, he says he is but an intruder into the groves of Parnassus. He never lived in a garret like a thoroughbred poet. Moreover, he expects no profit from his poems, and whether they succeed or not, it is highly improbable, from his situation and pursuits, that he will again condescend to become an author. So I suppose we are well off to have got so much from a man of his station, who does not live in a garret, but has the sway of Newstead Abbey. So I say let us be thankful, and bid God bless the giver, nor look a gift horse in the mouth.

" Byron's most dignified course would have been silence under such gross injustice, which would have recoiled upon the heads of the perpetrators. But there was too much littleness in the man for any such course as that. For the rasping, after all, he had afterwards cause to be thankful, as it roused his slumbering genius, and gave him his rank among the great lights of the age.

" He wrote his ' English Bards and Scotch Reviewers,' which is probably the wittiest, most caustic, and vigorous satire which has ever been written in the English language. But in the virulence of his temper he forgot to discriminate, and friends and foes went down alike under the relentless scythe of his satirical pen. I believe he was sorry for this afterwards, but it could not be recalled.

I would not advise you, however, young people, to cultivate an admiration for Byron. He was a bad man though
a great genius; and I do not think the style of his
writings healthy or profitable."

Margaret felt herself blushing. She was just at the
Byron age; and, as Mr. Williams spoke, felt conscious
that the perusal of his works had had the effect of strength-
ening her in the indulgence of the moody, melancholy
temper which had of late possessed her.

As their trip to the mountain-top was fixed for very
early the next morning, it was decided to disperse about
nine o'clock, which they did, and the whole party were
soon asleep. The last sound which fell on Margie's
sleepy ear was from Mary, saying,—

"I believe I will always sleep on a pallet, it is so
pleasant to feel that you can't fall out of bed,—ain't it,
Margie?"

As there was no response as an encouragement to
further conversation, Mary joined her sister in the land
of dreams.

"Goodness! how funny it seems to be waked up this
early!" said Margaret, rubbing her eyes, as Rachel at
last succeeded in making them understand that the whole
party would be waiting for them, and the sun would be
up before them if they did not make haste. It did not
take them very long to make their toilets; but when they
got down-stairs, they found Mr. Williams leaning over
the gate, and the boys rolling restlessly on the grass,
awaiting their arrival; and John pronounced them
"humbugs" because they took so long to dress.

They started forward, up the steep sides of the mountain, all for a race to the goal which was nearly half a
mile off. In her eager enjoyment, Margaret almost for-

11

got her mature fifteen years; but recalled to herself, she
assumed her expression of dignified consciousness, and
fell back; and Mr. Williams and herself followed the
others at a slower pace, though always in view of them.

It was a sight worth seeing, those country girls and
boys, with the agility almost of Highlanders, making
such speed up the precipitous side of the mountain, now
clinging to a tree or shoot, or holding on to a rock, or
planting the foot more firmly on the slippery path. Mary
was so light and active that she reminded Mr. Williams of
the fleet-footed antelope springing from rock to rock. She
outstripped even the hardy boys; and when Margaret and
Mr. Williams were still far below them, they saw Mary
standing on the topmost verge of a high rock which crowned
the peak, waving her hat to proclaim her triumph.

"Stand still a minute, Mary," called out Mr. Williams,
"and I will draw your likeness!" And hurrying past
Margaret, he said, "I would not miss that chance for a
scene on any account."

Mary, highly pleased at the idea of having her picture
taken, stood like a statue, while the artist got out his
drawing materials, and commenced rapidly to sketch the
pretty child with the glowing cheeks and laughing eyes,
and that wealth of beautiful hair. Just then the sun,
rising above the horizon, tinged with his earliest beams
the figure on the rocky peak, tinted the bright hair like
threads of gold, and lighted up the whole scene with magi-
cal beauty. How the young artist wished for the pencil
of a Rubens that he might do justice to his subject; and
how often, in after-years, did the memory of that beautiful,
fairy-like child come back to him as she stood there, looking down upon him with her coronet of gold sparkling in
the beams of the rising sun!

He had made but a rough sketch, but it was enough to

guide him. Mary exclaimed, with an artlessness which
made them all smile,—

"Ah, me, how pretty! And it looks like me, too!"

"Why, Mary, what a piece of vanity!" said Margaret,
in a shocked tone of voice which brought the crimson to
Mary's face.

"Indeed! indeed!—I did not mean—I did not say—I
—Pshaw! I meant the drawing was pretty!"

"We all know what you meant, my child," said Mr. Williams. "As I told your sister, last night, she is rather
hypercritical. Let her confine herself to assailable people,
like Byron and others, and not send the arrows of her criticism towards such harmless objects as you and myself."

"It seems to me," said Margaret, her eyes flashing
upon him, "that you are making a rather lame attempt,
Mr. Williams, to get up an edition of 'English Bards and
Scotch Reviewers' for my chastisement. I am much
obliged to you."

"Excuse me, Miss Holcombe. I did not mean to be
rude; but I could not bear that you should suggest a
consciousness to your sister, whose perfect freedom from
it, or assumption of any kind, is her greatest charm."

He had spoken in a low tone, so that Mary might not
catch his explanation; but Margaret was not appeased.

"You mean, I suppose, to insinuate, Mr. Williams, that
I possess the qualities which you esteem her for lacking?"

He did not speak for an instant, but seeing her waiting
still for an answer, he said,—

"I did not say so, nor do I think it could be fairly in-
ferred from what I did say. I have no right to pronounce
judgment upon you, nor will I consent to be forced
into it."

Margaret turned on her heel and walked away,—her
love of approbation was very strong, and she felt keenly

the implied reproof in Mr. Williams's words; but it did not do her the good it might have done, it only made her angry, and her uncandid comment upon the whole was, that Mary's beauty had turned her sober teacher's brain, and made him view everything she did in an exaggerated light; and then the old cry came back, "Oh, that I were beautiful!"

Breakfast was ready for them when they reached the cottage; but everybody was tired, and Margaret's brow had not yet smoothed, so it did not possess the charm of the supper the night before.

Each one was to follow the bent of his inclinations for the day. And the boys got out guns and fishing-tackle to provide *their family* with food, as they pompously announced; Mr. Williams was not well enough to accompany them, so he decided to remain behind, and as a proffer of peace proposed a game of chess with Miss Holcombe. The young lady in question declined, however, and went off into the grove to write letters. So Mary claimed his promise to teach her to draw. The morning was whiled away very quietly, reading soon superseding drawing and writing; at length, however, Mary becoming tired of her inertia started off on a tour of inspection. Some little time was spent in studying natural history by observing the birds and insects, and she was just wondering where Mr. Williams was that she might consult him about some of her discoveries, when her eye caught sight of a sapling. It was the work of a minute to pull it down and mount it,—and her delight knew no bounds when she found herself flying up and down in the soft breeze; ·the amusement suited her admirably.

There was an observer of her motions hidden from view by some undergrowth about ten yards off, and laying down his book he amused himself watching the feathery-looking little figure in her light draperies flitting up and down before his eyes; he felt impelled to join her and be a boy again, so vividly did the scene recall the days of his childhood. Just then, however, the crunching of the dry leaves announced the approach of another outsider, and he heard, without seeing, Margaret's tone of grave reproof and shocked propriety.

"Oh, Mary! I declare I never saw such a tomboy as you are. You forget how old you are, my child. Why, if any one were to see you they would be perfectly shocked at your appearance. Suppose Mr. Williams were to come up now?"

"I wish he would," said Mary, without slackening her pace; "I think he would like a ride himself, it is perfectly splendid, a great deal better than horseback."

"How in the world did you ever get up there?" said Margaret.

"Oh, nothing easier; you see it is so thin I just pulled it down to the ground and held on to it until I mounted. No one is about, Margie; just try it, you don't know how nice it is."

Margie laughed; she was child enough to like the fun, though not quite willing to lay herself open to the charge of inconsistency. As Mary seemed to have forgotten her expressed disapprobation, however, perhaps it had made no impression upon her.

"I have half a mind to try," she said. "Where is Mr. Williams?"

"I think he must have gone to the house. I'll watch and listen,—no one shall catch you."

A little longer struggle between the child and woman in the girl, and the child conquered. Mary got off, and obligingly held the steed down very low while her sister mounted, secretly exultant that now her frailties must meet with some leniency since the dignified young lady of fifteen was transgressing.

11*

In another minute Margaret was flying away in as full enjoyment as Mary's had been, and the recumbent figure among the trees, very much amused at the whole scene, was trying to roll himself farther out of sight, so that he might make his way to the house. To him they were merely two children at play, but he well knew that Margaret's wrath would be dire if he was caught, so his most earnest desire was to make his escape.

The very efforts he made, however, defeated his object; as the fair equestrienne made a higher flight than usual she caught sight of a moving mass among the bushes.

In an instant Mary's riderless steed sprang back to its position, and Margaret only managed to ejaculate "A man!" and buried her face in her hands. Mr. Williams, finding that he was discovered, came forward, not very much disconcerted; and Mary threw herself on the ground and laughed so that she could not speak.

"Forgive me, Miss Holcombe," said Mr. Williams, "it seems I am in bad luck to-day; this is twice I have fallen under your displeasure." The words were penitent, but there was a tone in the voice which revealed to her the fact that if he dared he would join Mary in her laugh on the grass.

Her answer was indignant in the extreme: "Mr. Williams, I scarcely expected to find you occupying the position of a spy. I thought you were a gentleman, at any rate. I shall let papa know as soon as I go home to whom he has intrusted us."

"I shall save you the trouble, my dear young lady," he said, his voice betraying none of the feeling which showed itself in his face. "I shall tell him myself; no doubt he will be very much amused at the whole incident."

The idea of being placed in the ludicrous position she

knew his story must put her was too much; words failed her and she burst into tears.

Mr. Williams, like all men, and particularly young men, had a dread of hysterics, and, besides, he was really sorry to see her so distressed; so, going up to her and speaking very gently, he said,—

"You asked me this morning if I thought you possessed the qualities of which I pronounced Mary so free. I will answer that question now by telling you why I was interested in the little scene I have just witnessed. I had not this morning quite made up my mind what I thought, and I lay there a little while since dissecting your character. Shall I tell you what I found?" He took silence for consent and went on: "I saw you making a great mistake, I said to myself. Oh, why will she not see that genuine childhood is the most beautiful thing in the world, and that she loses the best part of her life by assuming the airs and rights of a woman?

"To my surprise, however, in a moment I found that the child-nature was there, though in abeyance; and I watched with all the interest of a philosopher to find which nature was predominant, and almost felt a triumph when I found the real Miss Holcombe without the disguise she chooses to assume. I have so high an opinion of you in many respects that I have not been able to reconcile myself to what I must consider as a blemish in your character. Take my advice and don't thwart nature. She is more lovely in her operations than art will ever be."

He turned and walked hastily down the path leading to the house, rightly judging, if he gave her an opportunity to reply, pride, not quite conquered, might impel her to say something for which they would both be sorry; and he knew that if she were left alone her better self would conquer. When he had walked about three or four yards from the girls, he turned and beckoned Mary to follow him.

The result proved his conduct wise, as Margaret appeared at the dinner-table with a softened manner, the traces of tears not yet obliterated.

The rest of the visit was delightfully spent in various amusements, and nothing else happened to mar the pleasure of the prolonged picnic, and the party returned home with many regrets that another happy time was past.

They found everything as usual at Rose Hill, except that Lilias still appeared listless and languid. She wanted to hear all about the trip, but was so wearied before they got through that they had to stop. Her condition was beginning to excite some apprehension in Mrs. Holcombe, though no one else seemed to observe anything peculiar.

# CHAPTER XV.

## THE ANGEL OF DEATH.

"Mr. Holcombe," called Jean, as he started off on Festus the next morning, "I wish you would ask Dr. Campbell to come and see Lilias."

Mr. Holcombe turned quickly in his saddle and said, "What is the matter? There don't seem to me to be anything but debility, caused by this miserably warm weather."

"No, that is all; but still I feel uneasy. Perhaps she needs some tonic."

"Oh, yes, I dare say she does. I will call and tell the doctor; but, Jean, for goodness' sake, don't be so gloomy. You are a perfect Jeremiah. I have seen her this way before, and I know it is only a little lassitude. She will be well in a few days."

Jean smiled at him as he rode off, but could not adopt his idea. She went back to the room and looked at the little face almost as white and delicate as the gown which she wore, and she felt sure that there must be real ground for anxiety. Here she had two months more of warm weather still, and already so reduced; and yet no one seemed to see it but herself. The fact was the child had always been so much of an invalid that the rest of the family had become accustomed to it, and did not remark the great change which had taken place in a short time, and then, too, she never complained; indeed, she hardly seemed to have the strength to do so, but lay all day long like a blighted lily dying in the glaring sun.

"Betsy and Nelly" and the other members of her "family" lay all around, and she would look at them with her old tender smile without the old gladness. Even the pretty work-box was laid aside "until cool weather comes."

Jean read and sung to her, and Margie and Mary did the same, and the boys would come in with their burst of joyous health; but nothing seemed much to rouse her from the apathy into which she had fallen. Every one said, "Oh, she is always so during the heat of the summer months." And so matters had been allowed to progress. That morning Jean had called in old Mammy; and as soon as she saw her she said, "You had better send for the doctor, Miss Jean; she is a very sick child; don't mind what Mars' Ned say; he never will look at trouble till it come; she ain't never been so low down as this before."

Dr. Campbell had been the family physician of the Holcombes for the past thirty years: and his arrival was always hailed by the children as an era in their lives. Accordingly, when his sober old gray was seen coming out of the grove, on this morning, at least three witnesses announced the fact at Mrs. Holcombe's door; and even the sick child roused up to some appearance of interest when the old gentleman made his appearance.

"Why, what's the matter with Dame Lilias, hey?" said he, kissing the white little face which smiled up at him from the pillow. "At your old tricks, I perceive. Young woman, what hurts you?"

"There is nothing the matter with me, doctor; I feel right well."

"You do; then why don't you get up?"

"Well, I will to-morrow,—but it is so warm to-day. I like to lie here and have Nanny to fan me."

"Ah, poor little puss!—do you eat anything?"

"Yes, sometimes."

And this was all. And, after ordering strong tonics and perfect rest, he said "Good-by."

"Will you come to-morrow, doctor?" said the child.

"Oh, yes, if you want me." And as he raised up from kissing her farewell, Jean saw the moisture in his eyes.

She followed him out of the room, and said, anxiously,—

"Doctor, is there anything serious?"

"Oh, yes, madam; everything is serious with a little atom of mortality like that, with not the life of a flea in it. There is nothing to build on."

"Oh, doctor,"—and the tears came into her eyes,—"she will not die, will she?"

"God only knows that, madam. If a cool rain were to come up she might recuperate, and she may yield to the tonics; but no one can tell. But there must be some revival, and soon, for her blood flows but slowly now."

"Cannot something be done, doctor?" And the trembling hands beat the air as if the sense of helplessness was too great in the presence of such danger.

"Oh, yes, madam. Let her be perfectly still; and don't try to rouse her too vigorously. Rest is the best thing for her. No matter if she does not notice things, it is want of strength which causes it; and the strength she has will be best recruited by perfect quiet. She has no disease."

There is no sickness so trying to the nurse as that in which there is nothing to be done but to sit and watch. So long as the hands are busy, the heart finds relief; but to sit motionless, and see the pulsation flowing feebler each hour, is dreary work.

At first the tonics raised the pulse, and light came back into the blue eyes; but it was only the feeble flicker of the little rushlight which, it soon became apparent to all, would, before long, die out.

Mr. Holcombe was hard to convince on the subject, as he determinedly put conviction from him, and would sit beside her; and, whenever she waked, try to make her laugh. The most he could ever gain, however, was one of her soft, feeble smiles.

One night Jean and himself sat beside the little crib on one side, and Margie and Mary knelt on the other, while Mammy sat at a little distance; Nanny (her nurse) having fallen asleep from exhaustion.

The blue eyes were opened, and looked around in surprise at so many gathered about her bed. The expression of the face was so different from what it had been for some time past that Mr. Holcombe, turning to his wife, said, smiling,—

"There now, Jean, she is better; just see how bright she is!"

Old Mammy spoke. "Oh, Mars' Ned, so is the candle when it jumps up out of the socket jes before it goes out."

He turned around on her almost angrily.

"What do you mean, Mammy? The child is evidently better,—ain't you, my darling?" Stooping over her.

"I don't know;" and the little hand, trembling with weakness, went up to her head. "Am I very sick, papa? What does it mean? What are you all crying for?" And the blue eyes searched each face keenly.

"You have been very ill, my darling baby," said he, in vain striving to control the quiver in his voice as he spoke. "We have been very miserable,—but you feel better now. Tell papa, Lilias, you feel better." And the strong man broke down over the agony in the tones of his own voice.

"I did not know I was sick: I only feel tired. Margie, what are you and Mary doing here?" She was evidently becoming confused, and the girls withdrew to a little distance; but the anxious eyes were still wide open, restless, dissatisfied. At last she said,—

"Mamma, come here." And as she knelt beside her, the little arms crept around her neck, and she whispered,—

"Am I going to die?"

"You would not be afraid, Lilias, would you?" was the evasive answer.

"I don't know: tell me about it."

"You know you would go to heaven to be with Jesus."

"Say 'Suffer little children.'"

"Yes, He said 'Suffer little children to come unto me and forbid them not, for of such is the kingdom of heaven.'"

"I don't want to go by myself,"—and the clasp of the arms became tighter,—"I am afraid."

"Listen, Lilias! Don't you remember in your pretty book about the shepherd in the mountains, and the picture you thought so pretty, where he takes up the little lambs and carries them over the rocks?"

"Yes."

"Well, you are one of the little lambs, and Jesus is the kind shepherd, He will take you safely to the end of your journey."

"Are you coming, too?"

"After awhile, darling, when God is ready for me."

"And papa?"

Jean moved aside and made room for him close beside her.

"Papa, are you coming, too?"

"Oh, Lilias, stay with me! I don't know, my child."

"You must come, papa. I would stay if I could, but God wants me."

"Lilias," said Jean again, in her low, trembling voice, "do you remember, baby, in the same story of the shepherd, that sometimes, when the old sheep would stray away from him, he took the little lamb in his arms, and then the old sheep would follow without any more trouble?"

"Yes." And the eyes looked full of interest.

"Now, maybe when the Good Shepherd takes our little lamb we will follow Him in the same way."

"Yes, all must come. Papa, Margie, Mary, and John, —all come soon." She was very tired now, and they gave her a tablespoonful of brandy, and Mr. Holcombe sent off for Dr. Campbell.

The bright eyes commenced their wanderings again.

"Where is Mamie?"

"Here, darling." And Mary stooped over and kissed her.

"Mamie, take care of my family; don't let them get all broke up."

The promise was given. "And," continued the failing voice, "Margie can have my work-box, and John my Rollo Serious,—and mamma, you let Mammy have my chair, and give Nanny my ring,—that is all I have got." This was said at intervals as her strength would allow; then a long silence before she spoke again.

"Mamma, will I walk when I get there?"

"Yes, darling, you will leave this poor, little, suffering body behind you, and your spirit will be as bright and joyous as any other,—you will be very happy."

"Will I know anybody there?"

"Oh, yes; your mamma, about whom we have talked so often, and so many dear friends who died before you were born."

"Is that the 'Happy land, far, far away,' mamma?"

"Yes, darling; but not so far away now. I think you are nearing the river."

"What river, mamma?" And the voice grew alarmed.

"Never mind, dearie; it is a very shallow stream for you,—the Shepherd will take you over." And she was quieted.

"Is Margie there, mamma?"

Margie herself answered her. "Yes, darling, what do you want?"

"Sing, Margie, 'There is a Happy Land."

The voices of the two girls rose sweetly in the quiet of the room. The white lids closed over the violet eyes, and, when they opened, they saw "another land than ours."

When Dr. Campbell arrived he found them all gathered around the little lifeless form, while Jean was trying to convince Mr. Holcombe that she was gone. There is always something painfully striking in the contrast between the sobs and grief of bereaved friends around the dead and the marble stillness of the corpse. So thought the doctor as he entered the chamber of death,—there she lay with a smile on her parted lips like a child who had just dropped to sleep; while the sobs and cries of the children and servants sounded noisily through the room, and Mr. Holcombe tried in vain to command silence, insisting that it would wake the little slumberer. As Dr. Campbell entered, he said,—

"Oh, doctor, I am glad you are here, you can assure these poor frightened children that she is only sleeping."

And he tried in vain to maintain his composure by insisting upon this point. The doctor came forward, took the limp little hand in his, laid his other hand next the still heart, raised the closed lids of the now sightless orbs, and put his finger into the mouth. It reminded Jean of the old scene in the prophet's chamber, where the dead son of the house lay upon the bed, and the old prophet bent above the corpse, "But there was no sound nor hearing."

Turning to the bereaved father, and laying his hand on his shoulder, he said, " Be comforted, Edward, ' she is where the wicked cease from troubling,'—your little, weary one is at rest." And the sobs which had been suspended during the examination broke out again. While the little sleeper lay, regardless of the confusion, with the happy smile upon her lips.

> " She has learned the song they sing
> Whom Jesus has made free ;
> And the glorious walls of heaven still ring
> With her new-born melody,"

said Jean, as she kissed the white brow of the little sleeper; and, taking her husband by the arm, persuaded him to go with her out of the room.

Brother George and sister Annie came to them as soon as they heard of the trouble,—how different from the last gathering beneath the Rose Hill roof!

" It is better to go to the house of mourning than to the house of feasting," said good sister Annie, as Jean spoke of the contrast ; " some of the sweetest seasons of communion with my Saviour have been after the death of my most precious friends. He always makes up our losses to us by giving us more and more of himself,— there need never be a vacuum in the heart."

They stayed until the little empty casket was laid away

in its silent resting-place, then returned to their homes. Before he left, Mr. George Holcombe handed his brother the following lines:

"Say, have they spring in heaven, as we on earth,
　That tender buds should be demanded there,
That, from your flow'rets of terrestrial birth,
　One all acknowledged lovely, sweet, and rare
Should thus be called, and softly borne away
To ope its petals in celestial day?

"You have one flow'ret less, and He one more,
　But yours must know the cold, the blight, the storm,
His shall be nurtured where no tempests roar,
　No change nor death may touch the gentle form
Then do not grieve, when more to you are given,
To offer up one bud to bloom in heaven.

"Was she the loveliest?　Give the best to Him.
　Was she the dearest?　Fittest for the skies.
Was she the purest?　Never more may dim
　Sin with its taint the lustre of her eyes.
Was she the best-beloved, the fond, the true?
Then give the best-beloved, it is His due."

**12***

# CHAPTER XVI.

## MARGARET LEAVES HOME.

PERHAPS no member of the family felt the vacuum created by the death of Lilias more constantly than did Jean.

She had been so much with her, and was such a care upon her, that for weeks she felt perfectly lost. Her occupation was gone. And when the little crib was put away, out of sight, and the familiar clothing was no longer seen, she began to realize, for the first time, that "the child was not."

They laid her beside her mother in the family burying-ground, and the children used to keep the grave covered with fresh flowers until the frosts of winter stripped the bushes.

It is an easy thing to say, "Oh, she is so much better off!" and so they all know. But grief is a selfish thing, and is apt to dwell more on the empty chair in the house-hold than the shining spirit in heaven.

Mr. Holcombe, impulsive and sanguine in tempera-ment, suffered, as such people always suffer, very in-tensely. As old Mammy expressed it, "He took trouble monsus hard."

He could not, for a long time, hear her name mentioned. But Jean said to him one day,—

"My dear husband, I do not know how you can bear to let the name of our little one die out of the household.

( 138 )

Let us keep that alive, at any rate. I love to think and talk of her pretty ways and her quaint sayings. They recur to me all the time, and if you will only for awhile put a constraint upon yourself, I am sure you will find comfort in it."

He did make the effort, with success, and it became no uncommon thing to hear constantly in the household, "As our dear little Lilias said." It is true, the smile which accompanied the recollection was often sad, and accompanied by a tear; but after awhile her humorous sayings became quite household words. But it takes a long time for a wound such as that to be healed. And the children were more subdued in their enjoyments, and showed conclusively that little Lilias was not forgotten.

During the fall, the question of sending Margaret away to school was often discussed, and since there was no longer open war between herself and the other members of the family, and she was old enough to claim greater advantages than a home school afforded, Jean ceased to oppose the move. So that obstacle being removed, the arrangement was soon decided upon.

At the first mention of the plan, Margaret positively refused to listen to it, but when she heard that the school fixed upon was the same which Ellen Randolph attended, she soon became reconciled, and, with the pliability of youth, grew enamored of the idea, and would at last have been much disappointed if the decision had been reversed.

There was an excitement, too, in getting ready, which was very pleasant to Margaret. All the seamstresses on the place were busy in her service, and the shopping expeditions to C—— altogether made her forget the pain of parting with home and home friends.

Imagination was busy building castles which time would surely destroy. She could not help, however, some little uneasiness about her standing at school. And her pride and ambition led her to improve every moment of time under Mr. Williams, until he was astonished at her progress.

The day before she left was spent in roving over all of her old haunts—her grotto in the grove, over which the ivy she had planted was spreading so beautifully. Here she sat a long time with her head on her hand, and here she first felt that she was giving up much in leaving her happy home, for it was happy in spite of her *self-*made sorrows; of late, too, habit had accustomed, if it had not reconciled, her to the existing state of things. Lilias's death-bed, with the low-voiced comforter at its side, had made a great impression upon her; and while it humbled her proud spirit to think that, there, she had been obliged to give up the first place by the side of the dying child, at the same time she had more than once asked herself if Lilias had died the year before, who would have been there to guide the trembling little feet heavenward. Even her father had never given these things the position they should have occupied in his thoughts, and she—how could she have pointed to a path she had never herself trod? And her heart, always candid and truthful to itself, acknowledged the good which had come out of what to her at first seemed such unmitigated evil.

If she had only followed the impulse, which for one moment seized her, to confess all this where the acknowledgment was due, how much of suffering and sin would have been spared her! But that pride to which Margaret Holcombe was a prisoner utterly refused to allow her to make any humiliating concessions.

"What! go and humble myself before her and say, 'I have been a wicked, bad girl; I am so sorry, please forgive me!' That I can never do."

"But," said her better nature, "to think of being relieved from this load of self-reproach, of being able to go away leaving nothing but love behind you, and then the nobility of acknowledging a fault, of making reparation to one you have so grievously injured!"

"Ah, yes," whispered Pride, "and to have yourself held up to your brother and sister as a warning against ill-doing and its consequences." And Pride exulted over another conquest.

"I am going away so soon now it is not worth while to change my manner; but when I return I will show her, without saying anything about it, that my feelings have all changed."

This she considered quite a concession, and her self-approbation rose at what she looked upon as a self-conquest. "Yes, she would write to papa and send her love to her; that will gratify him so much, and it will show him that I think myself wrong without having to say it."

The rustic grotto in which she sat, and which was her favorite resort, was formed of immense blocks of limestone rock, partly a natural formation, but with some assistance from art; it extended around three sides, leaving a space in the center about nine feet square, which was surrounded by stone seats, while the green grass formed a soft, pretty carpet for the floor. A chance acorn had buried itself somewhere amid these old rocks, and from it had sprung a tree which spread its wide branches over the place, forming a beautiful and appropriate roof, while the evergreen ivy was fast cementing the fragments of the rocks together with its resistless fingers.

The tears came into Margaret's eyes as she stood in

front of this beautiful arbor, and thought how long it would be before she would see it again.

Her next visit was to the negro quarters, to tell the servants all good-by; and she finished her course at Mammy's cabin, where she received the usual warm welcome.

"So you is goin' away to-morrow, my child?"

"Yes, Mammy, I suppose so; my heart begins to fail me."

"Of course it do, my dear; and I kinnot say I sees the good of it."

"Well, Mammy, I can learn so much more at school, not only books but music."

"Why, law, honey, it do seem to me that, smart as you is, you ought to ha' learnt all that is in the books by this time."

Margaret laughed at Mammy's limited idea of the progress of literature, but she did not attempt the task of enlightenment; only said,—

"Well, papa wants me to go."

"Oh, yes; and he knows what he is about. It is all right. Don't you want to read your old Mammy a chapter in the Bible before you goes?"

"Yes, indeed. Where is the book?"

It was brought from an ample chest in the corner, carefully wrapped in a white cloth; and Margie heard, with exemplary patience, the oft-told story of how "old marster" give this Bible to her mother, and she left it to her.

She opened at random, and read from the gospels the teachings of the Saviour; and as her eye caught the passage "Suffer little children to come unto me, and forbid them not, for of such is the kingdom of heaven," the image of a white-robed little figure rose before her;

and she heard again the soft voice saying, "Say, 'Suffer little children.'"

She closed the book hastily, and burying her face in Mammy's lap, burst into tears.

"Yes, my dear child," said the old woman, patting the head which lay in her lap, "I knowed you was thinking about that dear baby. Well, she wouldn't change with us. He is took her in his arms, and carried her over the river; and, Miss Margaret, don't forgit, when you goes to that furrin school, that she told you to come along after her. She will be lookin' out fur you, 'long of your ma."

As it is not our purpose to follow Margaret through her two years of school-life, we will close her present history with her first letters home, one written the day after her father left her, under the subduing influence of home-sickness; also one written one week later.

"WOODBINE, November 14, 1856.

"MY DEAREST FATHER,—After a night of agony, I have risen before any one else to write to you. I cannot tell you how miserable I am. I know I never will get used to being here, where everything is so different from home. I feel as if it would kill me to rise up and lie down to the sound of a bell as big as a church-bell, to run here and run there, to be in time to the minute, to dress by candlelight, and study with my eyes full of sleep. Papa, let me come home. I know I have not been the daughter I ought to have been; but, indeed, I want to begin now. Mr. Williams is a first-rate teacher, and I know I shall do very well with him; and I will try my best to improve in my music.

"Oh, papa, suppose any of you should die while I am away, and I not get home in time! I laid awake all night imagining the cars running off the track, and killing you on your way home. Do write at once and tell me you are safe.

"Everybody is very kind, but I am very unhappy. Ellen Randolph tries to comfort me by telling me that everybody feels so at first, that she hugged her trunk for three days because it looked like home. But I know I never shall get over it: and I do hope you will write at once, telling me to come. I will not unpack my trunk until I hear from you.

"Tell George that I am not as backward as I expected, and when I come back I will study harder than ever.

"Tell Mary that I think constantly of our dear bright room. When I look at this great barn, with a bed in every corner, and then to dress and undress before all these strangers, I never can stand it. Suppose you let me ask if I can have a room to myself. It is all so different from what I expected. And then, too, it makes me feel so strange, for everybody to know each other so well but me; even Ellen seems farther off than she ever was before, because she has so many friends, and I have only her.

"The teachers are as kind as they can be, and promised to excuse me from school to-day, because they felt sorry for me, I suppose. But they will have to keep on excusing me if it is for that, as I know I *never* will get any better.

"But I must stop, *dear, dear papa*, in time for the mail, as I want to get an answer as soon as I can. Oh, how I wish I could go in my letter!

"Give my love to *everybody*. Don't forget, *everybody;* grown people, children, and servants,—I love them all. May God spare us all to meet again in health and safety, is my earnest prayer.

"Devotedly your daughter,
"MARGARET.

"P. S.—I am so sorry for everything I have ever said to you that was wrong and impertinent. Please forgive me."

"WOODBINE, November 22d.

"MY DEAR PAPA,—Your letter has just reached me, and I hasten to answer it. I was very glad to hear that you had such a pleasant trip home. You will think me very silly, I dare say, when I tell you that I was right nervous about you for a little while. I agree with you that it would be very foolish to come home now after making a start at school. Indeed, I feel that my advantages are so great here, that I would not be willing to resign them even to go back to dear old Rose Hill.

"I must have written you quite a homesick epistle, judging from your answer. I hardly know what I said, as I wrote in a great hurry.

"The teachers are so sweet and kind, I love them all; and the girls, especially my room-mates, are lovely. I did not like being in the room with so many at first, but I don't object now. You get so well acquainted with a girl by staying in the same room with her.

"I think I am going on very well with my music,—I practice two hours a day. To-day I commenced my singing-lessons, and I am happy to say Mr. Branger thinks I have a very good voice. I am thoroughly interested in all my studies, dear papa, and like the school as well as I could like any place away from home.

"It seemed so strange to me, at first, to hear a great big bell all the time. But I am used to it now, and don't object to it. It rings every forty minutes through the day. And the minute the first sound reaches us there is a stir through the whole house,—every class changes, and all of the pianos change their occupants. It is right

13

funny how we have to hurry to get to our places in time.

"Well, dear papa, it is time for me to go to study hour, so I must stop. Ellen sends her love to everybody. Give mine to each member of the household, and believe me your devoted child,

"MARGARET HOLCOMBE."

# CHAPTER XVII.

*July 1st.* I can hardly believe that nearly two years have passed away since I last made an entry in my diary. But one does not have much time with so much to do as I have. Since Mrs. Bascombe left, it keeps me pretty busy.

I find upon looking back that the last time I wrote in this book I recorded the account of dear little Lilias's death, whose place in our hearts can never be filled, though the precious gift our Father gave us some months after has been the greatest comfort to us. Though we mourn the loss of our dear little one, we have learned to bless the kind hand which drew her so gently and painlessly from our grasp, and now shelters her so safely in his bosom, having stripped her sweet spirit of its robe of suffering mortality, leaving it at liberty to soar in its joyous freedom through the realms of bliss.

And has not her loss been blessed to us, too, in being the means of leading my precious husband to his Saviour? I can never forget the long struggle he endured, and how he could never lose the impression of the little hand beckoning to him, and the tender voice saying, "You must come, too, papa."

And now how changed he is! and how happy! He has lost that restless fear of trouble which he used to have, which led him to put aside everything which seemed

( 147 )

to threaten it.   He has learned to see the rod, and Him who sends it.

Yes, I shall always think of that dear child as such a blessing to me in her life and death,—she was so quaintly amusing in everything she said and did.   She filled up so much of my life in that first year of my marriage, and then in dying she brought such a blessing to our household.   Blessed little angel, it used to be hard to see why she should have been born, just to suffer and die, but it is easy to see the "*why*" in it all now.

And I cannot help hoping Mary is a Christian too, though she has never joined any church.   She is so particular about her religious duties, and then her Sunday-school.   All last winter how she used to go down all weathers to teach the servants!   I do not think she could be so self-denying and exemplary were it not that she has some religious principle in her heart.   God grant that it may be so.

I think John has improved very much too; he is certainly a fine, brave boy, with a great many faults, but so many good qualities.   I can hardly realize that he is the same child that met me at the depot the happy old day I first came to Rose Hill, or that cut down the pear-tree, to be like George Washington.   This last is still a standing joke against him.   I shall always think Mr. Williams did John a great deal of good.   I am glad he is coming to see us this summer; I do like him so much.   He always seems as one of the family, being here, I suppose, at the time Lilias was taken from us, and feeling so much with us.   Those are ties one never breaks.   Death breaks a great many, but makes almost as many.

The idea of Margaret's coming home a young lady this summer!   It seems very strange.   I wish I was not so much afraid of it; but my life has been so quiet since she has been at school that I fear any change. When she has been here at her vacations I have seen but little of her. It seems to me, however, that she is pretty much the same, with so many fine qualities and so many blemishes.

" In thinking over all which has taken place in these past three years, I feel as if there had been more crowded into them than into the whole of my past life : my marriage, my introduction to my home, that delightful Christmas, our precious baby's death, so soon followed by my father's, my darling's birth, Robert's promise to visit me, upon which I am living now, and the blessed change in· my husband. I feel as if I must say, " How shall I magnify the Lord for all his goodness to me ?"

It has been a blessing, too, that baby has always been so good. He has never been sick a day since his birth, and consequently so little trouble, though, I suppose, if I did not have dear old Mammy to help me, I would find the difference. But I can just pack him off. to her cabin, and I know he will be taken such good care of. Dear old lady! she is not often able to come up to the house now, and I feel as if I could never do enough for her. I trust God will spare her for many years to come. I do not know what any of us would do without her; but she is getting so feeble I feel very uneasy about her.

13*

# CHAPTER XVIII.

## AN IMPORTANT ARRIVAL.

It was on a warm morning in July when the air, seemingly languid from the intensity of the heat, refused to stir even the leaves upon the trees. A strange lull rested upon nature. The oak-tree overshadowing Margaret's grotto might have been painted on canvas, for all the motion it showed. The ivy has clambered and climbed until the outside of the rocks is one mass of dark, green leaves; and the resistless fingers are putting their fibery touch on the old tree, which, strong as it looks, has no power to resist its soft and gradual encroachment.

Beneath the green roof upon the grassy carpet stands a young girl. The first glance shows us an old acquaintance. It is Margaret Holcombe! But the old longing is satisfied: "the ugly duck has become a swan;" so changed, and yet the same! There is the same lithe figure, but now so magnificently proportioned, from the falling shoulders and rounded waist to the arched instep of the slender foot; tall, above the ordinary height of woman; the flowing robe of the softest white muslin falls in waving lines from the waist, and disposes its superfluous length upon the ground, while the white arm and neck show purely through the thin texture.

The face is less changed than the figure; there are the same irregular features. But what matters the wide mouth when the lips are full and rosy, which at each motion disclose glimpses of the perfect teeth? Even the forehead, much too low for perfect beauty, is redeemed by the elevated coronet of raven hair which rears itself above it. The sallow complexion has given place to blood of the richest hue,—a complexion coming and going with every variation of feeling, like the shifting hues of the sky, no minute the same.

Beautiful! high-born! accomplished! and wealthy!— what more can be asked for? Yet, what means the dissatisfied expression about the mouth? The old longing has been gratified only to give place to another. She has not found happiness yet. She would have deeply resented it, if any one had told her that it was dissatisfaction with herself which gathered the brow together in a wrinkle, which so often made her shun society and seek solitude.

I said she was standing at the opening of her grotto, with the green branches above her head, the green carpet beneath her feet, and the old gray rocks in the background. She had risen at the sound of a footstep,—a gentleman—a stranger—advanced towards her, hat in hand. There was something in Margaret Holcombe's appearance which would take the hat off of any man's head, be he gentleman or boor. But this was a gentleman without mistake, in spite of the travel-worn appearance of the whole person, the dusty clothes, the heavy boots.

"Pardon me, madam, but am I in the road to Mr. Holcombe's?"

"Yes, sir; the house is but a step from here. I am just returning; I will show you the way."

The shrewd eye turned upon her, — consciousness brought the blood to her cheek.

"You are Miss Holcombe, I suppose?"

The haughty head scarce nodded an assent. He felt that he had taken a liberty, and hastened to apologize.

"Pardon me; but I cannot feel that you are a stranger. I have heard so often, through my sister, of you."

"Ah, indeed!" Some one of her school-mates she supposed.

But here they came in sight of the house; and the exclamations of admiration of the scene prevented all other conversation until they reached the door.

"Walk in," said Margaret. "Shall I call papa?"

But before an answer could be given, a cry "Robert! Robert!" broke upon them, and Jean was locked in her brother's arms.

No thirsty traveler at the sight of a stream of water, no starving man at the sight of a feast, could have felt more satisfying happiness than did this sister at the sight of her long-wished-for brother. It was the moment so ardently looked for, and the fruition was so full. Mr. Holcombe soon came in, and gave his glad welcome to the traveler; then Mary and John, all rejoicing with "mamma;" next the wee toddling boy—Master Ned, Junior, claimed acquaintance with his new uncle.

"Well, Jean," said Mr. Holcombe, "are you going to keep Robert here all day? Let him wash his face, at any rate. We won't let him leave us for a long time now we have him, so you will have time enough to see him. Ah, Robert, she will 'kill the fatted calf' now!"

"I am no prodigal son, though, I want you to understand," said Robert, as he got up to go to his room.

"Well, it don't make any difference," said Mr. Holcombe; "we like you just as much as if you were."

Margaret was completely taken by surprise. She had never even heard of Jean's brother; but she could not help sympathizing deeply with them both. And when

Robert turned towards his fair guide in leaving the room, her eyes were moist and her face radiant with feeling.

There was so much for the brother and sister to talk about that they were not seen again until dinner-time. Mary took the keys, and insisted that there was no necessity for Jean going down-stairs at all,—nor was there. The servants were too anxious to do everything for the newcomer, and the young housekeeper felt her responsibility too deeply to go wrong.

Meanwhile, in the library sat Mr. Murray and Jean Holcombe. He occupied an easy-chair, and she sat at his feet looking up and listening to him. As they sit there, we are struck with the contrast between the two. He being as far above the average height of man as she was below the ordinary height of woman. They were both Saxon, in their fair complexion and light hair; but he might have been one of those old conquerors of the Britons who lived before men were dwarfed and stunted by wealth and luxury. No one would ever have thought of calling him handsome; indeed, his face would have been pronounced homely but for the strength in it. There was a powerful irregularity in every lineament, and I believe nature is apt so to assert herself as the towering mountain with its frowning cliffs, "where the clouds stop to repose themselves in passing by," its turbulent streams and rocky crags convey an idea of strength so much greater than the smiling plain, where the glassy stream glides so quietly.

So in man,—strength of character and strength of mind is apt to show itself in strongly-marked, irregular features.

Robert Murray looked every day of his nine-and-twenty years: he had not led a life of luxurious ease. After Jean left England, he too found it impossible to remain, though he had never, so long as his father lived, called any other spot home; but after he grew to manhood his love of change and adventure led him far away from the scenes of his childhood.

He studied for two years in the universities of Germany: dipping deeply into their metaphysical investigations and mythical theories, he became tainted with skepticism, if not infidelity; leaving there, with mind and heart bewildered, he determined to travel on foot through Switzerland and Italy, and by constant contact with nature strive to throw off the apathy which possessed him after his years of hard study. He stood by the Lake of Como, but its peaceful quiet had not the charm for him which more rugged scenes possessed,—his home was among the Cheviot Hills, and all of his tastes were for mountain scenery. So he determined to follow in the footsteps of two of the greatest generals of history, and cross the Alps, taking his first glimpse of the fair plains of Italy from its summit,—this he did. And as he stood on the rocky boulder, which is all that remains of the wonderful bridge which Hannibal built, with the turbulent stream dashing with mad fury at his feet, and defying the touch of man, while the chasm above his head was spanned by the wonderful skill of the great Napoleon; here, in the presence of this greatest work of art, and with nature in her unequaled strength all around him, how puny did man seem! And there it seemed to him that the God of nature showed himself to him in all his power, causing him in the humility of his soul to exclaim, "What is man that Thou art mindful of him, and the son of man that Thou visiteth him!"

It was this life which had given such vigor to his frame, and it was this view of God in his works of nature and providence which had given strength to his soul.

But as he sat there in that pleasant room, with its shady, green blinds, against which the waving boughs outside cast their shadows, with that confiding face looking into his, and the old familiar touch of her arm resting on his knee, he was nothing but a boy after all,—they were living over their past together.

"And, Robert," said Jean, "tell me of my father again. Did he seem to want to see me very much?"

"Of course he did," was the answer. "I think if he had lived much longer, in spite of the madam, he would have made a pilgrimage to your shrine with me."

Jean's eyes filled with tears. "And was he happy, Robert?"

"Oh, yes; she was always good to him, loved him indeed. It was that very feeling which made her dislike us, she could not bear that anything should come between them, not even his children; she nursed him very faithfully, and I never saw greater grief than hers at his death. I forgave her everything then."

"Yes," said Jean, "and so do I from my heart,—it is so much easier to forgive everything with you by my side, Robert,—it has been such a sore trial to be separated from you."

"I know it, dear," he said, laying his hand on her head; "but you have certainly had a great deal to comfort you. I never saw a more interesting family—from Ned, Senior, to Ned, Junior."

"Yes; I think so, too; you met Margaret at the grotto in the grove, did you not? I hope she was kind."

He laughed. "Oh, yes; but I see you think there was cause for apprehension; well, we can pardon her queening it a little, it suits her so well. She is the most regal-looking woman I ever saw; but I should think she would blot you out entirely, my small sister."

"Oh, she does; though she tolerates me now,—at first it was dreadful; but she is a girl of warm feelings and generous impulses. I have seen her tried more than once."

"Well, I hope so. I confess my taste lies in another line from her, though I love to look at her; she has the finest face I ever saw. I should think she would excite a good deal of admiration."

"You know," said Jean, "she is just from school,—has not been home more than a few days. I have no doubt she will, she is very intellectual."

"Pshaw!" said Mr. Murray, "that is of very small value; she is very beautiful, that is her strongest point."

"I don't think she is, Robert; she has but two good features,—her eyes and nose."

"Which leaves mouth and brow; but I am not at all disposed to criticise: I have not seen enough of her for that; but I am artist enough to see that she is undoubtedly a beautiful woman."

"I don't think she cares for admiration at all."

"Don't she? Well, Jean, I would be willing to lay a wager that when she once sees her power she will be as insatiable as Alexander or Nero, who wished all Rome had one neck that he might be saved the trouble of killing them by piecemeal."

"I think you do her injustice, Robert. She is not the kind of girl to enjoy those things."

"My dear sister," said Mr. Murray, "it may seem like vanity on my part, but actually I believe I know your sex better than you do."

"That may well be," said Jean, laughing. "I know myself, and a few others, and there it ends. Your acquaintance is more extensive."

"Yes; and I have never met with more than one or two women, who possessed beauty, who would not use it as a weapon of offense and defense; and if I am any judge at all, this fair daughter of your husband's is a genuine daughter of Eve."

"Have you two people talked yourselves out yet?" said Mr. Holcombe, entering with Eddy in his arms. "I have exercised the greatest self-denial in keeping out of here all the morning, because I was not wanted. This wife of mine, Robert, has behaved herself so well in all these years that I am glad she is rewarded at last by a sight of you."

"I didn't know where you were," said Jean; "we wanted you here with us."

"No, I know your deceitful ways, and that you would pretend to want me, so I made for the woods; and came back just now to find this boy crying, as if he thought he was an orphan."

"I think you must have taken good care of this sister of mine, sir. She certainly looks very well and young."

"Oh, yes; we don't grow old up in these mountains; and besides, I think Jean has the gift of perpetual youth."

Mr. Holcombe drew up a chair to the party, and Eddy took an early opportunity of transferring himself to his mother's knees, from which position of security he was gazing at his new uncle with that wide-awake expression which babies assume on first meeting a stranger.

Mr. Murray tried all sorts of blandishments and bribes to induce him to come to him; but the big gold watch and the enticing smile were equally inefficacious. He clung more closely to his mother at every attempt to entice him from the familiar resting-place.

"You will have to wait awhile, Uncle Robert," said Jean; "Master Eddy is rather shy; but when he once gets acquainted he will be sociable enough, I promise you. But here is Robin come to announce dinner." And they all adjourned to the dining-room.

14

# CHAPTER XIX.

## THE FAMILY CIRCLE.

FOR some weeks after the events narrated in my last chapter, the usual quiet life at Rose Hill was exchanged for gayeties of various kinds. In the first place, the whole neighborhood, including the town of C——, turned out to acknowledge the *début* of Miss Holcombe. It was so long since there had been a grown daughter in the family; and the former reputation of the place as a gay rendezvous excited to an extravagant pitch the expectations of the younger part of the community, who were full of anticipations of a renewal of the "good old times" they had heard their parents talk so much about at Rose Hill.

Meanwhile Mr. Murray and Margaret, notwithstanding his uncomplimentary views of her character on the first day of his arrival at Rose Hill, progressed rapidly towards a friendship. She could not help admiring his magnificent physique, and the wonderful completeness of the entire man,—strength of body, mind, and will characterizing all of his actions; even his voice contributed to the impression: every tone was a deep bass-note full of music. It was one evening that Margaret sauntered into the parlor in the twilight, and finding the room deserted, seated herself at the piano, and commenced singing that air which seems never to grow old, or if it does, ever retains all the sweetness of its earliest youth,— "Bonnie Annie Laurie." Her voice was plaintive, and,

( 158 )

at the same time, powerful; but on this evening she was
singing for herself alone; the tones were subdued and
soft as a nightingale's, and her thoughts floated away on
the wings of her own music to her school-days,—the old
play-room where they used to meet in the evening to join
in the merry dance or the gay romp, and where she so
often acted as the musician for the others.  How often
she had sung "Annie Laurie" for that simple little audi-
ence!  Well, those times were past, never to return, nor,
with all her pleasant recollections of them, did she wish
it.  She was very happy now; and felt, too, that her life
was untying the tangled skein of her character, that,
after awhile, the thread would run smoothly and evenly.

Suddenly she became half conscious of a step in the
room; but before she could turn around a tone like the
deep notes of an organ accompanied her voice.

> "And for bonnie Annie Laurie
> I'd lay me down and dee."

She knew it could belong but to one person in the
world, and that one was Robert Murray.  It was no
longer a low warble which her voice sent forth: lifted up
and carried on by the strong swelling wave of those
magnificent tones, hers gave forth their full power, and
the whole house was filled with the delicious harmony.
The pleasant discovery of the mutual accomplishment was
a surprise to them both, and after that it became a regular
habit to practice together, generally in the twilight, or
after tea, while the rest of the family sat together on the
long portico, where the moon shone brightest, and caught
the delicious strains through the open doors and windows.

Nor was this the only amusement they enjoyed together:
there were long rides on horseback.  She took him to see
all the fine views in the neighborhood, and received in

return his graphic pictures of scenes in Switzerland and Italy.

This was probably the happiest time of Margaret Holcombe's life; her face lost the restless look of dissatisfaction, and the family looked on with surprise at her happy gayety; her temper lost its irritability, and she seemed to be returning to the demonstrative impulse of her early childhood. Mr. Holcombe looked at her with delight, and all his fears for her melted away,—she was developing so beautifully,—her rich gifts and sparkling qualities combining to form a rare character.

Jean had taken her brother to call on Mammy as soon as he arrived. And although he did not feel sure that he would ever get used to the constant presence of this "queer" people, he became much interested in their simple lives, and happy ignorance of anything beyond what those lives contained.

Mary came in one day very much amused from a visit to Mammy, and informed Mr. Murray that Mammy pronounced him "A fine well-growed young man."

"I am much obliged to her," said he, laughing. "Tell her that I am a mere baby in my own country. We belong to the Brobdignags."

"I shall take care not to tell her that," said Mary, "as I shall have to explain what Brobdignags are."

"And you can't do it, hey?" said Mr. Murray.

"Oh, yes, of course I know," said she, indignantly; "but as to going through Gulliver's Travels for Mammy's benefit, I could not think of it. I never could understand, anyhow, why such absurd stories should be so highly thought of."

"No. I don't suppose you have ever taken the satirical view of the book."

"The satirical view?" said she, inquiringly.

"Yes, it is intended as a great satire upon pigmies who think themselves the head of civilization and everything else, and big men who have nothing but their *bigness* to recommend them."

Mary did not look as if she quite understood yet, but would not ask any more questions.

Mr. Murray was in that favorite sitting-room of the family, the library, and had been reading occasional items from the "Baltimore Sun" for the edification of Jean and Margie, who sat at the window engaged in some bits of feminine work. Margaret's consisted of bright-colored worsteds, as fresh looking as the pretty morning toilet she presented, while Jean's was a dress for Eddy.

"I do think," said Mr. Murray, "that a larger number of literary outrages are perpetrated over the dead than in any other way. I have read this paper now every day since I came to this country, and I have not seen more than one or two copies which has not been adorned with such twaddle as this:

'Dearest Lizzie, thou hast left us,
    We thy loss most deeply feel,
But 'tis God who has bereft us,
    He can all our sorrows heal.' "

"Why, that is one of their best," said Margaret, laughing.

"Oh, we can stand it *once*," said Mr. Murray; "but to have it repeated every day is more than human nature can endure."

"It is easy enough not to read it, I should think," said Jean, laughing.

"Not so easy as you think. There is a fascination which draws my eyes back, in spite of myself."

"Talking of obituaries," said Margaret, "reminds me of a tombstone over a grave near Woodbine, where I went to school. The verse on the stone was this:

> 'Come, blooming youth, as you pass by,
> Pray on these lines do cast an eye;
> For once I bloomed as well as thee,
> Prepare for death and follow me.'

One of the girls wrote below it,—

> 'To follow you I'll not consent,
> Until I learn which road you went.' "

" But," said Mary, " I don't think that is as funny as—

> 'Here lies Jane Bent,
> Who kicked up her heels and away she went.' "

"I remember," said Mr. Murray, when the laugh had subsided a little over the unfortunate Jane's epitaph, "hearing of an amusing story a long time ago. There was a death in a little town in Germany of a composer of music, and his disconsolate widow erected a monument to his memory and put, as the inscription, upon it, 'He has gone where alone his works are excelled.' A very pretty tribute every one said, and the simplicity as well as the beauty of the thought was somewhat talked about. About this time a maker of brimstone-matches died, and his ambitious widow, not to be outdone, also erected a monument with the inscription, 'He has gone where alone his works are excelled.' "

"Here is my contribution to these valuable literary collections," said Jean, producing a slip of paper from her work-box. "I tore it out of a newspaper the other day: 'To the memory of Sarah, youngest daughter of John and Ellen Smith, aged six months and one day.

"'Sweet baby, 'twas hard to give thee up and see thee die, though your angel-face I never beheld till hidden 'neath the coffin-lid.

"'We have laid you at the foot of thy sweet little brother, who lies there a-sleeping six years ago. My word is to the parents and all the friends : Prepare to meet thy God.' "

" This is really making light of a GRAVE subject," said Mr. Murray ; " but it is very amusing to go through some of those old graveyards in England. Some of the monuments give a regular history of the survivors. I remember one in Cambridge, erected to the memory of some earl or other—I have forgotten his name—who died worth, the inscription goes on to say, '£100,000. His daughter married Lord ——, whose fortune amounts to £50,000.' And then another, which marked the resting-place of a tallow-chandler, and stated, for the benefit of all who wanted to know, that his widow carried on his business at his old stand, mentioning the address."

" I don't think," said 'Margaret, " when I die I want anything put over me, because I don't like the idea of people, a hundred years hence, laughing over the inscription on my grave ; and times change so that what would seem perfectly proper now may be very absurd to them."

" Well," said Mary, " Margie, I don't think it is worth while for you to make your final arrangements yet ; but we will try and be as brief as possible with your inscription, though I don't care a cent about a hundred years hence. If I can afford any amusement to my great-great-grandchildren, I am unselfish enough to be very glad."

" Does it never occur to you," said Mr. Murray, " to remember of how really little importance the body is ? I have just been looking at you two as you sit here talking so calmly about ' a hundred years hence,' and looking all the time so blooming that it is hard to connect the idea of death with you. Of how much more importance does it become us to inquire where our souls will be ' a hundred years hence.' "

This was giving a more serious turn to the subject than

any of them had expected; and Margaret looked up in surprise. She had never thought of Mr. Murray as a Christian; she liked him as an agreeable, intelligent man; but this was a new view of him, and one she did not altogether like, as it seemed to place a barrier to their friendship; and then, too, she said to herself, "I shall always be afraid that he is going to take me up in this way." She said, in her petulant, restive way, "Mr. Murray, I am disappointed to find you are that kind of person."

"What kind of person is that, Miss Holcombe?" said he, smiling.

"Oh, well, to force that subject into every conversation and talk at people, it throws a damper over every gathering. Now we were having such a pleasant time, and you come with your uncomfortable suggestions, and there is an end of it."

"Would it not be better, Miss Holcombe," he answered, "if we so arranged matters as not to find these subjects 'uncomfortable'? They certainly ought not to be excluded from conversation, particularly when the tenor of the conversation leads so naturally to it as it did to-day."

"I don't agree with you, Mr. Murray; we were in the midst of a conversation on amusing epitaphs."

"Yes, and you began to talk about the disposition you wished made of your body. What more natural than for me to speak of the disposition to be made of the soul, so far more interesting, more important?"

His manner was so earnest and even tender that Margaret was subdued by it; and she made no reply, but bent down lower over her work. He went on,—

"You will excuse me for saying so; but I cannot help thinking that your very sensitiveness on the subject shows that it is one which often intrudes itself upon you in spite of yourself."

"Of course," she answered. "I suppose everybody thinks of those things sometimes."

"Woe to those who never do!" he said. "To be let alone of God is the greatest curse which can befall man. God forbid that it should ever be said of any of us— 'Ephraim is joined to his idols, let him alone.'"

"Mr. Murray," said Mary, "why don't you study for the ministry? I should think you would make a splendid preacher."

"I don't know that," he said; "but I should certainly feel highly honored to be permitted to preach the gospel. Maybe I will some of these days." And so the conversation ended.

# CHAPTER XX.

" Papa," said Margaret Holcombe, going into his study one day, about the beginning of August, " I want to give an entertainment."

Mr. Holcombe put aside his book, and, it must be confessed, looked anything but pleased at the prospect.

" Now, papa," she continued, answering his look, for he had not uttered a word, " I know when you were young you used to like to go out and have company too ; and grandma gave splendid parties,—Aunt Mary has told me of them. And now I am the only young lady, and your first grown daughter. You ought to want to launch me into society with *éclat.*"

" Indeed, my child," he said gravely, " I have higher aspirations than that for you. I do not know that *launching you into society* is by any means the best thing for you."

" Papa," she said, " I don't believe any one ever became a Christian by having those subjects hurled at their heads all of the time. I just learn to think of religion as a something which is to interfere with every pleasure I have. It is very well for you, who have had your day, to be willing to give up everything now ; but I have a right to some enjoyment, and it is hard to have it all spoiled for me."

" Why, my daughter, this is a very unnecessary tirade you are giving. I have not said anything about interfer-

( 166 )

ing with your pleasures. On the contrary, I want to do everything to promote them. But you are mistaken, Margie, in thinking that being a Christian would interfere with any solid happiness. It would, on the contrary, give a zest to all rational pleasures."

"I dare say; but we may differ about what you call 'rational pleasures,'" said Margaret. "I think a party would be a very rational pleasure."

"I don't think there is anything irrational in it. I will consult Jean about it. When do you want to have it?"

"Oh, very soon. I want to return civilities. Ellen Randolph and Mr. Williams come next week. Suppose we have it as soon after that as possible."

"Very well," said Mr. Holcombe; "if your mamma chooses; of course her word is law in these matters.".

She did not resent this declaration, as she would have done two or three years before. She had happily become accustomed to seeing the perfect deference he showed to his wife's opinion in everything. Nor did she object to it. Her heart had long ago acknowledged to itself its errors, though her lips had not been equally candid. She always felt a little embarrassment, engendered by a sense of having committed a wrong; and so the coldness had never worn away. Her manner formed such a contrast to Mary's that it made her seem even colder than she was in reality.

As might have been expected, Jean had no serious opposition to make to the plan, though at first she insisted that she could not be present, as her mourning dress, which she still wore for her father, would excuse her presence. But Mr. Holcombe declared that unless she would herself matronize the party it should not take place. And with her usual forgetfulness of self she consented.

Mr. Holcombe engaged the services of a man from the

city to come up to Rose Hill and superintend the arrangements; as he said, if he "gave an entertainment, he was
determined it should be worthy of the place; that no one
of the older guests should be able to say, 'But, ah, you
should just have seen the preparations which old Mrs.
Holcombe used to make.'"

Mr. Murray proved a valuable acquisition at this time.
He remembered seeing an illumination in Germany, which
suggested some ideas to him, and he proposed that they
should illuminate the grounds around the house. All
that was wanting was a little ingenuity, and he thought
he could supply this.

Mr. Williams and Ellen Randolph arrived early in the
week, and the library was given up to the "Lantern Committee," as they named themselves. The ladies always
came supplied with their work-boxes, and the gentlemen
with knives,—while Nannie, now promoted to the position of lady's-maid, stood at a table and did the pasting.

With the help of a few paints and colored tissue-paper
they managed to vary the hues of their lanterns, so as to
make a pretty variety.

They formed them into various shapes: tulips, lilies,
bluebells of Scotland, indeed, any flower of a cup shape;
then there were huge heads with staring eyes and grinning teeth, and even rude attempts at statuary; of course
there was many a failure recorded, which excited much
merriment. Mary proved the most efficient assistant
Mr. Murray had, and was constantly at his side, improving upon his suggestions, or in her turn making happy
ones for new devices, until he declared himself completely
thrown into the shade by her more tasteful efforts.

Mr. Williams seemed to enjoy his return to Rose Hill,
and declared the year he spent there to have been the
happiest of his life.

"I think when Master Eddy grows large enough to learn his A B C's," said he, one day, "I shall petition to come back and be permitted to try pedagoging a little while; that is, if my country can do without me by that time, which privately I doubt."

"I suppose," said Margaret, "that like Mr. Weller you find it a dreadful thing to be so 'sought arter?'"

"Well, not yet, Miss Holcombe, not yet; but I know my merit cannot always remain unappreciated, and the time must come *soon*, when I will be rewarded for my long waiting. When I look at you young ladies, though, and think that I had a hand in making you what you are, I feel that teaching must be my forte."

"I should not think you would remember me with much pleasure, Mr. Williams," said Margaret, blushing. "I certainly was the most disagreeable child."

"That is *most* too strong, Miss Margaret," was the answer; "but your difficulty was in not being a child at all."

"Oh, Mr. Williams," said Mary, "will you ever forget the day Margie rode on the sapling, and you saw her?—it was too funny."

It was curious to see how Mr. Williams watched her face to see how much she would allow. She caught his expression and laughed.

"I know what you are thinking, Mr. Williams; and I don't know that I do like to hear of that adventure even now; but I see you are dying to give your account of it to the company, so I sacrifice myself on the altar of friendship."

Thus encouraged, he gave a very amusing account of the adventure in the woods,—and ended with,—

"I tell you I had to argue my case powerfully to obtain pardon. I wish I may ever be as effective before

·15

the judge as I was when I was the criminal, my client will be fortunate."

"If you have truth on your side, as you had then, Mr. Williams," said Margaret, "you will be,—every word you told me was true, and I knew it. Oh, how I did hate myself after that! I think I used to have the most humiliating views of myself after those attacks of arrogance. Actually, I have been afraid to go to bed sometimes because I had to meet myself face to face."

Mr. Murray turned around on her in surprise,—it was a new view of this proud-looking girl. He said, very quietly,—

"I should never have thought of you with such experiences."

"And why?" said she, quickly.

"Well, I don't know,—you don't look like it."

Her face flushed, and she answered, hotly, "I am always so unfortunate as to convey the idea to every one of being utterly wanting in humility."

It was very vexing for everybody to laugh, but very natural, as she stood there with the implements of her work in hand, and that proud young head thrown back.

Mr. Murray comprehended in a moment her sensitiveness, and said, "Well, it is true, Miss Holcombe, that I never saw any one whose appearance and manners indicated less of the quality named, and yet I cannot help believing that it is latent in you somewhere."

"Latent means where it can't be seen, don't it, Mr. Murray?" said John, mischievously.

"Yes," said Mr. Murray; "unless there is some influence brought to bear which will cause it to escape."

"Well, we will hope for the influence," said John, "on Margie's account."

It showed considerable self-command in the young girl

to be able to control herself; but she did, though her flushed cheek and moist eye showed it required an effort, —to change the subject now became the prime object of both gentlemen.

"How does the chess come on, Miss Margaret?" said Mr. Williams. "I bet I could beat you now."

"I expect you could," said Margaret. "I have scarcely played a game since we used to play together."

"By-the-by," put in Mr. Murray, "I met with a curious story about a game of chess, connected with an old German ruin in the Black Forest,—it was told me by a German countrywoman. And if you have any taste for the weird and horrible, I will tell it to you."

There was a general clamor for the story, and Mr. Murray began:

"As I was passing through the forests of Germany I come upon a curious-looking ruin of what must have been a large building,—it bore the marks of having been destroyed by fire,—and the wild, desolate appearance of the surroundings excited my curiosity to know its history. I stopped for the night at a tavern, only a few miles off, and finding my landlady very talkative, I asked for some information relative to it.

"I saw at once that I had touched upon a favorite topic, as she squared herself round, and, with great animation, told me the following story. But I have the manuscript."

He went out of the room a moment, and returned and read the following:

"'The castle of Guelhelm,' she said, 'was an old rambling building, which had been in the family of that name for centuries. In the time of my grandmother" (for I shall quote her own words) "the old baron died without heirs, and an Italian count, named Castorella, came and took possession of it. He was an old man, and his fierce black eyes excited the fears of the people around in the neighborhood, and then, too, stories began to be told of his strange behavior, until at last people believed he was wrong about the head, and were more afraid of him than ever. And he lived almost alone, up in the old castle, except every now and then my grandfather used to go up to pay him the rent for his land, and he says he was always glad to get away, that the place was so desolate. But he never was permitted to leave without playing a game of chess, of which he was passionately fond.

"Matters went on thus for years,—the old wolf leaving his den every now and then, and absenting himself for a month or two, and then returning wilder and stranger than ever. At last he told my grandfather one day, over their game of chess, that he was going to bring a wife home, and wanted to engage a number of servants, as he did not intend to lead the life he had been doing. Nothing could surpass the astonishment of the people at the idea of his being married, and you may be sure it was a difficult thing to get any one to take the place of servant at the castle. But the love of money will overcome almost any fears, and so they found enough to fill the different offices in the household. My grandfather's youngest daughter, Gretchen, was engaged as lady's-maid.

"But if the astonishment was great at the idea of his bringing a wife home, it was much greater when she made her appearance. She was a young girl of about eighteen, with soft, melancholy, black eyes, and Gretchen says she could see her shrink away whenever he came near her, though she tried very hard to keep him from seeing it.

"Well, her life must have been a very dreadful one.

At first he used to invite company to see them, but he was so jealous of her if she spoke to any one else that her life was miserable. And he treated the visitors so badly that they never cared to return, and at last, but for the servants, she would have been perfectly alone with her dreadful lord. Gretchen says she used to walk about within the walls which inclosed the grounds, and even then he would watch her from a turret-chamber where he spent most of his time.

"He used to make her play chess with him, and she always let him win, because it kept him in better humor. It used to make my aunt so sorry to see her growing thinner and paler, pining away like a bird in a cage, and all the time his eyes got fiercer and his manner wilder, and she could see the look of terror in her face every time he came into the room.

"Well, one day as Gretchen sat in a little antechamber, next my lady's parlor, the lord having gone to the woods, for a wonder, one of the servants ushered in a young man, and when the lady saw him, she fainted away, and Gretchen came in to recover her. She found the young man holding her in his arms, and kissing her and calling her all sorts of pretty names, and there she lay, not knowing anything, as white as the snow. At last Gretchen persuaded him to lay her down on a lounge in the room, and in a few minutes she opened her eyes and looked around her so wildly, and when she saw who was bending over her, she burst out crying, and said something to him that Gretchen could not understand, as it was in a foreign tongue; but she knew she was begging him to go away before her husband came back. He tried to persuade her to let him stay, but she was in such agony, and even pushed him away from her, that he got up to obey her. But as ill luck would have it, just as he

turned towards the door the old lord opened it. Gretchen
said she never will forget the look of his face as he saw
the stranger there,—she thought he must have lost his
senses from passion at once. It was in vain that my lady
tried to explain that her cousin from her own country had
come to see her. He knew better than that, and raved
like a madman, then drove him out of the house. Suddenly he grew calm, but looked like he was thinking how
he could get him in his hands again."

John here interrupted the speaker to ask what sort of
an expression that was.

"I don't know," said Mr. Murray; "I only give you
her own words. I am not responsible for her errors of
rhetoric.

"At last he disappeared, and the poor lady cried herself
to sleep. Gretchen sat by her fanning her all the evening. At last she heard the old lord calling up the servants. She crept to the door and found him dismissing
them one by one; she did not know what to make of it,
and as the lady still slept she was afraid to leave her to
see; so there she stayed until she heard the last one
leave, and knew her lady and herself were alone in the
house with the crazy lord. Presently she heard him hurrying along the hall, and he opened the door with a crash,
which waked the lady and brought her standing on her
feet.

"'Ha! ha!' he said, laughing his dreadful mad laugh;
'you wanted a lover, did you? Well, you shall have
him; I will keep him safe.'

"She clasped her hands and threw herself at his feet.
He only laughed at her and said 'he thought he was
coming to my lady's bower, where I sent Heinrich after
him with a message from you; and when he came and
waited he found the old man was too cunning for him,

and locks and bars would hold him safe enough.' And then he would laugh until the old walls rung again. Oh, how she lay there on the floor and wept and bewailed herself in her agony!

"Gretchen had remained a quiet spectator all this time, thinking what she could do to help her lady. She thought now if she could only get out of the room she might give the alarm and rescue not only her mistress but the young man, if he were indeed a prisoner. But then the danger of moving, as she did not think he had observed her yet. At last she determined to try, and crept along behind him to the door, though it went to her heart to leave her mistress alone in the hands of this man, no better than a wolf; but it was the only thing she could do. Just as she got her hand on the handle of the door, however, the madman turned around and rushed at her. Seizing her by the arm, he dragged her across the hall and threw her into his own bedroom, locking the door on her. She examined all of the windows and doors, but there was no place that a rat could have crept out, and there she had to stay, every now and then hearing that awful mad laugh; and once, as she listened at the door, she heard her mistress cry for 'Help! help!' as she seemed to be dragged up, up, as high as the turret-chamber. She shook the door violently, but it was no use. Again she rushed to the window, but it was all as still as the grave. The servants were too glad to be paid off and dismissed to linger about longer than they could help. She looked eagerly at all the windows of the castle. At last she caught sight of a human face across the court at a window almost facing hers; it was the unfortunate young man. She tried for a long time to catch his eye, but in vain. At last she bethought her of the old lord's dressing-gown of bright red, which she waved backwards and forwards before the window. He saw it; that was a little accomplished, but so little! She tried to open her window in vain; it was fastened down with strong iron bolts. She saw a like effort on his part, and a like failure. What was to be done? Nothing but watch and wait.

"After she had been thus shut up for about two hours, she was startled by hearing that mad laugh again; at first faint, then louder and louder, coming down the turret stair. My aunt said she never forgot the terror of that moment. What had happened?' The poor lady alone in the hands of that dreadful man! The laugh came nearer; she thought he was coming to the door of the room where she was; her heart stood still; but he turned off, and again the laugh grew faint, though it did not now come from above; he was going in the direction of the other wing. Involuntarily she again flew to the window; there was the face of the young stranger still. She tried to signal to him that danger was approaching, but he only looked puzzled; but some sound evidently attracted him; he turned away from the window. Oh, how she strained her eyes to see what was going on! but in vain. Once she saw a white face for a moment against the window-pane, a hand thrown up as if to make some sign to her, and that was all.

"Gretchen threw herself on the ground and shrieked aloud. Then a mortal terror seized her; but no escape, no escape!—to be mewed up like a rat in a hole!—dreadful! But again the fearful sound echoed through those long corridors; it approached more closely now, the steps were heavier, and ever and anon there was a sound as if something brushed heavily against the wall in passing. Again she thought the steps were coming towards her door, and again she was mistaken; they went upward, upward.

"Oh, if she only knew what was going on! Anything was better than this suspense. She felt as if it would be a relief even if the dreaded madman would come and tell her what he had done. She had hardly brought her mind to this when it seemed as if she was to be gratified, for she heard him descending the stairs.

"Now, Gretchen was a shrewd girl, and the danger she was in sharpened her wits. In one moment it flashed into her mind that she had certainly to fight for her own life, and perhaps for the others. Of course she had no strength to oppose a madman, so she resorted to stratagem.

"She picked up a book, and took her seat as quietly as she could, hoping that the sight of her sitting so might calm him, since she had often heard that mad people, like wild animals, can sometimes be managed by a quiet eye. So, there she sat, the footsteps came up the passage, a key was inserted in the key-hole. She fixed her eyes on the door, and when the old lord poked his head in, he met those quiet eyes; the expression of ferocity in his was near undoing her. But life was too precious to be abandoned willingly. She saw him try to withdraw his gaze, but could not; the calm eyes fastened him. He came towards her; she did not retreat an inch, but stood firmly, waiting his coming.

"'Ha, my pretty Gretchen! you here? I had forgotten you.' And he stretched out his arms to clasp her. One motion of fear now and all would have been over; but the brave girl stood still and looked at him, and said as naturally as she could,—

"'Where is my lady, sir?'

"The extended arms dropped at his side. She gathered courage from this sign of success.

"'Your lady! Ah, she has merry company to-night. She does not want you or me!'

"Her blood ran cold in her veins. What did he mean? She dared not ask: but managed to say, quietly,—

"'Indeed! Ah, then, if she is satisfied we need not be unhappy. Who is with her?'

"Again that laugh—mocking! weird! terrible!

"'Oh, she has her gay young lover by her side. She does not want more. She played her game of chess for him and won him; and now she has him!—ha! ha! ha! ha!'

"Without his seeming conscious what she was doing, or without taking her eyes off of him, she put out her hands and gently thrust him into a chair, and sat down facing him. Her only hope was to keep this control over him until weariness overtook him, and then to get on the other side of the door,—the key was on the outside. And there she sat, never moving, her eyes on his. She felt, rather than saw, the sun fading away; its light creeping over the floor. Now it touched her shoulder, now it was gone. Would she ever see it again? Twilight was coming on. She could not stay in the dark with him, that was impossible. She remembered a flint and a taper on the table beside her. Could she find it? She reached out her hand. The fiery eyes opposite burned into hers, and watched her motions. She simply said, 'It is getting dark, we had better light the taper.' How she did it she never knew; but done it was, and the fearful vigil was still unbroken. At last she saw the lids of those burning coals closing. It was gradual, interrupted, but he slept. She waited without motion until she saw that the slumber was real, and then, moving softly, gained the door. It was unfastened, but creaked as she opened it. She saw the wild head turn, and spring upward; but she was on the outside, and the great key turned in the lock.

"She heard him beating upon the door, but knew he was safe enough now.

"She flew up the stairs and reached the turret-chamber. It was locked. She shook the door; a shriek answered her: it was her lady's voice. 'For God's sake, my dear lady, tell me, are you safe?'

"'Oh, Gretchen,' wailed the voice, 'open the door!'

"'In a minute, my lady. Don't fear, you are safe!' And down she flew again, past the door where the beating still continued, down to the kitchen, seized an axe, and up the stairs two steps at a time until she again reached the chamber. Gretchen was a stout lass, and now she worked with a will, battering at the heavy door, every now and then stopping to say some word of encouragement to the poor lady inside. At last the lock gave way, and the door flew open; and the lady threw herself into her arms, crying, 'Gretchen! Gretchen!' and, without turning round, pointed behind her. The sight which met her eye she never forgot. There was no light in the room except what the moon threw on the floor; and there, in its light, lay the body of the young man with its white, dead face upward.

"'Take me away, Gretchen! dear Gretchen!' cried the lady. Nor had she any wish to linger. Down those long stairs, through the long corridor, by the door where they heard the gnashing and shrieking of the enraged animal she had caged, she dragged the unfortunate lady, —lingering only for a minute to get a mantle to throw around her,—and then out into the moonlight.

"The poor lady was perfectly passive in her hands, seeming not to know what she did, and to care less; every now and then her hand would go up to her face, as if to shut out some sight; but, except this, she showed no signs of consciousness.

"Great was the surprise of my grandfather and grandmother when Gretchen made her appearance dragging, rather than leading, the beautiful lady of the castle. She explained as well as she could what had happened, and a number of the men started off to the castle to secure the madman; but before they got half way there the way was lighted by the flames from the building shooting out in every direction.

"It was supposed that the old lord set it on fire with the taper Gretchen had left lighted on the table. Certain it is he perished in the flames, along with the body of his unfortunate victim.

"It was a long time before the lady of the castle recovered her reason: she had a fever of the brain, and it was pitiful to hear her begging Gretchen to take her away; then she would fix her eyes on a particular spot, and move her fingers, and call out 'check,' 'check,' 'checkmate;' and when she said checkmate, she would fall back and scream that she had won! she had won! She had a way too of looking behind her, and then, as if she saw something dreadful, would jerk her head round again and say, 'Oh, if he only would shut his eyes!'

"This state of things lasted for many, many weeks; but at last the fever left her,—they thought she might recover, but she faded away.

"The night before she died she told Gretchen her story, and asked her to bury her in the village churchyard, and put '*Helen*' on the stone.

"Her story was this: Her father was an Italian, whose noble name was all his wealth. She had lived all her life in an old chateau, and the only companion in her solitude was her cousin, Paulus Paola. As was to have been expected, they became attached to each other, and grew up with the idea that they would one day be married. She talked so prettily of their life together; how they wandered about the old woods, or studied or read together; how he, being the eldest, taught her everything she knew. Every now and then her father would go to Rome and be absent some time, and from one of these expeditions he brought back the Count of Castorella; but his arrival did not trouble Paulus and herself much, until her father took it into his head that Paulus must go to Rome to study with some of the masters there; of course this was a trial to them, but Paulus was devoted to painting, and delighted to be able to improve himself in the art; but his greatest pleasure in the prospect held out to him was, that he would be able to claim her for his wife as soon as he returned.

"Imagine her horror, though, when the day after his departure her father bade her prepare to receive this old count as her future husband. Of what avail was it that she wept and prayed?—it was determined upon before Paulus left. And what could she do, poor lamb, in the hands of two determined men? So she was married, and brought over to this melancholy old castle in the depths of the forest; and she never heard of Paulus again until that dreadful day when he appeared so suddenly before her. He told her that he stayed in Rome six months, and then returned, expecting to find her. What was his astonishment to learn that she had been married nearly five, and gone no one knew whither. And her father refused to give him any satisfaction, except that she had married the Count of Castorella, and was gone where he would never find her. Wild with grief he started out, and after incredible difficulties succeeded in tracing her.

"She also told Gretchen what happened to her after she was imprisoned in the room of the old count. She said that when she saw him drag her out of the room

16

she bethought her of a way through the antechamber by which she could reach the outer court, and, perhaps, send help to both Gretchen and Paulus; and she had actually almost reached the outer door, when she heard his steps behind her. He seized her, exclaiming that he knew she was only trying to make her escape to join her lover; and, after dragging her back to her own room, and taunting her with her misery, he exclaimed that he would have her safe enough, and, seizing her by the arm, he tried to drag her towards the door, but she threw herself on her knees and plead for '*mercy*,'—but she might as well have spoken to the winds,—and his only answer to her appeals was that mad laugh. She thought of nothing less than a violent death, when he caught her around the waist, and, lifting her from the ground, carried her from the room; then it was that she uttered that wild cry for 'Help!' 'help!' which Gretchen had heard.

"She was surprised to find herself borne upward, until the turret-chamber, that favorite resort of his, occurred to her. All the way up those stairs she wept and plead with him; it only excited his mad mirth. She thought he would put her up there and let her starve to death, and no one would ever hear of it. At last they reached the door; he opened it, and, throwing her upon a bed, he said, with a horrible imprecation, 'Now you are safe! now you are safe!' After gibing at and tormenting her for some time, he proposed a game of chess, and said he,—

"'By way of interesting you in the game, suppose we play for some stake. What say you? This gay, young lover—this kind cousin; if you beat me he is yours; if I beat you he is mine.' She looked at him for an instant; his eye was less wild; there was an appearance of sanity, at any rate, and so the dreadful game began, her excitement becoming so intense as she went on that she felt as if she was smothering. She could see him watching her with his fiendish eyes, but she did not care, the terrible stake for which she played absorbed all feeling; her trembling hand moved with caution from one piece to another, and at last she threw herself back in her chair and buried her face in her hands. The game was won! she had saved him!

"Long and loud laughed her mad husband. 'Ha! she played for and won him, and she should have him.' And she could hear him, as he went down the steps, repeating this over and over.

"She never knew how long a time passed before she heard the heavy footsteps returning. Ah, how eagerly she listened to hear if Paulus was with him! But no, only the one footstep coming up; now stopping, as if wearied, and now stumbling on again. At last the steps paused before her door, the key was turned; she saw the dreadful burden he bore, and fainted. When she came to herself, all was still; she lay on the floor; she tried to collect her scattered senses, looked around her, and, horror of horrors! close beside her lay that dead face, with the staring eyes! She shrieked until her voice sounded hoarse; but of what avail was it? No one would hear her except her jailer; even his presence, though, would have been a relief. She called upon him, entreating him to come and kill her, as he had done Paulus. No answer! She had thrown herself as far off from the body as she could; but every now and then her fascinated glance would return to that stolid face lying there in the moonlight, ever looking upward.

"At last came Gretchen's flying footsteps, and then Gretchen's voice.

"She died the next day, said my hostess, and they buried her in the burying-ground on the hill."

"How horrible !" ejaculated all the company as he ended.

"Yes, it is, indeed," said Mr. Murray. "I have no fancy for such stories; but I was tempted by your conversation on the subject of chess to give you this one."

"Do you suppose it is true ?" said Mary.

"In its main facts, yes," was the answer; "but I would not vouch for the entire truth of any story which has had half a century in which to grow."

# CHAPTER XXI.

## MISS HOLCOMBE'S DÉBUT.

At last the preparations for the feast were over, and the time arrived to which all looked forward with so much pleasure.

The day proved a lovely one, and was passed by the ladies in giving the finishing touches to the house, and by the gentlemen in disposing to advantage the fanciful lanterns and other ornaments for the grounds. Daylight never gives much encouragement to this style of preparation, as the colors, unaided by the light of the candle within, and in the face of day, look decidedly dingy; but the pretty little refreshment-tables set about under the trees, at each of which a waiter was stationed, were decidedly tempting. Every place was opened which could possibly be spared for the reception of visitors.

The invitations had been very general, and as it had been a long time since so large an entertainment had been given at Rose Hill, and all were anxious to make the acquaintance of the young daughter of the house on this her first entrance into society, it was expected that the attendance would be almost as general as the invitations.

"Look here, papa," said Margaret, sailing into the parlor where Mr. Holcombe was standing, with Mr. Murray, superintending the lighting of the rooms.

Her dress was, as usual, pure white, of some gossamer material, which floated around her like the cloud in which it is the fancy of painters to represent angels; but it was

16*       ( 185 )

a very human face which smiled above this cloud. The
wax-lights with which the rooms were illuminated lent a
softened tone to the brilliant style of her beauty, while
the bright eyes sparkled and danced with the anticipated
pleasure. She wore no ornaments except a simple pearl
pin which had been her mother's, and one magnificent
white rose, which shone like a star in her jet-black hair.

Mr. Holcombe was standing with his back to her as she
came into the room, but turned at the sound of her voice.
At the first glimpse of her he put his hands over his eyes
as if dazzled, and then folding his arms around her said,
with considerable emotion,—

"My darling child! you are startlingly like your
mother to-night; I can almost fancy that I am living
over the past again. God bless you, my child, and make
you like her in other respects than mere outward appearance; but I did not mean to give you so sober a greeting
on this your gala day; you took me by surprise."

Mr. Murray now came forward and said,—

"Now let me offer the greetings of the evening. I am
glad my rose met with sufficient approbation to give it so
honored a position."

"Yes, I was going to wear pearls in my hair, but decided that I would favor nature for this one evening," said
Margaret, smiling and blushing.

"Don't say for this one evening, but always; I am
glad you did not wear the pearls—youth is too rich to
need foreign aid."

"Have the lanterns been lighted?" asked Margaret.

"Yes indeed; have you not seen them? I expect
your visitors will imagine themselves transported to fairy-
land."

He gave her his arm as he spoke, and led the way to
the door. They met Mr. Williams in the hall, who in-

sisted that her first sight of the lawn must be from the lower end, and playfully proposed blindfolding her.

She consented, and he tied a handkerchief over her eyes, and thus reduced her to entire dependence upon her companion.

"Oh, I feel so helpless!" she said, reaching out her hands. "I don't like this; I don't like to have to trust entirely to anybody."

"That is doing yourself injustice, I am sure," said Mr. Williams; "you are no true woman if you are not willing to trust."

She put up her hand to remove the bandage, but it was taken possession of by a large one, in which her own felt completely lost, and Mr. Murray's voice said,—"Let me take care of you; you are not afraid to trust me, are you?" And without waiting for an answer he rested the hand gently upon his arm, guiding her steps with the greatest care, leaving Mr. Williams looking after them, with a smile upon his face.

"What are you looking at, Mr. Williams?" said Mary's voice behind him.

"At you now, Miss Snowflake," was the answer; "I am so glad you still have the good taste to cling to your childhood. Stand away, and let me see you." And, as she curtsied off, "Yes, you are very well worth looking at, but I think I would rather see you in that torn calico dress, with tousled hair, standing on the rock at 'Hawk's Nest.' You were a very pretty little child; it is a pity, though, that it was all expended at that early age; pretty children seldom make pretty grown people," said he, laughing down at her.

"I am much obliged to you, Mr. Williams," said Mary, looking puzzled and vexed; "but I don't think it is very polite in you to talk so to me."

"Well, you know, Mary, it would not be polite for any one else; but I am an old man to you; I can take those privileges which would be an impertinence in another."

"I wish you wouldn't, though," said she; "I don't think it is at all pleasant to be told that you are ugly."

"Oh!" in a shocked tone. "Excuse me, I never said anything so dreadful; I only want you to cultivate other qualities, and not depend on such a fading flower as beauty. And if you should happen to be pretty,—now remember I am only supposing an improbable case,—try and not know it."

"I think if I have *to try* not to know it, there won't be much reality in the ignorance," said Mary, laughing; "I dare say it is not of very much importance in a long lifetime, but still no one likes to be disagreeable-looking; and I don't believe you think I am, either." And she ran off into the parlors.

Meantime Margaret, with her guide, made their way down through the yard to the terraces, she begging to have her independence restored, and he enjoying seeing her in this novel position too much to agree to any such move.

"Indeed, Mr. Murray," said she, "I am afraid to venture down these steps; I don't know anything about your ability to take care of blind people. Just suppose you should go mad, like old Lord Castorella, and hurl me to the bottom of this place. Let me take this handkerchief off."

"You may, after awhile," he said, laughingly preventing her purpose; "but for the present I have you in possession, and don't intend to resign my privileges,—I may never have another chance."

"Mr. Murray," she said, hardly knowing whether to

be angry or not, "I never allow gentlemen to say what I shall or sha'n't do,—I generally do as I please."

"So I have perceived, Miss Holcombe; so much the worse for you,—it is time you had some one to take you in hand," was the imperturbable answer. He had drawn her down to the top of the last flight of steps, as a gentleman started at the foot. Hearing footsteps, Margaret took matters in her own hands, and drew off the bandage. The stranger bowed and passed on. Nothing could exceed Margaret's vexation; she let Mr. Murray see the material of which she was made,—blamed him without stint for placing her in an absurd position.

He seemed annoyed about it himself, but laughed-it off, telling her that he should seek the gentleman as soon as they returned and explain the little scene to him. "The statement of the familiar relations in which I stand to you is sufficient explanation," said he.

"I don't see why," she said, still indignantly.

"Well, as your stepmother's brother," was his answer.

"That does not bring us one step closer, I assure you," she said, and was sorry the minute the words were out of her mouth.

"Excuse me for advancing it as an argument on my side,—I am not ambitious of the honor of being your uncle, I assure you," said he.

She tried to laugh, but he did not respond, and their walk continued in perfect silence until they reached the lower end of the lawn. The scene was indeed beautiful. The house was illuminated from attic to basement, and the thick trees immediately around were studded with lights of all colors. On the lawn below, however, most of the labor had been expended, the center of the circle around which the carriage-road ran being fixed to represent a parterre; there were huge tulips of gaudy colors rearing their heads by the pure lily and bright bluebell, while the statuettes glowed prettily in every direction. The whole thing was pronounced a success; and as the carriages were heard rumbling in the distance, approaching the house, they turned their feet homeward.    Margaret longed to tell him that she knew she had been rude, but as usual her pride interfered, and she left him free to resent an implied affront to his sister, at which he would have laughed had he alone been concerned.

As soon as Mr. Murray returned to the house he hunted up the stranger who had made so malapropos an appearance on the steps, sought and obtained an introduction, and made an explanation to him of the circumstances, which must, to a stranger, have been a little puzzling.

"Not at all," said the gentleman, laughing; "I saw a little *romp* going on between——"

"You are mistaken, sir," said Mr. Murray, hotly; "there was nothing of the kind,—I was only guiding her to the end of the lawn, that she might see the lights to better advantage."

"In what relation do you stand to the young lady?" said the stranger, meaningly.

Mr. Murray felt disposed to knock him down for his insufferable impertinence, but he restrained himself, and said,—

"I do not know, sir, that the information is necessary to my object in seeking this introduction; I simply wished to explain on the young lady's account.

"Ah, yes, yes; all right.  I suppose you would not mind giving me an introduction, would you?"

But Mr. Murray was no longer by his side,—he had anticipated his request, and left before he should be called upon to refuse, as he most undoubtedly should have done, as the man's manner to him was disagreeable in the extreme.

He found himself beside Ellen Randolph, a sweet, gentle little girl, too diffident to make acquaintances easily, and with whom he had never advanced beyond a first introduction.

He had not recovered from the vexation produced by his last encounter, and as usual his face showed it, though he tried to conceal it by assuming a careless manner.

" Why, Miss Randolph," he said, "what are you doing way off in this corner? Let me take you into the gay world; you ought to know better how to take care of yourself." And he offered his arm.

" I wonder," said she, diffidently, "if I am ever going to get over this dreadful shamefacedness?—it is a positive annoyance to me."

" Oh, yes," said he, gently; "I suppose most young ladies of your age feel it,—it is not expected that a rose should burst into full bloom all at once; the bud which closes its leaves from the common gaze is, to my mind, much sweeter."

" Thank you, Mr. Murray," she said, "for a pretty compliment; but it is very uncomfortable to be a bud, I assure you. I have been looking forward to this party with so much pleasure, and as soon as I get into the room I feel perfectly out of place; I am as stupid as an owl."

He laughed, and said, " I had a young friend once who professed to be afflicted as you are, and she told me that she often tried to guard against these spells of embarrassment by making up her mind what she would say beforehand."

Ellen blushed and laughed, consciously.

" Ah, I see, Miss Randolph, that I turn a leaf in your experience."

His free, kind manner drew her out and encouraged her, and she laughed almost as merrily as Mary would have done.

"Tell me the candid truth," he said, bending down to look into her face.

"Well, yes, I own it," she said; "but nobody ever says just what I expect, so I am thrown out in the beginning and cannot find my place."

"Shall I give you a good rule to overcome this,—better than learning a lesson ?" said he, kindly.

"Please do."

"Well, look around and find some one who is in need of help,—perhaps suffering as you do, or in some other way, and try to relieve them, and you will find your own way infinitely smoother."

"You mean," said she, "that I must try and forget myself ?"

"Yes, exactly; you will pardon me, and understand what I mean, I know, when I say that the feeling from which you suffer is, after all, a little selfishness "

He doubted her understanding him, and feared he had pained her when he saw the flush mount to her cheek; so he hastened to explain,—

"Not selfishness in the objectionable sense of preferring ourselves to others, but in thinking of our own imperfections and indulging in the too earnest desire to shine,—it arises from a want of self-appreciation; but try my recipe. Your cousin does not seem to be annoyed by any such self-torment,—how well she graces her position !"

They were standing opposite Margaret, who was doing the honors to her guests with the most perfect ease. Just then Ellen saw a look of vexation cross Mr. Murray's face as a gentleman was introduced to her cousin by Mr. Williams.

"Miss Holcombe, let me present my friend, Dr. Burton."

"Who is he?" said Ellen, under her breath.

"I don't know," he said, "but I don't like his manners or appearance; I cannot imagine how he found his way here."

Dr. Burton leaned forward and said something to Margaret, and Mr. Murray saw the blood rush to her face and her eyes flash in his direction for an instant. He would have given a great deal to know what had passed, but could think of no way of finding out.

Jean came up, leaning on her husband's arm, and said, "I have not seen you all the evening, Robert; where have you been keeping yourself?"

"I have been taking care of this young lady for some little time," he said, smiling at Ellen. "Mr. Holcombe, who is that talking to your daughter?"

Mr. Holcombe turned to look. "He is a stranger, but has been very generally received by the good people of C——; I don't know much about him. He was here last winter, and this morning some one sent me a note asking for an invitation for him, as he had arrived at C—— last night;—of course I sent it."

Margaret had taken Dr. Burton's arm, and was going out into the grounds with him. Mr. Murray had never seen her so animated.

"Pshaw!" he said to himself, "what is the use of my worrying about her?—she is fully able to take care of herself without any interference of mine." But it was no use to argue,—he did worry every time he saw them together, which was almost every time he saw her at all. Her face was flushed and her eyes excited, and once or twice he knew they were talking about him. He was exceedingly vexed and curious, and then vexed with himself

17

for wasting a thought upon it; but the fact is, Margaret had interested him more than he had any idea,—the variety in her character gave him a constant desire to understand her. That she did herself injustice, at all times, he could plainly see, and that she only wanted some strong influence to develop her good qualities he could also guess; her father was too yielding,—too much afraid of provoking her irritable temper to oppose her; and Jean's influence, which might have been of benefit, she had utterly rejected.

It had occurred to him more than once,—what if he could be such a friend to her? It would be worth trying, at any rate. He was just beginning to hope that she would learn to regard him in such a light when the unfortunate little encounter of this evening took place, and now he saw a man whom he utterly distrusted apparently obtaining an influence over her.

"Hallo, Murray! what is the matter?" said Mr. Williams. "You are not in party trim, man,—you look as if you had lost your best friend."

"Look here, Williams," was the answer, "who is that man Burton? I heard you introduce him as '*your friend*' to Miss Holcombe."

"Indeed I don't know,—he is only my friend as of course everybody is whom I meet in this house. I never met him until to-night; but why do you ask?"

"Simply because I do not like the man at all."

Mr. Williams laughed meaningly, and said, "No, I suppose not; I should not, either, under the circumstances."

Mr. Murray turned on him and said, "What do you mean?—I am utterly at a loss to understand you."

"Well, I sha'n't explain, I promise you."

"It is not possible," said Mr. Murray, reddening, "that

you imagine for an instant that I am interested in that child?"

"Well, I confess I did have such an idea. She is no longer a child," said Mr. Williams.

"Nonsense; to me she is. She is not my style of a woman, I assure you, though I feel interested in her on account of her family."

"Please let me pass," said a voice. And they turned to find Margaret Holcombe behind them. She was very pale, but except that which might have been the effect of the cool night air on her,—for the gentlemen were standing in the door of the hall, and she must have come up the steps from the lawn the moment before,—there was no sign of discomposure about her. She bowed as she passed, in her queenly way.

"How unfortunate!" said Mr Williams.

"Exceedingly so, if she heard," said his companion.

"I am afraid there is no chance against that," said Mr. Williams. "But stop, here she comes again."

She came back enveloped in a large white nubia, which was wound around her head and neck. If she had been pale before, it was certainly a thing of the past,—she never looked so brilliant, her cheeks were almost purple with excessive bloom, and her eyes, as she again asked permission to pass, were flashing with wounded pride, but the voice was perfectly courteous and calm. They saw her join some one on the steps and wander off in the moonlight.

That moment was a revelation to Robert Murray. He knew that Margaret Holcombe was the only woman in the world for him; that it was not the wayward, proudly sensitive child who interested him, but the peerless woman, whom he must win for himself or be miserable.

"Where is Margaret?" said Mr. Holcombe, coming up just then. "They want to announce supper, and cannot do it until she is here to lead the way."

"She passed us just now," said Mr. Murray, "and went in that direction," pointing through the shrubbery.

"Can't you just step out there and call her for me? I have to go back to Jean."

He did not say it, but not for all the world would he have gone after Margaret Holcombe then.

"I will see she gets your message," he said, and went in pursuit of John, by whom he sent the message to his sister.

And then he went to look for Mary to take her in to supper, but he found he was too late, as she was already dancing along on Mr. Williams's arm. He turned to look for Ellen, but she, too, was provided for, and he had to console himself with a poor little lady who had adorned the corner, in which she stood, all the evening. Ellen whispered to him as he passed her,—

"I see Mr. Murray practices as well as preaches."

His next encounter was with Margaret and Dr. Burton; but they were laughing at some joke and did not seem to see him.

He heard some one say to her, "Oh, Margaret, you have lost your rose!"

"Have I?" she exclaimed. "Well, it don't matter,—I can easily get another."

His companion tried to chirp agreeably to him, and he made an equal effort to overcome his annoyance, but in vain, for wherever he looked there was Margaret, and wherever she was he saw the source of his discomfort.

The supper was very brilliant,—the pyramids of candied oranges and grapes, with the straw over them; the beautiful white cakes ; the sparkling jelly ; indeed, every-thing beautiful and tempting was found there, and the company did ample justice to the preparations.

They soon began to disperse after supper, and Robert Murray retired to his room, having learned a lesson which all Germany and the Alps had never taught him.

**17***

# CHAPTER XXII.

## THE TOURNAMENT.

MOST men in Robert Murray's position would have fled from the danger, but that course was foreign to his disposition. He conceived an idea strongly, and his iron will never acknowledged impossibilities.

The idea of going away now, and leaving the woman he loved to be carried off by a man utterly unworthy of her, he never thought of; indeed, to leave her at all, even to think of her as belonging to any one else, would be impossible. He made no confidants, nor did he, like an impulsive boy, rush madly forward into the heat of the battle, but like a wary, experienced commander he surveyed the field and bided his time.

He never avoided her, but he never sought her. It was like death to him sometimes to see Burton lifting her into her saddle and riding off with her; but he never interfered. He felt safe so far; he knew that though the impulse of the moment might lend a fascination to his attentions, that such a man as Burton could never satisfy the cravings of Margaret Holcombe's nature. There was one thing, however, which he did not know, and therefore could not take into consideration; but I will not anticipate.

Meanwhile Dr. Burton was a constant visitor at Rose Hill, and Margaret seemed to encourage his visits; but her temper was more fitful and wayward than ever. Mr. Williams returned home, and the household settled down to its usual quiet sobriety. I say the household; but there were exceptions to this rule. Invitations poured in from all quarters upon Margaret, Ellen, and Mr. Murray; entertainments were the order of the day ; scarce twenty-four hours passed without the carriage or riding-horses being ordered out.

Margaret engaged in everything with a zest which astonished her friends, as her character had never indicated this element. On the contrary, her love of solitude and rather brooding temper led them to expect a different course ; but now she was never satisfied unless she had something in prospect. Her belleship was firmly established ; her beauty and wit were the topic of conversation everywhere ; but notwithstanding the fact that she was constantly in requisition, that whenever she made her appearance in society she was the center of an admiring crowd, who flattered her vanity and laughed at her quick repartee, she felt that she was not altogether popular. Her own sex were disposed to search out and comment on the flaws in her character, because she absorbed so much of the attention of the other sex; and the gentlemen had so many of them winced under the arrows of her sarcastic tongue, that although they still, like foolish moths, buzzed around the dazzling light, it was always with a recollection that, beautiful as it was, the flame could scorch and singe their precious wings.

It was no wonder, then, that she often turned with a feeling of relief to Dr. Burton, who never allowed himself to be rebuffed, and was always, no matter in what temper he had last found his divinity, ready to return to the charge, with no vestige of recollection of ·former blows. Her general feeling with regard to this gentleman was contempt. A proud woman like Margaret Holcombe is not apt to conceive a real liking for anything mean-spirited in the other sex, and the imperturbable good nature and forbearance under such provocation as she often afforded him made her utterly careless with regard to her words and actions to him.

Meanwhile Mr. Murray watched her with the deepest anxiety; he saw that some wretchedness was tugging at her heart, and that this reckless course of dissipation was nothing but a cover for her real feelings; he remembered the day in the library, when she had spoken so candidly of her hours of self-torture, and he wondered if she were not now avoiding a meeting with herself face to face! With regard to Dr. Burton, he often doubted if it was not his duty to speak a word of warning to Mr. Holcombe; but then the feeling of delicacy engendered by b's own position with regard to him kept him silent, as he could not bear the idea of seeming to calumniate a rival.

A rival—the idea! Margaret Holcombe would have curled her lip contemptuously at such a suggestion. The cold, proud man,—she believed he really disliked her; or, as he had said that night, he felt an interest in her on "account of her family."

"More invitations!" exclaimed Mr. Holcombe, in comic dismay, as he walked into the breakfast-room one morning early in September and threw a pile of envelopes on the table. "There is no rest for the wicked; and if that be so, my poor horses must be the most wretched sinners that ever lived. Where is it, Margaret?" for Margaret had seized on her note and opened it.

"Oh, delightful!" was the answer. "Just hear."

"'The gentlemen of C—— request the pleasure of your presence in Clarke's Grove to a Tournament, on Tuesday next, at three o'clock.

"'*Committee of Arrangements.*—William Marshall, Charles Clarke, Henry Dandridge, John Tucker.'"

And Margaret and Ellen both expressed unqualified delight that, at last, there was some prospect of a variety in their amusements.

"Well," said Mary, her usually bright face clouding over, "I wish I was grown, too,—it is so dull to stay at home all by myself."

"Never mind, Mary," said John, "we won't go into such general society; we will be more select, and have a tournament all to ourselves,—I will ride for you and you for me, and then, you know, there is no danger of any bad feeling."

"Much obliged to you, Johnny," said Mary, laughing; "but that is very dull work,—I am too used to you,—I want somebody new to ride for me."

"Won't I answer your purpose, Miss Mary?" said Mr. Murray; "or am I too big, and not new enough, either?"

"Oh, no!" said Mary, clapping her hands, "that would be splendid, if I could only go, and have you for my knight; I would give you a blue ribbon, my color, to tie on your lance."

"Would you let her go if she had an invitation?" said Mr. Murray, turning to Mr. Holcombe.

"Well, I don't know; what do you say, mamma?"

"Well," said Jean, smiling at Mary's eager face, "I think for this once, as she goes away to school next month; but how can she go without an invitation?"

"Oh, I will manage that," said Mr. Murray: "nothing easier. I shall ride into C—— this morning to get admission to the knighthood, and of course they will be delighted to send an invitation to this young lady. I sha'n't ride unless I am permitted to ride for her."

In looking towards Mary his eyes fell on Margaret; her face was bent on her plate, while the blood looked as

if it would burst from her cheeks. She raised her eyes
for a moment and caught his gaze fixed on her with a
puzzled expression; the haughty head was thrown back
at once, and she said, "Oh, yes, of course Mary can
go; she will make a splendid Queen of Love and
Beauty."

"And oh, Margie," said Mary, in childish delight,
"what must I wear?"

"Time enough for that important decision, Mary," said
Jean, "as it is still nearly a week off."

Mary's invitation was easily obtained, and Mr. Murray
returned with the honors of knighthood upon him.

The place where the tournament was to take place
was a beautiful grove a short distance from C——; it
seemed almost as if nature designed the spot for some
such use as that to which it was now dedicated. It was on
the edge of the woods, and the trees grew sparsely,
leaving a wide space of level ground, with the waving
branches forming an arch above it.

The scene was a beautiful one. Seats had been erected
for the spectators on one side, near enough to give a full
view of the sport, and the gallant knights, with their
fanciful dresses, clustered together at the end of the
ground, while the bright scarfs of the marshals flitted
around gayly as their wearers dashed about among the
trees.

The seats were crowded with bright-eyed damsels,
whose gay dresses and laughing voices added to the general hilarity.

"Just look at Margaret Holcombe," whispered Jennie
Clarke to her neighbor, Annie Campbell; "she is evidently expecting to wear the crown to-night."

"She ought certainly to do it," was the quiet answer;
"there is no girl here who can compare with her. If I

were chosen Queen, of which I have no idea, I should abdicate in favor of the rightful sovereign,—she is perfectly regal to-day."

And so she was, in her simple, white muslin dress and rich, scarlet ribbons, with bright flowers in her hair, Margaret Holcombe possessed that advantage for want of which so many women of decided beauty throw away their claims to it,—she knew just what to wear and how to wear it. As long as the season would allow, her dress was pure white, because she knew that the contrast with her dark hair and eyes and brilliant complexion made it the most becoming for her. Exquisitely neat in everything, whatever she put on was the purest, the smoothest, and of the finest texture. No one ever saw Margaret Holcombe with anything on with a flaw in it. Dainty in all of her tastes, it became second nature to her to make her dress perfect in its simplicity and purity, and perfect in its adaptedness to her style of beauty.

Mary used to say that she believed Margie could jump over the house and come down without a wrinkle or a tear in her dress, and if she sat still in the house hers would be out of order in some way.

But the band begins to play, and the brilliant array of knights rode through the lists, their mettled steeds prancing and curveting or restrained by the grinding bit to the mincing gait of restricted freedom. They rode two and two, and filing in front of the seats occupied by the ladies, doffed their plumed caps and bowed low, with chivalrous acknowledgment of the presence of youth and loveliness.

They were a gallant company,—most of them sons of old Virginia, whose skill in the science of horsemanship is so justly renowned. Foremost of the band rode a kingly figure — a Saul among his fellows! — who bore

upon his breastplate the white and red roses of England
prettily blended, and the blue of his shoulder-knot had its
counterpart in the ribbons which adorned the dress of
Mary Holcombe. It was the Knight of St. George! And
happily had he chosen the name, for he wore well the
character of a Saxon knight, with his dress of blue and
silver and the long, white plume which drooped upon his
shoulder mingling with his magnificent beard.

Mary was wild with delight, clapped her hands and
laughed like the child she was. "Oh, Margie!" she said,
"my knight is the handsomest of any of them!" But
Margaret did not respond; her eyes were fixed upon the
orator of the day, a young lawyer of C——, Mr. Tucker,
who now stepped forward to deliver the charge to the
knights.

"Sir Knights," said he, "I have been appointed by you
to the pleasing duty of introducing you to the field upon
which you are about to exercise your prowess. The
knights of old, inured to hardship and danger, gladly
turned from the bloody battlefield to reap their reward at
the hands of the fair. You have no such stirring experiences as theirs, thank God! and grant that you never
may have; but nevertheless each one of you is daily
fighting the battle of life, in which, it is true, no blood is
shed, but in which heart and brain are deeply engaged.
From this field you turn aside, like true disciples of chivalry, to do your devoirs at the shrine of Beauty,—in a
cause, let me say, which always fires the heart and nerves
the arm of the brave.

"I see that each of you, in entering upon this contest
in imitation of the founders of chivalry, has assumed the
colors of the lady of his choice. Then let him remember that in so doing he assumes also a responsibility, for
her sovereignty in the Court of Love and Beauty rests

upon his prowess,—her eyes are upon him, with his success or failure she stands or falls.

"I therefore charge you, Sir Knights, in the name of chivalry, to be wary and watchful; let your earnestness in action attest your earnestness of purpose and your sense of the importance of the task you have undertaken, and I feel assured that your reward will be commensurate with your effort, in the smile of approbation from the rosy lips of her who shall wear your crown."

He bowed and retired, and the knights riding forward in the same order in which they had advanced, turned at the end of the ground and rode back again to the point from which they started, exchanging, as they passed, salutations with the ladies of their choice.

It might be remarked that three knights wore the scarlet ribbon of the shade which adorned the dress of Margaret Holcombe,—the Knight of Rose Hill (Mr. Campbell), the Knight of Virginia (Mr. Dandridge), and Brian de Bois Guilbert (Dr. Burton); but, like Haman of old, all of her honors were nothing so long as "Mordecai the Jew sat at the king's gate."

"How does it happen," said Mr. Tucker, taking a seat between Mary and herself, "that you have allowed this small sister of yours to carry off the prize yonder, in the person of the Knight of St. George?"

The tone was very indifferent which answered, "Perhaps I did not consider it a prize worth trying for."

Mr. Tucker laughed, and said, "Perhaps not; but I think you are a lady of too much taste to avow such an opinion. I never saw a finer-looking man."

"I don't estimate my goods by weight," said she, "fortunately for you, Mr. Tucker; I would rather have a small diamond than a large pebble."

18

"Hands off, now," said he, in pretended fright; "I won't be handled without gloves."

"Why, you have nothing to complain of," said she, laughing, "you are the small diamond."

"Ain't you ashamed of yourself, Margie?—you know Mr. Murray is—— is splendid," said Mary.

"We will be able to judge now," said she coolly, as the bugle sounded and the Herald called,—

"The Knight of St. George, come into the court!" And Black Festus, proudly arching his neck, moved forward, while his rider, poising his lance, bent his eye keenly upon the ring which hung midway of the lists.

"He stoops to conquer!" said Mr. Tucker, as the tall figure bent forward in his saddle.

"He stoops to fail!" said Margaret, as he rode off without the ring. The words were against him; the tone of disappointment which accompanied them betrayed her sympathies.

"That is too bad!" said Mary. "Never mind; I hope no one else will take it, either."

"You dog in the manger!" said Mr Tucker.

"The Knight of Ivanhoe, come into the court!" said the Herald.

"Here comes my young brother," said Mr. Tucker, "and he wears Miss Randolph's colors. Calm yourself, Miss Ellen. There! I knew he was good for it," as the shouts and music from the band announced his triumph.

"Brian de Bois Guilbert, come into the court!" cried the Herald.

"Now, Miss Holcombe, here comes the scarlet ribbons." And so each one of the knights rode in his turn with varied success. After six rounds the contest lay between the four most successful,—the Knight of St.

George, the Knight of Ivanhoe, the Knight of Rose Hill, and the Knight of Brandon.

Mr. Murray had never failed after the first time, and Mary was greatly excited.

"There, he has it again!" said she, clapping her hands. "I almost feel the crown on my head."

This time the Knight of Brandon and the Knight of Ivanhoe failed and were withdrawn, and the contest lay between Archy Campbell and Mr. Murray. They were so equally matched that no one could predict which would bear off the highest honors.

Time after time they rode and carried off the ring, until Mr. Tucker, becoming impatient of the delay, said, "Those fellows have become so accustomed to taking that ring they couldn't miss it if they were to try." But it was differently determined by one of the parties concerned. Robert Murray, tired of the long contest, and in his heart of hearts preferring his defeat to his success, determined to put an end to it, and as he rode up towards the ring dug his spurs into the side of Black Festus with such force as to make him swerve to one side, and the ring hung unharmed on the wire; but the mettled animal, enraged and frightened, dashed off among the trees at mad speed before his rider could regain full command of him.

"Heavens! he will be killed!" said Mr. Tucker, as the infuriated animal dashed on through the thick undergrowth. Mary hid her face in her hands, and the terrified girls all around shrieked, cried, or fainted after the manner of women. Mr. Tucker heard a sound beside him like a person choking; he turned around. Margaret Holcombe had risen and stood beside him; her face as white as the dress she wore; one hand pressed upon her heart, and her head stretched forward in the direction of the mad equestrian, while her breath came in thick gasps from her pallid lips.

"Safe! safe!" was echoed through the woods, and Margaret Holcombe sank into her seat and the blood rushed back to her cheeks.

"'Tis only a pebble, Miss Holcombe," said Mr. Tucker, turning to her and smiling.

Surely the pride must have been indomitable in the girl's heart who could answer with such a cool, sarcastic smile after such terrible agitation,—

"'Tis true, perhaps; and yet one does not like to see the useless waste of stones, even."

Mr. Tucker looked puzzled. She was an enigma to him; he could not pronounce her wanting in heart, because he had seen her face of agony. He said,—

"You women are curious creatures,—I can't find you out. I don't know any more about you now than when I began the study."

"I never knew one of your sex get on this subject before," said Margaret, "without quoting on us,—

> 'Oh, woman, in our hours of ease,
> Uncertain, coy, and hard to please,' etc.

I am so glad you did not. I have a much better opinion of you for the omission. I always cut an acquaintance who quotes trite poetry on me,—I can't stand it."

"You cut them sometimes without that grave offense," said he, laughing. "Poor Burton! I pity him sometimes."

"Reserve your sympathies for a more worthy object, Mr. Tucker. Dr. Burton wears a coat of mail no arrow of mine will ever pierce."

"And what is that?" asked he.

"Imperturbable good temper; he is a perfect example

to some of you hot-heads. It is such a relief to get with
a person you can say what you choose to and feel perfectly confident that there is no danger of their getting
angry; but the knight had better keep clear of me this
evening,—I am keeping a sharpened arrow for him."

"Why, poor fellow! you ought to sympathize with
him in his misfortune; but his riding was absurd." And
Mr. Tucker laughed.

"Yes," said Margaret, "I hate to see any one attempt
a thing and fail; he has no more idea of riding than if
he had never seen a horse. And the idea of placing himself in competition with these Virginia boys, who ride
like centaurs! And then, too, I confess, one does not like
to see their colors degraded. If he had worn any other
color I should not have minded half as much."

"Ah! ha! there's where the shoe pinches, is it?" said
her companion. "It was Miss Holcombe who was affected
by it,—Miss Holcombe's pride was hurt."

"Of course," she said, throwing up her head and looking like a full-mettled Arabian. "Miss Holcombe does not
deny her pride,—she always hopes to keep herself above
disgrace of every kind."

Just then Mr. Murray rode into the lists unhurt, though
a good deal out of breath from his contest with Black
Festus. Every one crowded around him to congratulate
him upon his escape. It had indeed been a very narrow
one, as the mad animal carried him through the thick
woods, and his clothes in more than one place showed
where he had been violently brushed against the trees.
He may be pardoned if he glanced towards Margaret
Holcombe to see if she had felt even an ordinary amount
of anxiety for him in his danger. His thought had been
of her through the whole of it, but he could not think

18*

she had even heard of it,—she looked so calm and uncon-
cerned as she jested with Mr. Tucker. Mary, on the
contrary, had not yet dried her tears, and more than one
of the young ladies prolonged their hysterics until his
arrival.

It was at once proposed that the last trial should be
taken over again; but Mr. Murray would not hear of it,
and seemed irritated at the suggestion. So Margaret
Holcombe won the highest honors.

It was decided to adjourn to Dr. Campbell's, where an
entertainment had been prepared, and the coronation
would take place.

The doctor lived at the entrance to the town, in a large
brick house; he had a good many children, and was always highly delighted to have his house full of young
people. He met them at the door with his hearty welcome, and was delighted to hear that "Archy" had won
the day, and, above all, had "shown such taste in the
selection of his queen," said he, bowing low to Margaret with old-fashioned, courtly grace.

"That is as much as to say I would not have made a
good queen," said Jennie Clarke, pouting.

"Ah, Miss Jennie, I'll ride for you myself next time,
if the old lady will let me." And he led the way into
the parlors, where Mrs. Campbell and her daughter
waited to do the honors. The girls went to work to im-
provise a throne, bringing into requisition all the bright
draperies the establishment could afford. It consisted of
a platform made of some convenient pieces of furniture,
covered with a bright-green carpet, upon which was
placed the doctor's large arm-chair, which was covered
with crimson draperies, and green wreaths hung in every
direction.

At eight o'clock the four successful knights stepped in,

each one with a wreath of flowers. Mr. Tucker rose, and taking from Archy Campbell his coronet formed of scarlet verbenas, said, speaking to Margaret,—

"The Knight of Rose Hill bids me crown you, lady, as Queen of Love and Beauty. My part is a meager one,—I can only place the crown upon your brow, where nature has been beforehand with me in stamping the impress of sovereignty."

Margaret bowed her head, and he placed the beautiful wreath upon her coronet of dark hair; then turning to Mr. Murray, he received from him a wreath of white rose-buds, and said,—

"It is fitting that the fair sister of our noble queen should occupy the position nearest her person, and the Knight of St. George presents this, the highest honor in his gift, to Miss Mary Holcombe. Kneel, fair lady."

Mary, with a face of perfect happiness, knelt before him, and rose up crowned with the simple flowerets.

The next was a wreath of green ivy-leaves, and receiving them, he said,—

"The Knight of Brandon thus greets the lady of his choice. Had fortune favored him she would have graced the throne."

Here Jennie Clarke knelt and received her crown.

The next was a wreath of violets and heart's-ease. He said,—

"The modest violet has been appropriately chosen by the Knight of Ivanhoe to deck the brow of Miss Ellen Randolph. How well she deserves the compliment we can all vouch who have seen her efforts to conceal herself, until drawn into notice by her friends."

Then came the royal quadrille to the simple music of the piano, and the evening progressed merrily.

"Ah, Miss Holcombe," said Dr. Burton, coming up to

Margaret as she had just seated herself in a recess, out of breath with dancing, " at last I manage to get near to you.   I have not been able even to congratulate you upon the success of the day, in which, as usual, your star was the brightest."

" It is of not the smallest consequence," said she, elevating her eyebrows; " I thought you had done so."

The doctor looked rather mortified.

" Or rather," he said, willing to give a complimentary turn to her remark, " you know so well what I think that you may well imagine what my speech would be."

She only bowed her head haughtily.

" But, ah," he continued, " if the honor had only been mine to place that crown upon your head! but, alas! the fates were against me."

" Say rather you were against yourself," said Margaret, curling her lip. " I believe you did not take the ring once."

" No" was the answer ; " the fact is my horse was such a miserable affair——"

" That he furnishes you with an excuse for failure," said the young lady, finishing his sentence.

" You think I needed one, I suppose ?" said he, making rather a lame attempt to be amused.

" Indeed I do," said she ; " you remind me of all sorts of——well, of all sorts of uncomplimentary things."

" What, for instance ?"  said Dr. Burton.  " Don't spare me, you know I like to see you amused ;" but it must be confessed he looked rather uncomfortable at the license he had allowed.

" Well, since you want to hear, like a poor boy at a frolic ! a fish out of water !" And she felt like adding, like a presumptuous fool who aspires to a position for which he has no vocation.

" You are hard on me, Miss Holcombe ; you should not visit my misfortunes upon me."

" I only visit your folly upon you, Dr. Burton ; I would not eat my breakfast if I did not think I could not do it well ; and besides, I was unfortunately concerned in your failure, as you dragged my colors down with you."

" Forgive me, my dear Miss Holcombe," he said.

But she interrupted him with " Never mind appending an adjective to my name, I don't like the habit."

" Excuse me," he said ; " you are so very particular."

· Then followed a long silence, in which Margaret's conscience began to annoy her,—it was one of those dreaded controversies with herself.

" How rude I am !" she said to herself. " Here is this poor little man who has disgraced himself in an effort to honor me, and I add to his mortification by my taunts,—how mean that is ! I wonder any one should like me."

The impulse led her to turn to her companion with the most winning smile she could command and say, gently,—

" Dr. Burton, I wonder you do not resent my rudeness to you sometimes,—you are a perfect miracle of patience and forbearance. I don't know any one in the world who would bear with me as you do."

" And can't you guess the reason, Miss Holcombe ?" said the doctor, eagerly.

She knew what was coming now, but it was too late to stop it.

" Because," he continued, interpreting her silence into a permission to go on, " there is no one in the world who cares for you as I do. I would rather suffer your displeasure than absent myself from you. Oh, Miss Holcombe, *say*, is there no reward in your heart for my devotion ?"

"I do not care for you except as a friend," said Margaret, in a low voice.

"But that is a good foundation for a warmer feeling," he said; "I can wait for the rest."

Margaret Holcombe's manner was strangely cool as she raised her eyes to his face and said, "You do not know what you ask, Dr. Burton. I would make your life miserable with my imperious temper,—there is not the shadow of a chance for happiness to any man who marries me." And a tone of sadness entered her voice.

"Well, no matter; if I am willing to risk it, no one has a right to object. I would make you happy, at any rate,—you should never have a wish ungratified."

"In short," she said, her lip curling again, "you are acting Claude Melnotte to perfection; but I am no devoted Pauline."

He did not seem to heed her sarcastic tone, but went on, earnestly,—

"Miss Holcombe, I know you better than you think: you are very willful, and do not like to be thwarted. I promise you, on my honor as a gentleman, I will never interfere with your wishes in any way, but the aim of my life shall be to gratify you in everything."

She smiled, and was silent for some minutes; and when she spoke it was as if she recalled her thoughts from some far-off region. She said,—

"I would rather marry my master; and failing that, I suppose it is best to take my slave." And then changing her tone, she said, as she bent her eyes upon him,—

"Dr. Burton, is it possible that, knowing me as you do, and telling you candidly as I do, that I do not love you; that I feel I should make you miserable; that the only thing which could induce me to think of marrying you would be that I know—that I feel—I can never be happy, because I am not the *style* (she said this as if it was a quotation) of woman to win the only sort of man who could make me happy? Knowing this, if I married you, it would be that I might have my own will in every-thing. Are you still willing to marry me?"

She would have given anything if he had said "No." She almost thought he would at first; but he had no such idea,—there was too much at stake for that. He an-swered, passionately,—

"Margaret Holcombe, knowing all this, I ask you to become my wife. I will win you by my devotion,—I do not fear."

She put her hands over her eyes, as if to shut out the light, or perhaps to hide from her view a noble figure which just then entered the room, and sought her out with his eyes. Perhaps if she had seen the shadow of suffering which came into his face as he saw her com-panion, she would not have said, as she did, in that low tone,—

"Well, take me, if you want me."

"Thank you; ah, thank you!" was the answer.

Mary Holcombe had been asleep for some hours that night, when, turning over suddenly, she caught sight of Margaret sitting before the window with her head buried in her hands. She had not undressed, and the wreath of scarlet flowers, all limp and fading, still adorned her head.

"Why, Margie," she said, raising up, "what upon earth are you doing up this time of the night?"

"I am coming now, Mary," said she, rising and keep-ing her face turned from her sister.

She forgot the mirror which she faced, and which showed Mary a tear-stained face and pallid cheeks. She respected her evident wish to be unnoticed, and said nothing more ; but her mind was so busy with what it could be that could make her sister cry when she had just been crowned Queen of Love and Beauty, that she did not feel again like going to sleep, but lay there very quietly until Margaret put out the light and took her place at her side, and then she said,—

" Margie, you forgot to say your prayers."

" Never mind me, Mary, go to sleep,—I can take care of myself," was the answer ; but it suggested to her the thought that she dared not kneel before God and ask Him to prosper her in what she had that night undertaken.

And long after Mary had ceased to wonder at anything, and lay dreaming happily at her side, did Margaret toss and moan.  Daylight was creeping in at the windows before exhausted nature found repose.

# CHAPTER XXIII.

## ASKING PAPA.

IT was during the progress of breakfast the next morning that Uncle Robin, answering a call at the door, brought in a note to Mr. Holcombe, which that gentleman turned over and over, looked at through and through, examined the seal, and at last wondered who in the world it could be from.

"Papa," said John, laughing, "what is the reason people always do that? It would be so much easier to open the letter at once, and see who it was from, than to guess all over it that way."

"That's true, General," said Mr. Holcombe. "Well, I have tried my way,—I will try yours now." So he broke the seal. Now Mr. Holcombe was, besides growing a little gray, beginning to hold his letters and books at a considerable distance from him when he read, and in the seclusion of his study he even used glasses,—so that it was some time before he made out the contents of his note, and he interlarded his progress with exclamations which considerably whetted the curiosity of the company to know its contents.

"Well," he said, when he opened it, "what on the earth does the fellow want with me? 'Important business!' I have none with him, that's certain. 'See me at my earliest convenience.' My earliest pleasure would be fifty years from now. Indeed, I would be rather pleased never to see him again."

"Mr. Holcombe," said his wife, laughing, "please relieve our curiosity and tell us who your correspondent is."

Mr. Holcombe read aloud:

"My dear Sir,—What time may I have a private interview with you? I have some important business to consult with you about, and would be glad to see you at your earliest convenience.

"Very respectfully, etc.,

"William Burton."

"Well, I suppose there is no help for it." And he rose to answer the note.

Any one who had glanced at Margaret Holcombe's face as her father read this note, would have had no difficulty in guessing that in some way or other she was concerned in its contents. There was one person at the table who generally kept himself informed as to the changes in its expression. This person glanced at her now; saw the blood rush in torrents over her entire countenance, even down to where the neat little collar clasped her throat, and then recede, leaving her as pale as death. He thought for an instant she was going to faint, but she did not. Exerting wonderful self-control, she recovered herself before any one noticed her; and, though she did not venture any remark, her silence was not noticed except by Mr. Murray. His heart beat painfully against his breast. In all the cause he had had for anxiety in the past few weeks, now for the first time his courage failed him,—he had trusted so implicitly to the true nature somewhere hidden in Margaret Holcombe, which in a decisive moment must assert itself over the vagaries of her willful temper. But this was going further than he had ever imagined she could. Of course

Dr. Burton must have her permission to seek this inter-view, and but one inference could be drawn from her having given it. He had been blind, but now it was no longer possible to hide from himself the danger. He went out from the dining-room, and, hastily snatching his hat, walked rapidly away in the direction of the grove.

It is in the nature of men, even the best of them, to value what is hard to gain,—the unattainable is the object of their greatest efforts. Now, if Robert Murray had found Margaret a pliable, loving girl, ready to respond to his earliest efforts to win her affections, in all proba-bility his feeling would never have attained any great de-gree of strength; but the experience he had suffered since he first obtained a sight of his heart, had caused this feeling to gather intensity in proportion to the difficulties he saw to the accomplishment of his desire. He flattered himself that he could bear the disappointment for him-self; but to see her so false to herself,—to see her seal the misery of her life by a union with one so utterly unworthy of her, as he believed Burton to be, was hor-rible.

It may be asked upon what he founded this opinion. As our story has touched but meagerly on the doctor's character, it must be confessed that Mr. Murray had a prejudice against the gentleman to begin with, dating from the night of the entertainment at Rose Hill, on ac-count not only of his insolence to him, but because he felt sure that he had made a representation to Margaret during the evening which had produced the cloud between them,—which cloud everything since had tended to in-crease. But this was not all: there was a cringing, un-manly manner about the man, when with Margaret, which disgusted him; and once or twice he had caught a sinis-ter expression about his eye when she would make one of her quick retorts to him, which altogether belied his manner, and convinced him that he was acting a part, for a purpose. Margaret Holcombe was no despicable match for any one, apart from her own attractions, and literally nothing was known of Dr. Burton; so what more probable than that his addresses were paid to her dowry rather than to herself. All of these thoughts plied steadily through Mr. Murray's brain as he paced backward and forward in the grove. The heart of this strong man was heavy indeed. The situation was complicated. His great hope was in Mr. Holcombe, whose pride of birth and every other consideration would, he thought, oblige him to withhold his consent, at least, until something could be learned about the gentleman; and if this were the case, it would give him more time to counteract the plans of the gentleman, and "who knows but the lady herself might recover her senses?" And his hopes revived.

He was aroused from his reverie by the sound of horse's hoofs, and in a moment the figure of Dr. Burton appeared, riding in his own ungraceful style on a gray horse. He showed his white teeth as he passed, and was soon out of sight.

We will now transfer ourselves to the library, where Mr. Holcombe awaited his unwelcome visitor. It seems strange that Mr. Holcombe had never feared this result of Dr. Burton's constant visits; but the fact is he had never thought of his daughter as eligible for matrimony; or if he had, his confidence in Margaret's pride was such that the idea of her placing her affections upon a nameless stranger was without the range of his conjectures; so that the expression which met the doctor when Robin ushered him into the library was totally unsuspicious of the object of his visit.

This was rather unexpected to the gentleman, as he thought that his attentions must have made themselves understood in all quarters. He took his seat, fidgeted around, looked contemplatively at the ceiling, and at last said,—

"Fine weather this, sir." And clapped his hands as if in congratulation at having at least made a commencement.

"Very," was the brief reply, as Mr. Holcombe sat quietly waiting this important announcement.

"Planted your wheat yet, sir?"

"I am *sowing* it now, thank you."

A long silence followed this last essay, and again the little man's eyes sought the ceiling.

Mr. Holcombe found this slow work,—he would have to assist.

"I understood from your note, sir, that I could help you in some important business."

"Yes, yes, sir; I do wish to consult you—in fact—hm—your—rather Miss Holcombe permitted me to seek you—to seek—this interview in order—in short, sir, to ask for your consent to her becoming my wife."

If the sky had fallen over them at that moment Mr. Holcombe could not have been more astonished.

"Margaret!" he ejaculated, "permitted you to seek me for such a purpose? Who are you, sir?"

The tone was not complimentary, nor calculated to encourage a timid aspirant for matrimonial honors. He answered, rather faintly,—

"Who am I? What do you mean, sir?"

"I mean, sir, to ask you to tell me what claim you have to make for my daughter's hand," said Mr. Holcombe.

19*

"Her permission to ask you for it," said the doctor, with some appearance of offended dignity.

"That is not sufficient, sir ; we do not give our daughters away in Virginia upon such slender claims as that. I must know not only who you are, but who your parents were. Had you the wealth of John Jacob Astor to back your suit it would weigh nothing in your favor. Show me that you are worthy in yourself, and that my daughter in going to you would not be degraded below the station in life in which she has been brought up, and if I find her happiness depends upon her marriage with you, I will consider your proposition. Until then consider yourself banished from Rose Hill. I shall command my daughter to hold no intercourse with you."

The doctor's face was a study during this calm exposition of Mr. Holcombe's intentions ; wrath, indecision, and fear chased themselves over his countenance, and, mingled with all, the necessity of concealing his feelings. At last he managed to say,—

"I am from Massachusetts, sir."

"Which in itself is nothing in your favor," said Mr. Holcombe, coolly.

"You speak, sir," said Dr. Burton, with temper, "as if Massachusetts could not furnish as good gentlemen as Virginia."

"I said nothing of the kind, sir ; but I must be assured that Massachusetts has sent out the best man she has before he can take Margaret Holcombe. I have seen first-rate men in Massachusetts, but they, for the most part, stay at home, or, emigrating to another State, bring with them such credentials as will establish their claims to be received as equals in the community in which they make their residence. Perhaps Dr. Burton has such? I am ready to consider them. In the mean time, I think it is useless for us to continue this conversation. I must see my daughter before I speak any further on this subject,—I feel sure that there must be some mistake."

After the first burst of surprise Mr. Holcombe's manner had been perfectly cool and collected, and he now bowed Dr. Burton out with all the calm politeness which usually characterized his manner; but the moment his back was turned he rang the bell with a vehemence which startled the servants in the kitchen and brought an answer to his summons at once.

"Go and tell your Miss Margaret I wish to speak to her," said he to the boy who appeared at the door; and then to his impatient spirit it seemed an hour before he heard the light footstep coming slowly down the stairs; and when Margaret Holcombe opened the door she found him impatiently awaiting her on the threshold.

In an instant his heart was touched by her pallid face and evident agitation,—so different from Margaret's usual demeanor.

"My dear child," he said, "what in the world does this fellow Burton mean by saying that *you* have promised to marry him ?"

"He speaks the truth, papa,—I have given him such a promise."

Mr. Holcombe almost groaned aloud. Margaret looked up hastily, and said,—

"Is there any reason for your objecting, papa ?"

"So much that I would rather see you laid in your grave than that it should ever take place," said her father, solemnly.

"Give me your reasons, sir." With the return of calm her old defiant manner began to assert itself.

"In the first place, my daughter, you know nothing about him. Suppose you were to marry him, and he should take you into an entirely different sphere from that in which you move,—you would be miserable. Next, he is not the person to make you happy,—he is inferior to you in every respect; and you, of all women in the world, should marry a man of strong intellect and strong will. You will be governed by one you love, and by that one alone, and if you should be united to one for whom you had not the most unbounded affection, I dread to think what a wreck your life would be. I do not, my child, make it a necessary proviso that your husband should have wealth,—you will always have enough to meet your wants from your mother's property; and besides, the Holcombes, without despising wealth, have always placed other things above its considerations. I hand down to my children a name unsullied through its whole course by anything which they would blush to know,—an honorable lineage,—and I do desire that the stream may be kept pure; it is the one thing you owe your name." He stopped and waited her answer.

"You speak, papa, as if you knew Dr. Burton to be unworthy."

"No, I know nothing about him; but I have told him that before he enters this house again he must bring satisfactory evidence that he is a worthy suitor for my daughter, and that I should forbid your seeing him until the matter was settled."

The proud head was thrown up and her eye flashed as she said, "Did I understand you to say, sir, that I was to be a prisoner,—my movements coerced?"

"You know you did not, Margaret," he answered, indignantly. "You are only under my commands that you shall not allow Dr. Burton to seek you until he complies with my requisitions. That is reasonable, and I shall exact obedience."

It was not often that Mr. Holcombe spoke so decidedly to his children ; but when he did, they knew him to be in earnest, and did not venture to disobey. But Margaret said, excitedly,— .

"Am I never to be considered out of leading-strings? If I married for nothing else, it would be that I might be permitted to exercise the right of self-government."

Mr. Holcombe smiled as he said, "A new motive for marrying, Margaret. The man is the head of the woman, as Christ is the head of the church,—is that your motive in marrying Dr. Burton?"

Margaret was seated before the large table which oc-cupied the center of the room, with her face turned towards her father; her elbows rested on the green cover, and she seemed to be exercising the greatest diligence in tearing a piece of paper into even squares, which she threw on the table. The only answer that she now gave was a gesture of the hand, which let fly a perfect shower of these little snowflakes.

"Because, let me tell you, young lady," continued Mr. Holcombe, "I know my sex better than you do, and whatever Dr. Burton may promise now, he will be sure to exercise his prerogative after marriage ; and an obsti-nate fool is worse than ten men who can give a reason."

"But he *has* promised, solemnly," said Margaret.

"Then he has lied solemnly," said her father, "and I have a worse opinion of the man since I know it. He tries to entrap you by flattering,—what any fool might see is your weak point,—and in the attainment of his purpose does not hesitate to make promises which he does not mean to keep."

"You are unjust, papa. Dr. Burton is an honorable gentleman, and I know it is best for me to marry him. I am not calculated to make any one happy, and he is the only person I know who is willing to run the risk of marrying me."

"What makes you think, Margaret, that you are not calculated to make any one happy?"

"I never have," she answered ; "my unhappy temper is always interfering. In order to be happy I must not be so continually thwarted ; it keeps up the irritation in me, and makes me miserable." And she burst into tears.

Mr. Holcombe was surprised ; indeed, Margaret had surprised him all her life. She never did just the thing he expected, and now her passionate tears were an enigma to him.

"My precious child," he said, drawing her to him and taking her on his knee, "and for this were you going to throw away your life? Depend upon it, what you want is such a marriage as will make it a joy to you to surrender your will. The evil should be curtailed, and then eradicated, not encouraged and strengthened. You think it would make you happy never to be opposed, but you are mistaken,—you are too true a woman not to be miserable when you know you are violating the most beautiful prerogative of your sex."

"Which is submission to yours," said Margaret, laughing through her tears.

"Well, I didn't make it so, Margie," said he, glad to see her natural once more ; "though I confess I would rather belong to the ruling sex."

"Manlike," retorted Margaret.

# CHAPTER XXIV

DR. BURTON, CONTINUED.

MATTERS went on quite smoothly for some days at Rose Hill. Nothing more was seen of Dr. Burton, and although Mr. Murray did not know what had happened, he hoped much from his continued absence. Determined not to allow himself to be defrauded again, he sought Margaret more than he had done; supplied himself with a pile of new music, which he proposed their practicing; but he could not flatter himself that he progressed very rapidly, as she was always embarrassed in his presence, and once he was sure she avoided him. She was evidently, too, nervous and anxious; a step would make her start and send the blood to her cheek.

John and Mary started off to school, the first of October, their father accompanying them. Mary was almost broken-hearted at leaving home and going among strangers, though of course she was not without pleasing anticipations of the pleasure in store for her in her new life. Ellen Randolph also accompanied them as far as her home.

It was on the evening after their departure, while Mr. Murray and Margaret were engaged in practicing some new music, that Dr. Burton walked into the room. His approach had been so noiseless that even Margaret's sensitive ears had not been startled by it, and he stood beside her before she had any idea that he was near. She started to her feet and said,—

"Oh, Dr. Burton, how you frightened me!" And truly there was a greater exhibition of excitement than the occasion seemed to warrant.

"Yes," he said, "you evidently had no expectation of seeing me."

"Of course not," she said; "I thought you would wait until papa returned."

Here Mr. Murray, feeling himself *de trop*, left the room. He caught Margaret's eye as he opened the door, and almost paused at its expression of earnest desire for his presence; but, as she said nothing, he went on.

"And why should I wait for Mr. Holcombe's return, Miss Holcombe? After the insults he heaped upon me the other day one would imagine that I would not willingly find myself under the same roof with him. Nothing but your being here would ever have drawn me again; but, unfortunately to my misery, I am forced to return to you."

"Not at all, Dr. Burton," said Margaret, stiffly; "I assure you I did not consider you bound. My father did not approve the step I took, and dissolved the relations between us, and I of course submit to his determination."

"Margaret Holcombe has given up her lofty independence of character, then, and subsided into the yielding, submissive girl? I wish I could congratulate her upon the change."

Margaret's face flushed with indignation at his tone, and she answered, with grave dignity,—

"Dr. Burton would have cause to do so were the change such as he supposes. Miss Holcombe desires nothing better than to be able to give her submission where it is rightly due, though she cannot yet felicitate herself upon such a happy change in her disposition."

Dr. Burton saw he had made an error, and could not in a moment decide what would be his best course to repair it; flattery, however, he had always found potent.

"Forgive me," he said, with every appearance of candor, "but you have stood so alone in my esteem for the very qualities you possessed, in which most of your sex are lacking, that I must regret any evidence of their waning strength."

"What elements of character are they which have elicited Dr. Burton's admiration?"

Unawed by her coolness, he answered, throwing as much fervor into his tone as he could,—

"Independence of action, strength of will, and firmness of purpose."

He could see that at last he had made some impression, and he continued, "And when the other night your promise was given me, I said to myself, Now my happiness is secured,—she, of all other women in the world, will not allow herself to be swayed by the opinions of others. Even when insulted by your father, my confidence in you supported me, and enabled me to bear it with patience."

"Dr. Burton," said Margaret, "you have twice made use of that expression, 'insulted by your father.' I would like you to explain yourself; it is certainly a thing hard for me to understand, that papa could have been guilty of a rudeness to you for no greater offense than a high appreciation of his daughter."

"Nevertheless it is so, Miss Holcombe; he asked me, in the most contemptuous manner, 'Who are you, who dares to aspire to my daughter's hand?' And when I told him that I was from Massachusetts, he said that was a strong point against me, and intimated that a gentleman of Massachusetts was beneath the notice of a Virginian;

20

and in the most galling manner told me he did not believe my assertions of equality, and I must prove them. I assure you, Miss Holcombe, if any other man than your father had spoken so to me I should have knocked him down." And the wrathful little man looked as if he would like to make his words good at once.

"I am sorry," said Margaret, gently, feeling as if in some way she would have to atone for the ill treatment of the rest of the family. "Papa did not mean, I am sure, to express himself so strongly; but he was taken by surprise, and only intended to convey to you that you must bring to him some evidence that—that——"

"That I was a gentleman," he said, finishing out the sentence in which she had become hopelessly involved. "I am not accustomed to have that questioned by any one,—so long as my behavior lays me open to no suspicion I expect to be received as I always have been."

"You know we Virginians require something more," said Margaret, smiling.

"Yes, because you think yourselves better than the rest of the world?" he said, inquiringly.

"No, I don't know that; but we are entitled to our peculiarities just as another State,—Massachusetts, for instance."

"But we have no such peculiarities," said the doctor.

"Perhaps not," was the answer; "but you have others which are just as objectionable to us. I am sorry that your feelings were hurt, though, in this house, and feel sure that I should be authorized to apologize to you by papa if he knew your interpretation of his words."

"Thank you, it is not necessary," said he; "I would endure that, and a great deal more, to win you. If I only accomplish that, everything else will seem as nothing."

"That is an idea, Dr. Burton, which you had better

give up at once. I told you the other day that I did not love you, though I was willing to marry you for the most selfish considerations; but it would require a stronger feeling than that to induce me to meet the opposition I should have to encounter."

The doctor was nonplused,—her change of mood was inexplicable. The fact is, the carrying out of this scheme of his had become absolutely necessary,—there were wants which were becoming more imperative than the want of a wife, but in meeting which a wife could help him. The immediate cause of his visit to Rose Hill just now was some very important letters which had reached him, containing severe threats if he did not at once furnish satisfactory evidence that his affairs were on the highroad to fortune; and he found it necessary to hurry matters, if possible. It was rather embarrassing, then, to find his affairs so much out of gear. But one recourse remained to him. He thought he had made a discovery on the first night he met Margaret, which he might use to advantage. But with how much care and circumspection must each step be taken! He almost feared to begin, but the case was desperate.

"Miss Holcombe," he said, fixing his eyes keenly upon her, so as to note every change in her countenance, "I fear there is an influence at work which is more powerful than your father's commands."

Her startled eyes flashed upon him, for a second only, but in that second he read the truth of his conjectures. He must still be wary; but much was accomplished by those few words. As she did not answer, he went on,—

"I have suspected this, my dear young lady, since the first time I met you. Some chance words of—of the person concerned led me to think of it first, and ever since then matters have gone to confirm my suspicions."

He stopped now and waited for an answer. Of course she must break the silence or confirm his doubts.

"What do you mean, Dr. Burton?" she said, recovering her composure with an effort.

"Ah, Miss Holcombe, it is a strange thing to say to you,—beautiful, young, accomplished, with everything to win the heart; but already you feel your life a failure because you suffer from an unrequited attachment."

He was startled at the flame of anger which met him from those flashing eyes, as she said in loud tones, clear as the sound of a clarion,—

"Dr. Burton, what have I ever done that you venture to take this liberty with me? I am fallen, indeed, in my own estimation, when my very presence does not protect me from insolence."

Dr. Burton hid his face in his hands as he said, "Ah, Miss Holcombe, how I suffer under your displeasure! How I had hoped that in the calm, peaceful lives I had planned for us, this delicate subject might remain untouched! And now nothing but the hope that I might be the humble means of promoting your happiness, though you cast me off, induced me to brave your anger. But, my dear young lady, can you not trust me? Can you not have confidence in me? Surely the promise you gave me but a few nights since was sufficient encouragement for me to flatter myself that my position, as your friend, was at least a high one."

Margaret was still silent, and when he looked up he found her sitting opposite to him with a face as white as the dead: with expressionless eyes, the lips moved, but no sound came. He started up, and brought her from the table a glass of water; she took it mechanically, and drank it without saying anything.

He went on: "My dear young lady, I did not know

that the mere mention of this thing would be so dreadful; my reason for referring to it was that I thought I could do some good by gently hinting the state of your feelings to Mr. Murray,—the mere suggestion, I am sure, would be enough——"

"Dr. Burton," said Margaret Holcombe, rising from her chair, "leave the house; I cannot stand this any longer! Leave my affairs alone; I can manage them for myself." She was a queen to the last, he acknowledged that bitterly; but he knew he had gained the day. He knew that the fear which would hang over this proud woman would be a nightmare until she had his promise of silence. His tone was very humble as he said,—

"And do you forbid my return? I cannot give up the hope of making you happy." He held out his hand; there was a moment's hesitation, and then hers was extended.

Dr. Burton did two things on leaving the house: he sang as he went through the grove, and he wrote a facetious letter to his threatening correspondent, telling him that he had reached that point in the affairs of men where, it is said, the tide leads on to fortune; and he need have no fears, he would fully meet all of his obligations, and, besides, show him the handsomest and proudest wife Virginia ever produced.

Margaret fled up the stairs, locked herself in her own room; and when the servant went up to announce supper, answered, through the door, that she did not want any; her head ached, and she would not be down during the evening.

Nannie came afterwards with a light, but she declined letting her in.

Had Margaret Holcombe been a Catholic, her impulse would have led her to bury herself in a living death,

20*

where the mind, in its endless journey around and around the dull daily routine, feeds on itself for want of other nutriment; but having no such recourse, she lay in a torpor of despair, until desperation made her reckless. What was her one life at last? Far better to sacrifice it than to submit to the humiliation which threatened her. If she was miserable,—and she knew she would be,—other people had been miserable before, other women had lived through loveless marriages, and gone down to their graves honored by all. Her very trials might make her better: that might be the way she was to become a Christian; and then God would take her to heaven, where, poor child, her best anticipation was the meeting with the idol of her childhood—her mother. She could sob out her troubles on that gentle bosom. She forgot the humanity that had to be put off, she forgot the "no tears in heaven," she only thought of it as an elevated earth, where she would meet her mother.

Poor child! for, after all, she was nothing more than a child. She always thought, in after-life, of this night with a thrill of suffering,—there was so much concentrated in those long, dreary hours,—everything is so much worse at night: one lies awake under a threatened danger, and nerves and brain seem to combine with the imagination to paint everything in its most exaggerated colors, until the mind is terrified at the vividness of its pictures. She heard Dr. Burton insinuating his suspicions to Mr. Murray; saw his look of annoyance; heard him again say, "She is not the style of woman to please me." All this was as vivid to her as if it had been real. Then her plans for preventing the dreadful denouement were endless, and most of them by the light of day would have looked perfectly impracticable. But reason had no sway in those dark hours,—the slight frame tossed from side to side of the bed in weariness and discomfort. Would daylight never come? Oh, the dreary study of the horizon for the first streak of the god of day! At last! at last! a pale light begins to creep in at the windows,—the phantoms of night take their flight, and the figure on the bed, from sheer exhaustion, falls into a heavy sleep. For some hours she lay in a perfect torpor,—it was kind mother Nature interposing; even dreams were forbidden to visit her,—the poor brain rested at last; but the sun would not be kept out. Darting one of his beams into her face, and striving to get under the closed eyelids, he broke the blessed rest. She started up,—seemed trying to collect her scattered thoughts. Oh, they are at work again! She sees the precipice once more, but with less of the horror which the visions of the night had brought,—day was more the time for action than thought. For a few moments she lay down again, face hidden in the pillow, and then slowly rose and commenced her toilet.

"Why, Margaret, are you sick?" said Jean, as she took her place at the breakfast-table, startled at the dark rims around the eyes, and cheeks which had gone back to the sallowness of their childhood. Mr. Murray looked at her in alarm.

She tried to smile, and assure them that she was well, but the effort brought the tears to her eyes, and she owned to having a headache.

Ah, what a scapegoat the head is! How it bears off the sins of omission and commission! Is one afflicted with ennui, "it is a headache;" does one want a convenient excuse for indolence, "it is a headache;" does the heart ache to its core, ah! how carefully is the secret to be guarded, while the long-suffering head is made responsible!

Jean suggested getting the carriage,—a ride might do her good.

No, she thought not,—she only wanted quiet. And yet when Mr. Murray announced his intention of riding into C—— during the morning, she became eager in her desire to practice some of their music together, until, puzzled by her nervous earnestness, he gave up his projected trip.

"He had never seen her so brilliant or so unapproachable as she was that morning. The color had returned to her cheeks, and now burned with feverish intensity; and once when their hands came in contact, in arranging the music, he found they were as cold as ice.

"Miss Holcombe," he said, "you are evidently not well,—lie down; indeed, you are not fit for this exertion,—your hands are cold as ice." And he took one of them in his, as a brother might have done, though the brotherly affection must have been very tender which looked with the anxiety which he did as he urged his advice that she would lie down.

But no; she laughed as she said she was "too poor company to seek solitude."

"Then," proposed he, "go into the library,—it is quiet there,—and I will read to you."

This proposition met with more favor,—she would have him safe then. So they adjourned to the library, and he piled up the cushions, and she reclined upon them, while he read and talked until the red spots paled in her cheeks and a less anxious expression looked out from her eye.

"Mr. Murray," she said, interrupting him in his reading, "if I should go to sleep, will you sit right where you are till I awake?—it quiets me to see you so still with the book in your hand."

He smiled at the childish request, and said, laying his cool hand on her head, " I would sit here for a week, poor child, if it would give you one moment's pleasure."

One moment she allowed herself to rest under that soothing touch, and in that moment the thought came, oh, how sweet it would be to die with that hand upon her brow ! But no, she had to live first, and not betray herself again, as she had already done. So she turned her head restlessly away, and was soon asleep, turning to him as her eyes closed to say, "Now, remember, you promised." He smiled his acquiescence, and in a moment more she lost her consciousness.

Hour after hour passed, and still he sat there, book in hand, but closed, for he had a volume of far greater interest before him,—he was trying to decipher the troubled lines in the young face; but in vain. He traced out all the familiar lines in the features; could tell just how those brows elevated themselves to express sarcastic doubt; fitted expressions he had heard her use to the peculiar turn of countenance he was imagining; saw the graceful head thrown back,—it was such an hourly gesture with her; the very tones of her voice came back to him so familiar, and he knew now how dear.

And then conjecture began to be busy again with her evident distress. What was the influence that man Burton exercised over her? If he only knew he would soon put an end to it. And again he recalled, with a pleased smile, how she had wanted him to stay at home,—how she had begged him not to leave her while she slept. And Robert Murray was very young as he built his castles on this airy foundation; but it was easy, happy work, with that young face before him, and he by her own request acting guardian over her.

Once she moved, and half opened her eyes,—only remained conscious long enough to smile at him, and murmur, "Thank you." And sleep claimed her again.

"She must have been awake all night," said he to himself,

as he connected her appearance at breakfast with her present heavy slumber. "What can it be? what can it be?"

Presently there was a knock at the door. No soft-footed woman could have moved more lightly than did this gigantic man; the mouse in the wainscot did not even pause in his gnawing, gnawing, and the sleeper remained undisturbed as he softly unlatched the door, and, with finger on lip to enjoin silence, received from the messenger a note.

It was from C——, and in a gentleman's hand. If ever Robert Murray was tempted, dishonorably, to withhold property belonging to another, it was then,—he knew it was in some way connected with Margaret's uneasiness; and as he held the delicate missive in his hand he could almost have cursed the pen as an instrument of more evil than good.

If he had known it was an answer to a note from her sent off very early that morning, he would have been still more puzzled and troubled; but, at any rate, he determined to make the letter he held an excuse for speaking more plainly to her than he had ever yet done. This determined upon, he sat quietly, keeping his vigil.

Morning had given place to noon, and noon was an hour old before Margaret Holcombe opened her eyes. She started up and said,—

"Oh, Mr. Murray, how selfish in me to keep you here all this time! How long have I slept?"

Mr. Murray looked at his watch, and said, "About three hours. Are you better?"

"Oh, so much! thank you; my head feels quite clear. I got nervous last night, and did not sleep. Has no one been here since I laid down?" There was a shade of anxiety in the question which went to his heart. Now he must put this half-won peace to flight.

"Yes, Ned brought you this note." And he handed her the little scented, sentimental-looking envelope,—bearing even on its face, he thought, a likeness to Burton.

She crumpled it in her hand, and was starting up to go to her room, when he stopped her.

"Child," he said, taking her by the hands and putting her back on the lounge, "read your letter there; I will take my book across the room." And he went over to the window, while she resumed her recumbent position.

What had become of the proud, willful girl? She was nothing more than a submissive child in the hands of this man. She seemed to lose all disposition to resist, or power of resistance; and, stranger still, she did not dislike the manner he was assuming over her,—it was a rest to her troubled, tossed spirit for him to call her child, and command her actions in that way.

Robert Murray turned around when the rattling of the paper ceased, and found, as he had anticipated, the transient expression of peace gone, and the same goaded look she had worn in the morning.

"Margaret," he said,—"let me call you so for this once,—cannot you tell me what this trouble is which is tossing your spirit about so terribly? Let me help you." But she waved him off, and tried to say he was mistaken,—it was nothing; but the habit of truth was too strong,—she left her sentence unfinished.

"I do not want to pry impertinently into your concerns," he said, "but believe me, no one in the world can feel a greater desire to serve you,—you are very dear to me."

That was too much. Then, too, he suspected. Oh, terrible, he was about to take pity on her! She sprang from the lounge, and said, with an earnest, excited manner,—

"Mr. Murray, I have been very imprudent; don't mis-interpret my desire to have you with me this morning,—I was nervous and sick, and hardly knew what I was doing." And before he could detain her she was gone.

She had seen his intention then, and, meaning kindly, had prevented the full avowal of his feelings. The dis-appointment was great, but he could not yet feel that the matter was settled,—he could not and would not believe that she could care seriously for Dr. Burton.

# CHAPTER XXV

THE DEVIL HELPS HIS OWN.—A FUNERAL.

THE note Margaret Holcombe had written in the morning ran thus,—it lacked an address at the beginning, but was not less welcome for the omission:

"ROSE HILL, October 3d, 1858.

"I have been a good deal annoyed in consequence of your conduct yesterday evening, and write this morning to beg that you will never mention your ridiculous suspicions to myself or any one else again. You have no right to entertain them, and I have a right to command your silence.

"MARGARET HOLCOMBE."

The answer returned was as follows:

"C——, October 3d, 1858.

"MY DEAREST MISS HOLCOMBE,—Your note has been this moment received, and I hasten to answer it. Don't allow yourself to be troubled for an instant by my imprudent disclosures last night. I assure you I have deeply repented speaking to you as I did. It never shall be repeated. Could I avoid it, your life should never know one pang. I will do all I can to make you happy. When may I see you?

"Ever devotedly yours,
"WILLIAM BURTON.

"P.S.—Trust me implicitly with your secret, and believe that I will only use it for what *I* regard as your happiness. Yours, W. B."

21 (241)

It is said that the devil helps his own, and surely he must have helped in the concoction of this letter. Under the guise of the greatest devotion Dr. Burton managed to let Margaret know that at any time the dreaded revelation might be made. Mr. Murray's words also increased her distress. And she hid her face in her hands and actually groaned with shame at the idea of his suspecting her miserable secret.

The fact is, to understand fully Margaret Holcombe's self-torture during this time, one must comprehend her proudly, sensitive nature; when a thought, which cuts like a knife, seems to present itself over and over again with wanton cruelty, holding its victim like the malicious spider does the buzzing fly, returning again and again with its poisonous sting, and then retiring to gloat over its agonies; when, too, such a woman loses control over her nerves, she succumbs more quickly than one less highly strung to the touch of a dreaded evil. Then, added to this, Margaret was no longer well,—her body was sympathizing keenly with her distress of mind. And when her father came home he was shocked to see the change in her. Upon inquiring the cause, he went at once into C——, and had an interview with Dr. Burton, in which he told him, in his impulsive way, that after his violation of his express stipulations that his status was established, and did the whole of Massachusetts pour down its credentials, he would still stand in the position he now occupied,—the rejected suitor to Margaret Holcombe.

Mr. Holcombe would not have flattered himself so complacently that the trouble was over if he could have seen Dr. Burton's countenance after he left, with its expression of malicious triumph, as he brought down his fist upon the table and said, as though answering an unseen antagonist,—

"Yes, with all your boasted Virginia aristocracy, my lordly gentleman, I'll teach you the lesson that a Massachusetts Yankee is more than a match for a Virginia aristocrat."

Meantime Mr. Murray kept a steady watch over the unhappy girl; but she as steadily avoided him, unless she found that he had an intention of going into C——, and then every blandishment was put forth to prevent his carrying out his purpose. Once or twice Margaret was betrayed into an expression which almost persuaded him that he might afford to hope for a return of his devotion; but this was always followed by such long seasons of coldness and avoidance that he was completely nonplused.

One day, near the middle of November, when the Indian summer—that beautiful season in our climate—had thrown over all nature its misty veil, and was breathing its balmiest breath as a farewell before consigning us to the cold embrace of hoary winter, Mr. Murray was standing on the porch, which extended along the front of the house, with that potent consolation, a cigar, in his mouth, when Margaret Holcombe and Jean came out, evidently prepared for some expedition.

"Where are you bound this beautiful day?" said he, throwing away what remained of "his consolation," and coming towards them.

Jean explained briefly that Aunt Aggy had lost one of her children,—a boy of about six years old,—and they were going to the funeral.

"May I go with you?" said he. "I was just consumed by ennui, and wishing for a companion in my solitude, when, lo! in answer, as it were, to my invocation, you two make your appearance."

The required permission was given, and before they

had gone many steps Mr. Holcombe joined them, and, putting Jean's arm in his, left Margaret to Mr. Murray. Their way lay through the little settlement called the Negro Quarters, and along the base of a hill to a clump of trees, which almost merited the name of grove, where the rude head-boards and unmistakable little hillocks, now covered with dead leaves, which had not yet lost all of the brilliant tints of autumn, marked the simple burying-ground of the negroes. Here they had been laid for three generations past, and two or three gray stones, of unpretending appearance, proclaimed the extraordinary faithfulness and attachment of the humble dead who lay beneath.

The solemnity which always attaches itself to these " cities of the dead," however lowly they be, subdued the voices and checked the smiles of our pedestrians as they entered its precincts. The noble old forest trees, with their gnarled roots and bare branches, waved a requiem above their heads, while the few leaves which had still clung fondly to the parent from which they had sprung in their fresh greenness, now fluttered one by one to their feet, contributing, as their predecessors had done, to form the funeral pall which covered the face of the ground.

As the procession in honor of the dead had not yet made its appearance, Mr. Murray led Margaret to one of the gray stones of which we have spoken, and read aloud the inscription roughly cut in the rude surface:

"TO THE MEMORY OF

"AUNT DOLLY,

" Who died September 16th, 1840, aged 106 years, most of which time was spent in faithful servitude to the Holcombe family."

"One hundred and six years!" exclaimed Mr. Murray. "What a pilgrimage!"

"Yes," said Mr. Holcombe, who had just come up, "one hundred and six years; and I assure you, at the time of her death she was as active as Margie here. I remember her appearance so well,—she was a little, tightly-made woman, with a brisk movement and a quick manner of speaking. She always had her linsey-woolsey dresses made in the fashion of seventy-five years ago, with a tight jacket and a little, short skirt behind.

"She was the mother of our old Mammy; indeed, almost all of the negroes on the place are descended from her. We children used to delight in getting her to tell us some of her experiences in the Revolutionary war, and how she once saw 'Gineral Washington, when he come to old marster's, after Mars' Cornwallis had to surrender.' And how, when she was a 'slip of a gal,'— though she must have been nearly thirty at the time,— 'she used to go with her old mistus to *Jimtown*, when Governor *Buckley* used to have all the *quality* thar at court.'

"But," added he, "I see the procession coming. I want you to look at this stone before they get here." And turning to one similar to that before which they had been standing, he read:

"Sacred to the memory of WILLIAM, who died May 18th, 1836, aged seventy-six years.

"'Well done thou good and faithful servant.'

"This old fellow," continued Mr. Holcombe, "accompanied my mother's brother to Canada in the last war, where he fell fighting bravely at Lundy's Lane, and William bore his body off of the field and himself laid it in

21*

the grave; and, when he returned, brought his watch and purse with him."

Just here they were interrupted by the arrival of the funeral procession. The coffin was made of rough deal boards, and was borne by two men, while the parents followed close behind.

The negro is an impulsive, affectionate creature, and Mr. Murray was touched by the evident grief of these children of nature. At any other time he would have smiled at the rude attempt at mourning habiliments; but now he felt no desire to be amused, for the head, though it was adorned by a bonnet of a fashion many years back, was bowed with sincere sorrow, and the red handkerchief, so little in unison with the rest of the dress, wiped away genuine tears.

Uncle Armstead conducted the services. He was a fine-looking old negro, with tall figure still unbent by age, but whose long white beard gave him a venerable and majestic appearance.

They joined with the group which assembled around the grave, and the little coffin was lowered to its last resting-place. After singing their own version of the hymn,—

"When those we love are snatched away," etc.,

Uncle Armstead stepped in front of the others and said (I give you his peculiar pronunciation, because I wish to be perfectly truthful to nature),—

"My dearly-beloved bredren: we is met here dis day to commit to de dus' our deceas-sed bruder. Dus' to dus' en ashes to ashes, till de great resurrection day, when we shell all arise white en pure en clean, like an angel of God in heaven.

"But now, my dear bredren, let us not mourn for dis, our deceas-sed freu, as dus sum others, 'cause our good

Marster is dun took him to hisself, to live wid Him fru de endless ages of eternity; en you kno', my dearly-beloved bredren, dit we is told what a happy home heaven is, wid its golden streets en its golden harps forever a-ringing, en whar they ain't no mo' sno' en rain, en no mo' burnin' suns; but whar it is always sweet en mile like to a bright summer's day. So, my frens, dey is lef' us an essample dat we shell follow in dar steps.

"Now, my dearly-beloved bredren, our deceas-sed fren' who lays here before us, *doo* he was young, was a very good boy. Let us all try en do like he did, dit when de time come de Marster will sen' our summons en fine us ready.

"En now jes think of the change to little William Henry. Yestiddy he was sick en suffrin',—to-day he ain't sick en suffrin'; yestiddy he was crien' en weepin',—to-day he ain't crien' en weepin'; yestiddy he was sinful,—to-day he ain't sinful; yestiddy he didn't know nuffin' but how to eat and drink,—to-day he know how to read en rite en cipher.

"While I was a-sittin' by him yestiddy, he open his eyes en look at me so pitiful-like, en den de Marster jes' cum en call him, en he flopped his wings en flowed away.

"I ain't got nuffin' more to say at present, my beloved bredren. Jim, you en Ned kin fill up de grave."*

Mr. Holcombe, and afterwards the whole party, went up to speak to the mother and father; and Mr. Holcombe told them in different, but not more sincere, language, of the blessed exchange their child had made, and that after the toils and cares of life were over they would go to meet him at the right hand of God.

---

* Taken from one of their funeral discourses.

"Yes, marster, yes, marster," was the answer. "I knows all dat; but it is hard to give up you chile; but de Lord's will be done."

As they walked away, Mr. Murray said to Mr. Holcombe, "Don't you ever have to punish your servants?"

"Oh, yes," said Mr. Holcombe, "we are obliged to be a law unto ourselves. Of course there are many hard characters among such numbers, and as a white criminal would be punished by the laws of his country for stealing, lying, and disobedience, so the masters punish for like offenses."

"But I should think," said Mr. Murray, "that this allowed great license to a bad-tempered, tyrannical master."

"It does," was the answer,—"it is too much of an unlimited monarchy; but so does the power allowed to a husband over his wife,—a father over his child. Because a husband has been known to kill his wife, should you argue that no man should be allowed to marry?"

Mr. Murray laughed, and said he did not think it a case exactly analogous.

"No, not exactly, I admit, but a good deal so. I say that the institution has innumerable evils, but none so great as to set this poor, helpless people free, perfectly incapable, as they are, of self-government. We accept the least of two evils, and keep them in their light bondage, rather than to set them free and seal their destruction. The Anglo-Saxon race would never permit them to live on an equality with them, and they would certainly in the end be exterminated."

"We hear of a great many bad masters, though," said Mr. Murray; "it seems dreadful for a bad man to have the power over so many sentient beings."

"I agree with you, perfectly," was the answer; "but I

also know that there would not be nearly so many bad masters if there had been less legislation on the subject of slavery ; if the feeling of irritation and bitterness were not kept up by the interference which is continually going on with our domestic concerns by the fanatics of the North—— But here we are at home again. Uncle Armstead is a fine preacher, ain't he ?"

"Rather rambling in his style," said Mr. Murray, smiling; "but *they* seemed to understand him and to appreciate his efforts."

"Oh, yes ; old Milly always has hysterics whenever Armstead preaches."

Here Jean and himself went into the house, and Margaret, turning to her companion, said, nervously, "Mr. Murray, I want to speak to you, please, before we go in."

He offered her his arm, and they continued their walk. It was so seldom now that she did not avoid him that he was surprised at her request.

They walked for some time in silence, and then she said, timidly,—

"Mr. Murray, I want you to do me a favor, and not ask me any questions about it."

"These are hard conditions," he said, smiling, "but the pleasure of being able to do you a favor is sufficient reward for compliance."

"You are always so kind," she said, looking down.

"Ah, Margaret——," he began.

But she put up her hand, and looked annoyed.

"I am not going to say anything which will give you pain," said he ; "I will promise you that ; do not avoid me hereafter on that account. Let me be to you an elder brother, and I will not seek to be more if it pains you."

She looked at him gratefully, with tears in her eyes, and repeated,—

"You are very kind; but I wanted to ask you, please, if you meet Dr. Burton at any time, don't have anything to say to him."

Mr. Murray looked at her in surprise. Could that man have excited her fears by threats towards him? That might be the solution of this mystery.

"Margaret," he said, "of course I have no reason to have anything to say to Dr. Burton,—he is not sufficiently interesting to me to induce me to seek him out; but have you any objection to telling me if you apprehend danger to me from him? I think, if that be the case, you ought to let me know."

Her answer was quick and unhesitating. "Oh, no! of course not; *you* are not in the least danger from him; but still, I want you to promise me this; and likewise, if you should get a note from him, you will not read it,— will you, Mr. Murray?" And her eager face was raised to his.

"Of course, my child," he said, smiling at her earnestness. "You may make yourself perfectly easy,—he shall not nod his head to me across the street, if you do not wish it. I am glad of the excuse not to let him speak to me."

She drew a long sigh of relief, as if one burden were off of her heart, and then was brighter and more like herself than she had been for a long time.

"All this is a mystery to me," he said, presently, "and one which I would give a great deal to solve; but I suppose I must wait your pleasure in the matter. Now don't begin to get excited about it,—I am not going to try to find out; I won't even want to know if you don't wish it. But, my dear little sister, if you won't let me help you, I wish you would let me point you to the best source of help which any of us can have in trouble."

She looked up to him,—so longingly, so differently, from what she had done a few weeks since, when he broached the subject in her presence,—and said,—

"Oh, Mr. Murray, if I only could be made ready to die, and just go to heaven now!"

He was so startled by the hopelessness of her tone that he seized her hand as if to hold her back from the grave, for which, though so young, she was longing.

She gently disengaged her hand, and went on: "I have felt in the last few weeks, for the first time in my life, that I wanted to have a counselor and guide in my perplexities, for which there is no human aid,—won't you tell me what I must do, Mr. Murray?"

Was this, indeed, the proud Margaret Holcombe,—this gentle, teachable girl,—asking so humbly for instruction? Yes, she had proved her own weakness and insufficiency. All of her boasted strength was gone; she was groping about in the dark, and asking to be led.

Mr. Murray pointed her to the Saviour of sinners, who alone could help her; and all the time those deep, earnest eyes were fixed on his face, drinking in the instruction.

They had extended their walk to the grove, and now stood in front of "Margaret's Grotto." He turned towards it and said, smiling, "And here I first saw you, Margaret. I thought I had waked up a wood-nymph, as you stood there looking at the dusty traveler coming down the road."

She smiled sadly, and said, "I feel as if a lifetime had passed since then; life looks so differently."

"Ah, well, it will look differently again when this cloud

has blown over. After awhile you will wonder that you let this mysterious secret, whatever it is, trouble you at all."

Margaret shook her head.

Just then a step startled them both, and before they had time to wonder what it was, Dr. Burton stood before them.

"Miss Holcombe," he said, "please excuse my abruptness; but I must speak to you for an instant."

Margaret turned frightfully pale, and clung so desperately to Mr. Murray's arm that he thought she wished him to refuse for her, so he said,—

"Miss Holcombe is far from well, Dr. Burton, and can have nothing very private to say to you. Whatever you have to communicate can be done here, I am sure."

"Well, perhaps so," he said. "Have I your permission to speak in this gentleman's presence?" he said, turning to her.

"Oh, no! no!" she answered, and then tried to laugh, as she disengaged her hand from Mr. Murray's, and said to him, in her gayest tone, "Excuse us, Mr. Murray, Dr. Burton and myself have a little matter to talk about which even you must not hear."

The flippancy of her tone hurt him more than anything else,—it was in such strong contrast to her face of distress and anxiety.

"Margaret," he said, "don't do it,—your father does not wish it; throw off this influence, whatever it is. Let me take the liberty of sending this gentleman about his business."

She hesitated, standing between the two.

"Do, Miss Holcombe," said Dr. Burton; "I am ready to lend my aid, *you know,* in accomplishing your happiness. I am ready to speak this minute, if you wish it."

"No, I do not," she said, clasping her hands; then, turning to Mr. Murray, said,—

"Mr. Murray, don't misjudge me about this,—indeed, I am doing nothing wrong; I will not be gone many minutes,—please wait for me."

"Your pleasure is mine, Miss Holcombe," he answered, coldly, walking away.

Dr. Burton offered Margaret his arm, but she declined it, and said, haughtily, "Dr. Burton, this is too much! What do you mean by pursuing me in this way, when you know my father has forbidden my speaking to you?"

"Miss Holcombe," he said, "I was obliged to see you. I wanted to know for myself if this terrible disappointment is sapping your life. The change in you is worse than I anticipated, even. Ah, I entreat you let me speak,— I could do it without compromising you in the least."

"Dr. Burton," said Margaret, "I do not know what your object is in this; but that you have one I am well convinced. Let me hear it at once; perhaps I may be able to bargain with you for my freedom. What do you wish?"

Her manner was stinging in its cold sarcasm. Oh, how it made that man long for her possession, that he might break that spirit to his will! But there was too much depending upon his success in this interview for him to allow her to guess his real feelings. He had prowled around Rose Hill constantly for two weeks, and this was the first chance fortune had thrown in his way,— he could not lose it. Assuming a manner of the deepest dejection, he said,—

"This is the hardest trial of all. For weeks my every thought has been of you, and of how I could minister to your happiness, and now to be misunderstood and calum-

22

niated! I can stand this no longer; farewell, Margaret Holcombe! You may find friends with more ability to serve you, but none with a more honest purpose."

"Dr. Burton," she said, with one of her old fits of repentance, "please forgive me! I believe you do mean kindly; but, indeed, I think you take a wrong way to show it: the best thing you can do, is just to let me and my affairs alone. My life will work itself out, not happily, perhaps,—that, I think, I am not fitted for,—but with contentment. This is all, I believe."

"No, not all," he said, "I will write to you to-morrow, and make you my final proposition. I cannot stand this state of things any longer."

"Very well," she said; "but remember, though I may receive your letter, I shall not answer it."

"Well, perhaps you may change your mind when you get it." And before she could prevent him he seized her hand and kissed it, and walked rapidly away; and she joined Mr. Murray, who coldly offered her his arm, and silently walked by her side. She was the first to speak,—

"Mr. Murray, you do not know how to sustain your character as a brother."

He felt the truth of her remark keenly; he did not, truly, where she was concerned. "Why, Miss Holcombe?"

"In the first place, you call me Miss Holcombe,— brothers never do that; and then you do not trust me at all. I know appearances are against me; but won't you rejoice with me when I tell you that everything is clearing away? I begin to see my way through my perplexities." And she looked up at him with so bright a face that he was effectually won over by it.

"Well," he answered, "if this unaccountable interview

produces that, I shall feel that it was lightly purchased by the anxiety of the last few minutes. You know, I suppose, that Dr. Burton has been forbidden by your father to see you ?"

"Oh, yes, I know it, and I don't ever expect to see him again. After to-morrow I will try to be Margaret Holcombe once more."

# CHAPTER XXVI.

## FORTUNE FAVORS THE BRAVE.

"ROBERT," said Mr. Holcombe, meeting Margaret and Mr. Murray as they returned home, "I shall have to leave my family in your charge again for a few days. I have just received a letter from Richmond compelling my presence there immediately, and to-morrow sees me on my journey."

"Well, my dear sir, I think I can undertake the responsibility," said Mr. Murray, laughing; "I don't think either Jean or your daughter here will give me a great deal of trouble. Eddy is about the only difficult one of the family to manage, and with old Mammy's help I will even undertake him. How long will you be gone?"

"Not more than a few days; but it is a terrible bore to have to go away from home. I believe I could live my life out at Rose Hill, and never ask to go beyond. But what is the matter, Margie?"

"Oh, nothing, papa, except I hate you to go away," said she; then added, laughing, "As Mrs. Toodles said about the coffin, you are 'a convenient thing to have about the house.' I believe I would rather go myself than for you to."

"By-the-by," he said, "suppose you go with me,—it will do you good; your Cousin Jennie will be so glad to see you."

"Oh, no, thank you, papa, I could not go now,—I am going in February to pay a longer visit there, and to Williamsburg; but I am not ready for a trip from home."

( 256 )

" Miss Flora McFlimsey, I suppose," said he, pinching her cheek. " I wish you would get your roses back again : it worries me to see you so pale."

" Ah, well," she answered, " I will cultivate my garden while you are gone, and will have a good supply by the time you get back.  I know I am going to get quite well now."

She seemed so full of innocent gayety that her father looked at her with delight, and replied,—

" Very well; I intrust you to this young gentleman, and while this fine weather lasts you must resume your rides on horseback; that always does you good.  Come in, and let's have some music.  Robert, did she ever sing you that song written by my father :

"' Oh, breathe me that air yet again ' ?"

" No, I do not think she ever did," said Mr. Murray.

"Well, it was written to a young friend of his, who sang very beautifully.  She lost her lover, and could not be induced to resume her music, and this was an appeal to her from my father.  Come, Margie, let us have it."

They adjourned to the parlor, and Margaret, throwing back her wraps, seated herself at the piano, and sang the following verses, to the old tune of " Meet me by Moonlight alone":

" Oh, breathe me that air yet again,
    So buoyant and lightsome and free;
It bounds like a roe o'er the plain,—
    It bounds like a bark o'er the sea.
I have heard the sad song of despair
    From the lips of affection's sweet child,
And have wept from a being so fair
    To hear accents so plaintive and mild.
            Then breathe me that air yet again,
            Then breathe me that air yet again.

**22***

"A Peri, that loved her, was near,
    And caught the dear sufferer's sighs,
And whispered these notes in her ear,
    And wiped the sad drops from her eyes.
And now her enlivening strains
    Are buoyant and lightsome and free ;
They bound like the roe o'er the plains,—
    They bound like the bark o'er the sea.
            Oh, breathe me that air yet again,
            Oh, breathe me that air yet again.

"Oh, thy melody, woman, was given
    To soothe the sad heart with its strains,—
To lift the despondent to heaven,
    While it leads him a captive in chains.
Sweet consoler of others, then why,
    Since you lighten man's pilgrimage here,
Should your bosom e'er swell with a sigh,
    Or your cheek be profaned by a tear?
            Then breathe me that air yet again,
            Then breathe me that air yet again."

"Beautiful!" exclaimed Mr. Murray, as she ended. "I don't know which should have the highest praise, the poet or the musician. That gift for writing poetry seems to run in your family."

"Yes, but it never ran my way. I never could make two lines rhyme in my life, and George can turn any thought into pretty verse. I remember when I was a young man in love, I used to sit with my face in my hands for hours, trying to find proper rhymes for eyes, lips, nose, and love, and when I found the words the sense would not come ; for instance, eyes, flies ; lips, dips ; nose, hose ; love, dove. It was the great trial of my younger life. You need not laugh, Margie, it is a fact.' For Margie and Mr. Murray were both laughing at his youthful reminiscences.

"Ah, papa," said Margaret, "you do yourself injustice. I have mamma's album, with a piece in it from you."

"No, indeed; I assure you I had to go to George in my difficulties, and he wrote it for me."

"Worse and worse," said Mr. Murray; "it is like getting some one else to write your love-letters for you."

"Yes, it is a good deal like it, I confess," said Mr. Holcombe; "but in those days almost everbody wrote poetry, or what went for it; it was a common thing for invitations to be written in poetry, and playful controversies; and it was really a serious trouble to me that I could not. In this prosaic age it don't make any difference. But let's have some more music." And so the evening passed. Jean joined them after tea with her work, and the bright log fire on the hearth threw a cheerful gleam over the party.

"I declare," said Mr. Holcombe, as they rose to separate for the night, "I never did hate to leave home so much before." Margie came behind him, and, putting her arms around his neck, stooped down and kissed him. He took her hands in his, and said,—

"Remember, Robert, take good care of these treasures of mine; don't let any wolf get into my sheepfold. I shall certainly be back by the end of the week."

Mr. Murray gave the required assurance, and goodnight was said all around.

Before she retired for the night, Margaret knelt humbly by the side of her bed, and for the first time in her life besought the divine guidance, and thanked God that the clouds which had encompassed her were brightening; then lying down she slept more quietly than she had done for many weeks.

The next morning all was hurry and bustle. Mr. Holcombe was obliged to get to C—— very soon after breakfast, and everybody about the house had to be engaged in helping with his preparations.

The carriage was announced and the "good-bys" said ; but after it had actually started Margaret ran down the terraced walk, and, calling to the driver to stop, got in, and, putting her arms about her father's neck, whispered,—

"You dear old papa, I could not let you go without another kiss, and saying to you that——." And she hid her face against his shoulder. "I hope you will forgive me for everything I have done wrong to you, and that I will try to be a better child to you in future."

He put his arm around her, and kissed her fondly, while the tears stood in his eyes. In another moment she was gone, but her father could not forget the little scene.

"It is so like the child she has always been," said he, smiling, to himself, "sinning and repenting, and willing to make any confession, except in the one instance ; but I trust that has all blown over now."

The cars were just whistling in the distance when he drove up to the depot, so he had to hurry out of the carriage and run across to the track. As he stood there a moment a man brushed past him, brushed so vehemently past that he almost threw him forward ; and just as Mr. Holcombe was about to ask the meaning of his apparently intentional rudeness, turned around with a bow and broad smile, "Ah, Mr. Holcombe, pardon me ; I had no idea you were going from home,—be gone long, sir?"

"No, sir, I will be back immediately," said Mr. Holcombe, stiffly, and added, with considerable meaning, "Meanwhile Mr. Murray has charge of my family."

Dr. Burton, for it was he, showed his white teeth again, and there was no time for more, as Mr. Holcombe was obliged to take his place in the cars. Before they started, however, he tore a leaf from his memorandum-book, and, calling the footman, wrote hastily a line and told the man to hand it to Mr. Murray as soon as he got home. It ran thus:

"DEAR ROBERT,—I have just encountered that fellow Burton at the depot, and feel sure he rejoices in my absence. If he should dare to go to Rose Hill, you have my authority to kick him out of the house.

"E. H."

There was an observer of his actions at a little distance ; and as the cars moved off the footman felt himself tapped on the shoulder, and turned to encounter Dr. Burton's smiling face.

"My good fellow," he said, slipping a quarter into Ned's hand, "Mr. Holcombe handed you a note for me, did he ?"

"No, marster," said the man, holding out the note, " 'tis for Mr. Murray."

"I think you are mistaken," he said, as he took the little slip of paper without any direction, and, opening it, glanced at its contents. "Ah, I see you are right,— he will write to me when he gets to his journey's end, I suppose. Good-morning." And he went off smiling, and rubbing his hands, up the street.

"He would have me kicked out of the house, would he ? Much obliged to my good father-in-law. I shall take care that he never enters mine. Well, this opportune journey assists my plans wonderfully,—'Fortune favors the brave.'" And, still smiling to himself, he went up the street towards his boarding-house.

Towards evening of the day that Mr. Holcombe left for Richmond a letter was brought for "Miss Margaret

Holcombe," from Dr. Burton. She was in her own room at the time she received it, and, opening it, she read as follows:

"C——, November 14th, 1858.

"My dear Miss Holcombe,—I told you in our brief interview, on yesterday, that I would write you fully to-day. I now seat myself to do so.

"I have felt for some time past that it was necessary that some final decision should be arrived at with relation to our affairs; not only because it makes me unhappy to be thus separated from the only woman who has ever won my heart, but because your happiness, which is so infinitely dearer to me than my own, is so deeply involved in it; and I cannot bear that you should become the common topic for the gossips of society. You see, my dearest young lady, I am as proudly sensitive for you as you are for yourself; and when I hear it said (which I am forced to say has been the case more than once) that 'Margaret Holcombe is pining away,—a poor victim to unrequited affection; that at last her haughty head is made to bow,' I feel as you would, if you heard it yourself,—angry, pained, humiliated! and as if I would sacrifice anything to be able to stop these impertinent tongues. But, alas! I am powerless without your connivance.

"In our two last interviews I have tried to tell you this; that I know it to be a fact, that your affairs were at present furnishing the 'tea-drinkings' at C—— with conjecture and excitement; but, for the life of me, I could not see the pain I should cause. I am a very coward where you are concerned; so I determined to write it,—for, like a kind physician, I am willing to give pain to save the life of my patient.

"Now, my dear Miss Holcombe, you know that there is no wish so ardent in my heart as to call you my wife.

I have told you that too often for you to have any doubts
of its truth; and if you would only trust your happiness
to my keeping, I feel sure it would be secure. I repeat,
that I feel sure of this, in spite of the fact which I know
so well, that your heart is wholly devoted to another.
But what one of your sex does not succumb to kindness? Some of the happiest marriages I have ever seen
have been founded upon the wreck of an early affection.
And even if you should never love me with passionate
devotion, I would rather have your friendship and respect
than any other woman's love; and I know I could win
and keep that.

"And now for the other side of the question, for I do
not unduly urge my own claims. I know, that although
I could give you a peaceful, quiet, nay, a happy life, yet
of course you would know a higher degree of delight
with the man to whom you have given your heart, and
who, I am sure, is a worthy object of your affection.
That he does not now love you I am afraid; but that he
could help becoming attached to you when thrown daily
and hourly within your influence, I do not for an instant
credit. He looks upon you now as a mere child, and
upon himself too much as your uncle and protector to
allow a thought of a tenderer relation. But did he, for an
instant, suppose that the rich treasure of your heart was
at his feet, believe me, I know my sex well enough to
say with certainty, that his would respond instantly and
gladly.

"I confess that I do not see why you should let your
delicacy and pride come in here. You must know that
your secret is in the hands of one to whom your delicacy
is as dear as his own would be under like circumstances,
and who, by his manner of handling it, could accomplish
his full object without implicating you in the slightest

degree. Can you not trust me, dearest friend ? And will you not ?

"The two sides of the question are now open to you. I have pondered both of them, deeply, seriously, and I will tell you the positive conclusion to which I have come.

"I may startle you, my dear Miss Holcombe, by seeming to presume too much,—by taking hold of both horns of the dilemma with my own hands; but I have never been able, since the short time which elapsed in which I had your promise to be my wife, quite to feel that I had nothing to do with your fate, and I have determined to act for you if you refuse to act for yourself. You must either marry me, and so rescue yourself from the gossiping tongues of C——, or you must marry Mr. Murray, which will effect the same result.

"Unhappily, with regard to me, your father is so prejudiced against me—why, Heaven above only knows !—that I may not hope for a consummation of my wishes in the midst of your own family; but I have friends, to whom I could take you at once.

"Now, listen to my first proposition : I will be at Rose Hill to-night, between the hours of eleven and twelve, with a suitable conveyance. If you will meet me, in a few hours I will place you under the care of a lady who will be to you a mother in every sense of the word, *until* I can myself claim the full right to protect you. And your father, *you know*, as well as I do, will forgive you as soon as the matter is a fixed fact.

"But, on the other hand, if you cannot make up your mind to take this step, and I confess that your loss in decision of character of late leads me to fear this, I candidly tell you that I will to-morrow let Mr. Murray know that your heart is entirely devoted to him, and then I will disappear from the scene, as I do not think, dear as your happiness is to me, that I could stand by and see it accomplished in that way.

"I think this is all I have to say to you at present. I shall await you under the oak-tree, to the left of the house, between the hours of eleven and twelve, either to take charge or to take leave of you, whichever you please.

"I am, as I ever shall be,

"With the truest devotion, your friend,

"WILLIAM BURTON."

For a long time Margaret Holcombe sat with this letter open upon her knee and her head leaning against the back of her chair. One week ago, if it had been received by her, in her reckless mood, in all probability she would have thrown away her life upon an impulse; but to-day she was stronger, not in her own strength, but in that to which she had committed herself. And yet it was a fearful temptation to her, unknowing, as she did, the character of the man with whom she had to deal. "A quiet, peaceful life!" She did, indeed, long for it. And then the other alternative. Well, there was one thing,—she could refuse to marry Mr. Murray, and she would. It would be a life-long misery to feel that she had been thrown at the head of the man she married; that pity was the strongest feeling in his heart. And again her mind reverted to the unselfish devotion of Dr. Burton, for it must be so. What did he have to gain? Her fortune would be nothing to him, for he was far wealthier than herself,—he had been perfectly frank about that!—and his lavish expenditure of money confirmed his statement; and he was even willing to resign her to his rival, that she might be happy. And her heart melted to him, and she almost felt that she could be happy with him,—at least she could reward him for his goodness by making him an affectionate, self-denying wife.

The idea of noble self-denial is very attractive to such a woman as Margaret Holcombe.. There are times when self-abnegation reaches such a degree with them that no regard is paid to personal needs,—they can resign anything. It was such a mood as this which possessed her this evening; and if Dr. Burton could have looked into her heart he would have gloated over his prospect of success. But there was a power standing even then within the innermost recesses of this young heart, and saying to the waves of sin and sorrow which were dashing and surging against her spirit with such wild fury, "Thus far shalt thou come, and no farther, and here shall thy proud waves be stayed."

"Mr. Murray," said Margaret Holcombe, as he took his usual seat beside her at the piano in the twilight of the same day, "do you believe in ever doing evil that good may come?"

"Certainly not," he said; "the Bible expressly tells us 'whose damnation is just.'"

"Well, Mr. Murray," she said, "if you had everything to dread in pursuing the right course, if you knew you would be miserable, humiliated, shamed, would you still go in it?"

"Margaret," he said, and his voice grew very gentle as he spoke, "is it not the very path our Saviour trod before us? Suppose He had shrunk away because of the shame, the humiliation, the cursed death of the cross,—oh, what would be our hope to-day? No, dear—sister, I know not what your trial may be, and cannot do much to help you; but take it to Him,—He will bear it for you when it gets too heavy for you to carry. God knows, I would willingly take the burden myself, if I could; and oh, don't I know by that He would also? for He is gentle and pitiful, and full of compassion. But I had hoped the trouble was all gone,—I thought you were to be the real Margaret Holcombe to-day."

"I fear that was a vain boast; *that* Margaret Holcombe is a thing of the past." And the long eyelashes shaded the white cheek. "I am going through the deep waters of temptation, now, Mr. Murray; pray for me, that I may be supported through them."

His only answer was to repeat, "'When thou passest through the waters, I will be with thee; and through the floods, they shall not overflow thee.'"

"Thank you," she said; "that is very sweet. Now let us sing some of our songs." The thought passed over her, with a chill, that it might be the last time.

"What a sighing note the wind has to-night," said she, in one of the pauses in the music; "it sounds so mournfully!"

To change the sad currents of her thoughts, he said, "I'll make it sing for you, and then it will soothe, instead of making you sad."

"How?" said she, turning to him in surprise.

"Well," was his smiling answer, "get me some sewing-silk from that wonderful work-box of yours, and some wax, and I will show you."

She ran off to get what he wanted, very much interested in his mysterious preparations. By the time she came back he had supplied himself with two slender sticks, around which he wrapped some threads of the silk, very well waxed, and going to the window he inserted the sticks between the two window-sashes, stretching very tightly the threads of silk, and immediately a soft musical note breathed through the room.

Margaret clapped her hands in delight. "I know," she said, "it is the Æolian harp; oh, how sweet,—and so simply made! Now, as a reward for it, I am going to read you a beautiful piece of poetry on the Æolian harp."

"By Mrs. Hemans, I suppose?" said he.

"No, indeed,—by that wonderful grandfather of mine, though he quotes a verse from Mrs. Hemans at the beginning." She brought from a table in the room an old, brown leather-backed book, and, turning over the leaves, found the poem, and was about to read it, when Robin announced supper.

"A pleasure deferred is not a pleasure lost," said Mr. Murray, as they went into the dining-room. "I insist·upon your reading to me after this important duty is done."

She readily promised. And when they were all gathered around the center-table, Jean, Mr. Murray, and herself, after tea, with the bright light between them, and the Æolian harp singing its plaintive song in the window, he claimed her promise, and she read the following beautiful lines, which are well worthy to be preserved as a gem of poetry:

"APOSTROPHE OF THE ÆOLIAN HARP TO THE WIND.

     "'Wind of the dark-blue mountains,
       Thou dost but sweep my strings
    Into wild gusts of mournfulness
       With the rushing of thy wings.'

    "When the gale is freshly blowing
       My notes responsive swell,
    And over music's power
       Their triumphs seem to tell

"But when the breeze is sighing
  There comes a dying fall;
Less, less indeed exulting,
  But sweeter far than all!

"It seems to tell of feelings,
  And youthful pleasures fled;
Of hopes and friends once cherished,
  Now mingled with the dead.

"And oh, how sweetly touching
  Is the sad and plaintive strain!
Recalling former pleasures
  That ne'er can live again.

"Once more thy breezes freshen
  And sweep the Æolian strings;
And again their notes are swelling
  With the rushing of thy wings.

"They seem to cheer the drooping,—
  To bid the wretched live;
And with their sounds ecstatic
  His withering hopes revive.

"Alas! and in life's drama,
  Howe'er man plays his part,
Hope is forever breathing
  On the lyre of theheart.

"Hope is forever touching
  Some chord which vibrates there;
While bitter disappointment
  Mars the delusive air.

"Alternate joys and sorrows,
  Obedient to her call,
Now breathe a strain exultant,
  And now 'a dying fall.'

"But how unlike the measures
  Breathed from the Æolian string!
These soothe the heart that's wounded,—
  Those plant a deeper sting.

23*

> "Then, wind of the dark-blue mountains,
> Still sweep my trembling strings
> Into sweet strains of mournfulness,
> With the flutter of thy wings."

"Exceedingly beautiful!" he exclaimed, when she had finished, as he took the book from her hand. "What a rare gift he had! Do you inherit it at all?"

"No; I am afraid I could give almost as deplorable an account of my efforts in that line as papa did. Now, Mary scribbles all the time, though I don't think it amounts to much."

"Oh, Margie," said Jean, "you are unjust. I think she writes very sweetly, sometimes."

"Oh, yes, sweetly, I admit; but I have never seen anything from her which was not mediocre, decidedly. Now, anything mediocre is bad enough, but mediocre poetry is execrable. Unless I could write like Mrs. Hemans, or Mrs. Browning, I would not write at all."

# CHAPTER XXVII.

## A NIGHT VISITOR.

MRS. HOLCOMBE'S chamber and dressing-room occupied one corner of the first floor in the house at Rose Hill, and Margaret's room was directly above it.

It so happened on this night that her baby had not been very well, and her slumber, always light, was broken by his heavy breathing. She started up, as he stirred uneasily, and was bending over his little crib, when her attention was caught by the sound of carriage-wheels, as if some vehicle approached the house by the gravel-road, which extended around the lawn.

Alarmed at the unusual sound, she sprang up, and, throwing on dressing-gown and slippers, she flew into the dressing-room, and, opening the window, pushed back the shutters. Her first thought was of Mr. Holcombe, whose absence from home of course increased her nervousness on his account. Drawing aside the white muslin curtain which hung before the window, she gazed out into the night. The moon was at its full, and the sky was as clear as crystal, and she distinctly saw a vehicle draw up at the foot of the walk, and a man spring out. Very much alarmed, she was about to call out, when she recognized Dr. Burton, as he cautiously approached the house. At the same moment she heard Margaret's step crossing the room above her head, and the creaking of her shoes told her that, although it was so late, she had not yet undressed. The window above was cautiously raised, and Jean heard him say,—

"Are you coming?"

"Yes," she answered, "in a few minutes,—have a little patience."

Quick as lightning Jean flew up the stairs and into her brother's room, rousing him with "Robert Murray, get up, quickly, and save the honor of my husband's house! Margaret Holcombe is about to elope with Dr. Burton!" And in a second she told him what had happened. "Go down the back steps, through my room, out into the back porch," she said; "don't come the front way,—I will keep her there. If she once gets out of the house, nothing will stop her!" And without giving him time to reply, away she flew down the steps, and, taking the key from the front door, rushed into her room and lighted the lamp. She had hardly done so before she heard Margaret's foot on the stair. Taking the light in her hand she walked out into the hall, and confronted her, cloaked and hooded, ready for her expedition. Very much startled was she at meeting the pale face of her stepmother, as she walked towards her, waving her hand.

"Back! back!" she said, "Margaret Holcombe, before you bring disgrace upon your father's name by this mad step."

All of Margaret's old spirit rose within her at this opposition, and she said, coldly and calmly, though she was white even to her lips,—

"Let me pass, madam,—I do not require your guardianship."

Jean put her light down on the table, and stood firmly before the angry girl.

"Margaret Holcombe," she said, "I have your father's happiness in my hands, and I tell you, as your natural guardian while he is away, that you shall not pass through that door this night, to your destruction. You are mad, and should be treated as such."

Margaret walked to the door, tried it, found it locked and the key gone. This necessitated a pause, which gave her a moment in which to recall her new-made resolutions; and the recollection coming to her that she might explain matters, she turned and said,—

"Mamma, you are unduly excited, believe me. What do you imagine I want to do?"

Jean heard the noise she had been listening for,—the turning of the knob of the door in her room. In another moment all would be safe. Robert was already out in the night.

"Margaret," she answered, "unfortunately, I can have no doubt on the subject. I heard Dr. Burton ask you if you were coming, and you answered 'Yes.'"

She smiled.

"You thought I was going to elope with him?"

"Yes, what else?" said Jean.

"No," she said, "I was going to tell him that I would never see him again; but"—turning to the door—"I hear voices! Who is talking to him?"

"It is Robert," said Jean.

Margaret's frightened face turned toward her companion, as she said,—

"Does he, too, think——".

There was no time to say more,—the voices without became louder, as if in altercation.

"For God's sake, mamma, open the door!" said she, clasping her hands. "Suppose anything should happen to Mr. Murray!"

The idea of danger to Robert had not occurred to Jean before; but now she received it in its full force, and, rushing into her room, came back with the key; but before it could be turned in the lock there was the report of a pistol, a scuffle, a groan, and Margaret Holcombe dropped upon her knees. Jean never knew how she opened the door; but she heard wheels grating over the gravel as the vehicle moved rapidly away. And as she flew down the steps she saw, lying on the grass, a dark figure, with the moon shining on its white face. It was Robert!

Now Jean was a woman of great self-control on ordinary occasions; but when she saw this precious brother lying there, to all appearance dead, life seemed to stand still in her heart and veins. In an instant she knelt beside the prostrate body, and shrieked forth her anguish.

"'Let me pass, mamma," said a voice beside her, clear and sharp in sound as an alarm-bell, and terrible in its calmness; "this is my right. What though I have killed him by my folly,—I loved him more than you or any one else in the world could have done." And Margaret Holcombe almost thrust Jean aside; and, sitting down on the grass, raised the still head upon her knee. Then came a broken wail. "Ah, he knows all now,— my darling! my darling!"

Had her voice the power to wake the dead, or was it an echo which repeated my darling! my darling! as the blue eyes slowly unclosed and looked into her face with such joy in their expression as man seldom experiences more than once. Then strength failed her, and Margaret Holcombe fell back and fainted.

But now the servants had caught the alarm, and came running up to the scene of action. Robert Murray did not again lose consciousness, and with some assistance was able to walk into the house; but Margaret, still in that dead faint, was borne up to her room, and every means used to recover her, but for a long time without success. The doctor had been sent for at once, but before he arrived Robert Murray told Jean of what had happened after her visit to his room.

He said that, although appearances were so sorely against her, he never had the least doubt that they were deceptive as regarded Margaret Holcombe; that even in her most reckless misery, he did not, for an instant, believe that she could so far do violence to her character as to consent to such a step as an elopement; but his conversation with her on the evening before convinced him that the mystery which had seemed to pursue her for some time past had reached its culminating point, and the time had arrived for him to interfere, armed with the authority vested in him by Mr. Holcombe. So, following Jean's directions, he crept quietly down through her room, and so out into the night. Going around the building, he found Burton looking anxiously up at the house. He was evidently a good deal startled to see him, and made a step towards his vehicle, which waited for him; but, catching him by the arm, Mr. Murray demanded to know what he was doing there at that time of the night.

"I am master of my own actions," said he, doggedly; "and shall not make myself accountable to you."

"You are not master of your own actions on these premises," said Mr. Murray, calmly, "since the owner has forbidden your appearance here, and has given me full authority to expel you,—forcibly, if need be."

"Yes," said Burton, maliciously; "but there are orders more potent under which I act,—those of his daughter."

"I believe that you lie, villainously," said Mr. Murray; "but whether that be so or not, Miss Holcombe is under my care, and I shall not permit her to see you. Now, you can go."

"Not at your bidding," said he,—"I'll see you in h—ll first. I see your game,—you wish to marry her yourself."

"Whatever I wish," said Mr. Murray, "is not now a point under discussion. I shall know how to choose my confidants. Good-evening, sir."

An expression of baffled malignity passed over the man's face, and, before Mr. Murray guessed his intention, he had drawn a pistol, and, putting the point at his breast, said, with a terrible oath, "Then you shall not have her!"

Mr. Murray had only time to start a little to one side, which saved his life, though he was perfectly insensible until he heard Margaret's voice.

Jean longed to ask him if he had heard what she said, but felt that it was a matter of delicacy with which she could not intermeddle.

It was decided between them that Margaret's connection with the tragical affair must rest with them, and that, to secure this the more effectually, it must never be known that Burton was the perpetrator of the act.

"There is no fear," said Mr. Murray, "of his further molestation; take my word for it, he will disappear after to-night, for he thinks he has killed me, and will make all haste to escape the hands of justice. So we are freed from that trouble."

When the doctor came, his first care was to examine Mr. Murray's wounds, which Jean had bound up, to the best of her ability, but which demanded instant attention.

"By George!" he said, "the rascal aimed at your heart! A very narrow escape!—very narrow, indeed!"

The movement Mr. Murray had made had thrown the point of the pistol farther to the side, and given the ball a slanting, instead of a direct, course; it had grazed the ribs, and gone through the fleshy part of the arm, just above the elbow, thus inflicting two severe flesh-wounds, but with which, as there was no danger, Mr. Murray was very glad to compromise.

The doctor, of course, was full of curiosity about the affair, and his questions were rather embarrassing.

"Well, what kind of a looking man was he?"

Mr. Murray gave a general description, which would have covered the appearance of half the men in the world.

"Would you know him again, if you saw him?"

"Oh, yes," was the answer, "I think I should,—the moon was so bright, I saw him distinctly."

"Ah, well, then, we may hope to catch him yet." And then followed a long string of depredations which had been committed in the neighborhood, which Jean interrupted by proposing that the doctor should see Margaret, as she still seemed to be suffering from the effects of the fright.

"Fainted, did she?" said he, in surprise. "Why, I had no idea Margie was one of the fainting kind; but women always will faint if they get a chance."

Jean explained that Margaret had not been well, which accounted for her being more easily affected than she would otherwise have been.

When they went into her room they found that she had so far yielded to remedies as to open her eyes; but, further than that, she showed no consciousness.

"Strange!" said Dr. Campbell, as he felt her pulse and examined the dilated pupil of her staring eye. "There

24

is more the matter here than mere fainting,—her brain is interested."

Jean's heart beat quickly at the unexpected intelligence.

He leaned over her and called, "Margaret, Margaret." There was a movement of the eyes and a slight contraction of the brows at the familiar sound, but no answer.

He ordered a cool cloth laid on her head, and administered an anodyne; then, turning to Jean, he said, "I may be able to tell better by the morning; but," lowering his voice, "I think, at present, my dear madam, that her symptoms are alarming. Everything depends upon keeping her quiet and composed. Send for old Judy,—she is the best nurse in the world, and can live without sleeping." So Mammy was sent for, and took up her station beside the bedside of the patient.

When the doctor came in the morning, he found her still in the same condition, with wide-open, staring eyes. She had experienced no relief from the anodynes, though she lay still, except occasionally a restless movement of the head and the constant motion of the eyes, as they searched each face, earnestly, intently.

The doctor advised that Mr. Holcombe should be telegraped instantly of her condition, and promised to attend to it himself, upon his return to town.

"Halloo!" he said, going then into Mr. Murray's room, "last night was a sort of Walpurgis night; every place seems to have had an adventure. Here the whole town is in a state of excitement about the disappearance of that fellow Burton; or, at least, he has not yet returned. It seems he hired a buggy at Long's livery-stable, and told him to send for it to Marshall's Creek this morning, and when the man who stays over the stables came out at daybreak, here was the vehicle and horse standing tied at the door, and the money for its hire wrapped up on the seat of the buggy. And his landlady says she heard him come in, about half-past twelve o'clock, and go up to his room, and then return, and go out of the front door again. And when she went up this morning, she found a note from him, inclosing the money for his board, in which he stated that he had been called away suddenly, and might not return. By-the-by," he exclaimed, as if a new idea struck him, "what time did this fracas take place here?"

"I did not look at my watch," said Mr. Murray, evasively.

"Is it possible that the two things could be taken in connection?" asked the doctor, thoughtfully.

"Oh, I should have known Dr. Burton," said Mr. Murray," so naturally, that the doctor was thrown off the track, and said,—

"Oh, yes, of course you would, of course you would; but how are your wounds this morning?"

"I feel very little inconvenience from them," answered Mr. Murray, "except a stiffness of the tendons of my arm, and a want of strength, which I suppose is due to loss of blood."

"Oh, yes, you lost a good deal; but you are doing very well, and have great cause to congratulate yourself on your escape. I never saw one more narrow. I wish the rascal could be found. I am afraid that poor child up-stairs will not get off so easily as you are doing."

Mr. Murray turned to him in alarm. "You do not mean Miss Holcombe, I hope, sir?" For Jean had purposely kept the account of her illness from him.

"Indeed I do," said the doctor; "I am afraid she is going to be seriously ill. There is, evidently, some severe tension of the brain, and the anodynes have had no effect, as yet,—she has not slept at all. I shall telegraph for her father as soon as I get back to town. But, good-morning,—I shall return this evening again.'

Mr. Murray was infinitely shocked at the unexpected intelligence, and Jean coming in just then, he announced to her that he intended to get up and go himself to visit the patient, as he must judge for himself of her condition.

"Oh, Robert," remonstrated Jean, "there is no necessity,—you could do nothing if you went; Mammy is there, and the doctor said, particularly, no one else must go into the room. Besides, if she should recover her senses, I do not think she would be pleased at all to see you there."

"Perhaps not," said he, perfectly unmoved; "but I shall go, nevertheless. As to there being any impropriety in my going into Margaret Holcombe's room, that is non-sense. *You* must know, after what passed last night, that the tie between us two no longer rests on mere conventionals. She will be my wife as soon as I am permitted to claim her, and this I shall take care is understood by all who need know it. My place is certainly by her while she is in danger."

In a few minutes after, he walked to the door of Margaret's room, and, knocking softly, obtained admittance.

Mammy looked somewhat shocked at this invasion of her prerogatives; but he said, gravely and quietly,—

"It is necessary that you should understand my position with regard to this young lady. First, her father has committed her to my charge, and next, she will, God willing, be my wife; so my place is here." And the old lady bowed her acknowledgments of his rights.

His calmness was almost overcome, however, when

those bright black eyes turned upon him with their restless search; but they stopped in his face.

"I do bleave," said the old woman, "dat she is found
what she been looking for."

It did seem so. For the first time the eyes rested, and
a look of quiet crept into their expression.

He reached out and laid his cool hand over their burning lids. They closed; but when the pressure was removed they opened again; but she was decidedly more
quiet, keeping her eyes, whenever they were opened, on
his face, but never speaking an articulate word, though
the lips would move every now and then, as if the brain
was instructing the tongue; but no sound came.

The doctor came in the evening again, and was surprised to find Mr. Murray assuming the position of nurse;
but he quietly explained his claims, and when he saw
that he was doing his patient good, he no longer ob-
jected.

The fact is, nature was asserting her rights terribly
upon this young girl. She had been defrauded too long
to bear it quietly, and for a weary time the physician
watched and waited without being able either to give or
receive much encouragement.

Mr. Holcombe was much shocked to find the telegram
awaiting him on his arrival in Richmond, and at once returned home. How constantly his mind reverted, during
the journey, to her "good-by;" and his eyes overflowed
when he thought that perhaps it was the last word she
would ever speak to him.

Ah, the return home after a summons of this kind!
The tension upon the nerves seems to increase as the
distance lessens, until at last it amounts to perfect
agony.

Dr. Campbell met him at the depot, and, although

there was not much hope in his account, it was something that she was yet alive, and her case, though desperate, not hopeless.

Jean met him at the door, and made him at once master of the situation in full. He was prepared, therefore, to find her self-appointed nurse at her bedside, administering her medicines and nourishment with the tenderness of a woman, and he looked on with wonder at the power which this comparative stranger had over her. She was restless and irritable with others, but a request from him was seldom denied, and she would take nothing from any other hands.

It was a long, dreary time they had to watch, without encouragement. Indian summer had ceased to flatter with its balmy breath, and cold winter had come, with its white finger clothing all nature in its snowy garb. And still they dared not hope with any degree of confidence. It was a sad Christmas.

She was no worse, was all the doctor could be induced to say. Mr. Murray caught what rest he could during her brief snatches of sleep, but was nearly always ready to fill the vacuum for those restless eyes.

It was during one of these rare seasons that he lay down on a couch in the next room, ordering that he should be called if she waked, and fell into a sound sleep. To his surprise, he found, upon waking, that several hours had elapsed, and, rising hastily, went into the next room. There she was, still sleeping, with the lips parted, and the gentle breath coming softly between them. This continued for at least an hour longer, and then the eyes opened, and, for the first time since her sickness, he heard the sound of her voice.

He was sitting behind her, so that the first face her eyes rested upon was Mammy's.

"Where am I?" she said, putting up her trembling hand.

"Here, in your own room, my child," said she, without expressing any surprise.

The eyes closed for a minute, and then opened again.

"I can't remember anything."

"Don't try now. Here, take this," holding a spoon to her, "and go to sleep again." But she put it aside, and then Mr. Murray, thinking to enforce it, offered it to her. She looked at him in the greatest surprise. The blood mounted to her thin cheeks, and, trying to draw the cover more closely over her, she said, without speaking to him,—

"Oh, Mammy, don't let him stay in here!"

She was thoroughly conscious now, he saw, and the first result of the improvement was his banishment from the sick-room. He did not remonstrate, because he knew it would be of no use; nor was he very much surprised at it, because he had looked forward to a renewal of her self-torture with a return of reason; but it was, nevertheless, a great trial to him. He had been head-nurse so long that he did not know, in the first place, what to do with the idle time it left at his disposal; and then, too, he could not bear to think of any one else performing for her those offices it had been so sad a pleasure to him to perform during her illness. So he wandered about, looking very disconsolate, nor did the accounts brought him from the sick-room tend to console him very materially.

The patient progressed but slowly towards recovery, and her state of depression tended to confirm the idea in the minds of her nurses that some causes were operating still upon her mind which retarded her recovery. Jean had found Dr. Burton's last letter in her room when Margaret was first taken sick, and, without reading it herself, had handed it over to Mr. Holcombe upon his return. This was at once a key to the mystery; but how to meet the present difficulty in her weak condition was perplexing. Mr. Murray was confident that if he could only have a personal interview with her, he could remove the trouble; but to manage this required considerable skill. He wrote a letter to her, entreating that he might be permitted to visit her; and Jean told him that, so far from having a happy effect upon her, she was ill from nervous excitement at what she considered an unprecedented impertinence on his part. Nor did she recover from this for some days.

It ended in Dr. Campbell's being taken into their full confidence, and he announced to her one day that her removal from that room was absolutely necessary. It was in vain that she wept, scolded, and entreated by turns,— the old doctor was inexorable; so, making her toilet as well as they could in her present weak condition, old Mammy threw over her white wrapper a crimson flannel dressing-gown, and Mr. Holcombe, taking her in his arms, bore her, very tenderly, down to the library, and laid her on the lounge.

Now, we have seen enough of Margaret Holcombe's natural disposition to guess that this opposition to her wishes was not borne with angelic patience; but she had no physical strength to oppose to the move, and so was forced to submit, though with all the nervous irritability attendant upon her weakness of body. She cried from the time the preparations commenced until she was, as we have related, laid upon the sofa in the library.

She could not help, however, feeling some enjoyment in the cheerful aspect which this favorite sitting-room had assumed for her welcome,—the heavy dark-green curtains falling in folds to the ground, the bright carpet, and all the familiar books looking down upon her from their niches in the shelves, filling her with a longing to be well enough to resume her readings, and then the ruddy glow of the bright fire over everything. She closed her eyes with a feeling of comfort which she did not like to acknowledge. Then, too, she had so dreaded encountering Mr. Murray if she left the sanctuary of her own apartment; but there was no sign of him anywhere, so she grew much more quiet; and Mr. Holcombe, getting a book from the shelves, sat down at the head of the lounge, with his cool hand upon her head, ready to attend to any expressed want. Thus a feeling of peace and security took the place of nervous irritation and apprehension, and this, added to the unwonted exertion she had made, with the fatigue consequent upon it, made her an easy victim to the slumber which crept over her before she was aware of it.

She slept soundly for a long time, and was only dimly conscious of the closer drawing of the curtains, so as to throw a deeper shade over the room, and the click of the lock of the door; but, before she could rouse herself to see if her father was leaving her, the cool, soothing pressure was resumed on her head, and she gave herself up again, without further struggle, to the blessed slumber. It must have been two hours before she stirred, and still that patient nurse sat beside her, bending over, ever and anon, to look into the face which still exhibited such sad traces of her illness. And fervent were the aspirations which went up from his full heart, that this precious life was given to their prayers.

At last nature was resuscitated, and the repose was broken. Half-raising her head, she said, before her eyes became accustomed to the darkness,—

"Oh, papa, what a nice long sleep I have had!—and

you, dear, patient old nurse, have been sitting here all the time." And she turned towards him to reward him by a kiss; but her purpose was changed when she found it was not her papa, but Mr. Murray, who occupied the chair at the head of her couch.

Indignation at the trick which had been played upon her, and embarrassment in his presence under the oppressive recollections which filled her mind, strove for the mastery, and she buried her face in her hands and burst into tears.

"Why, my darling, what is the matter?" said Mr. Murray, leaning over her, and trying to take her hands from her face.

She raised up, and said, angrily, "Mr. Murray, I cannot imagine what can give you a claim to take such a liberty with me, unless it be a recollection of the absurd scene on *that* night, and I beg you will attribute it to illness, insanity, or any reasonable cause; but, remember, I do not choose that you should ever presume upon it."

"Margaret," said he, "it gives me a claim over you that nothing in this world shall ever dissolve, thank God! Would you take from me the greatest happiness which this life can afford me,—the bliss of knowing that my devotion to you meets with a response?"

There was no doubting the tone of feeling, — the expression which beamed upon her from his eyes, as she raised hers to his face. The hands he held ceased their struggle for freedom, and the blessed conviction that he loved her with all the fervor of his being, took possession of her heart.

"Oh, Mr. Murray," she said, in her surprise, "can this be really so?"

"It does but little credit to your discernment, Margie," said he, smiling, "not to have made the discovery long ago. I certainly tried every way in my power to let you see it."

"But you said that I was not your style of woman,— that you could never love me."

"That unlucky speech of mine!" exclaimed Mr. Murray. "Yes, I said so, and at the time I believed it; but not half an hour after it was made I had a deeper insight into my heart than I had ever been blessed with before, and I knew then that the only woman I could ever love was this one." And he stooped over her and kissed her brow. "Do you believe me now, darling?"

"It seems almost too strange to believe it all at once," she said; "but oh, Mr. Murray, how much trouble might have been saved if I had only known!"

"Don't let us murmur at the trouble," he said; "it has worked out its own end, I expect. It has done us more good than all happiness would have done. Let us take the blessing which God gives us, and cherish it as the best earthly gift of his hand, and, God willing, all the trouble, as well as the bliss, which life has in store for us, shall be shared together hereafter."

# CONCLUSION.

SPRING had again triumphed over gloomy winter, and was rejoicing in her victory, decked in her freshest green robes, when we look our last at Rose Hill. But what is it which gives the old place such an air of busy preparation? Perhaps only the spring upturning, which is so important a time with Virginia housewives. But no! as we come nearer now we see it must be something more, for around at one side of the house tiny white tents dot the green grass, and again the colored lanterns of fanciful patterns hang like luminous fruit of strange species from the trees. Shall I whisper a word in the ear of the reader, or does he already guess that once again the doors of Rose Hill are thrown open to welcome acquaintances, relations, and friends upon the occasion of the bridal of the eldest daughter of the house?

We recognize several old acquaintances among the guests. There is kind Mrs. Mason and her daughters; Mr. and Mrs. Randolph and theirs; Mr. George, looking almost festive enough for a Christmas occasion, and on his arm leans a fair, graceful woman, whom he introduces to everybody as "my wife;" then, in that tall young man, with the groomsman's rosette on his shoulder, we trace a likeness to fun-loving George; and that great boy there, whom they all call "General," can be no other than John, who is perfectly charmed at the idea of being a groomsman also. But here flits in a fairy little figure, with long golden hair and dancing eyes, who summons

( 288 )

the bridal party into the closed parlor; and instantly there is a cramming and jamming into the other room, and expectation even fails to subdue the crowd into silence until the folding-doors are thrown open, and a beautiful tableau bursts suddenly upon the sight.

We have no difficulty, fortunately, in recognizing those two central figures,—we have become too well acquainted with them during the progress of these pages to doubt their indentity; and surely they are a royal-looking couple. He still holds his rank, head and shoulders above his fellows, and, methinks, the noble head rears itself a little prouder than usual for the burden which leans upon his arm. He glances down once at that coronet of dark hair, around which glimmer, like stars in the sky, the pure wreath of orange-blossoms, over which the rich veil of lace is thrown, which, falling in such ample folds, even to the floor, envelops the whole of the graceful figure, and through whose gossamer texture the pure shimmer of the rich silk is seen. But the murmurs of the crowd cease for an instant as the minister delivers his charge to the married couple. Let us also hear what he says:

"God, in mercy to our race, smooths the rough pathway of our lives, and lights up its dark places, with these beautiful domestic relations, these endearing ties, where two natures, fitting and blending into one, develop and improve, each the other; and thus they attain to the highest degree of earthly happiness and usefulness. And if, as is the case with you, my friends, God has blessed you with a still richer gift,—even a sense of his continual presence and guidance,—your happiness increases through the endless ages of eternity.

"Hereafter your walk will be side by side,—your happiness dependent each upon the other. Your hearts are,

25 .

even now, saying the one to the other, in the beautiful poetry of Scripture,—

"'Whither thou goest, I will go; where thou lodgest, I will lodge : thy people shall be my people, and thy God my God: where thou diest, will I die, and there will I be buried : the Lord do so to me, and more also, if aught but death part me and thee.'"

www.ingramcontent.com/pod-product-compliance
Lightning Source LLC
Chambersburg PA
CBHW060604030726
47498CB00005B/1527